# PRAISE FOR HILAR

## HER LAST BREATH

"A black sheep family drama becomes a deliciously paranoid psychological thriller from the always-thrilling Hilary Davidson. Brilliant!"

—Adrian McKinty, *New York Times* bestselling author

"One part thriller, one part domestic suspense, and one part family drama result in a fantastic story of love and betrayal, loss and redemption. Tightly written, compulsively readable, with flawed characters I both rooted for and feared for. I loved this book."

—Allison Brennan, *New York Times* bestselling author

"Hilary Davidson brings her A game in this stand-alone thriller about a woman's search to find her sister's killer. With a twisty Agatha Christie plot, complex psychological threads, and deep, dark family secrets, *Her Last Breath* is a genre-bending page-turner!"

—Wendy Walker, bestselling author of *Don't Look for Me*

"Before you start *Her Last Breath*, be sure to take a deep one. Davidson starts her tale at full speed and rarely comes up for air."

—Linwood Barclay, *New York Times* bestselling author

"Absorbing, complex, and satisfyingly twisty, *Her Last Breath* is an addictive page-turner. Hilary Davidson knows how to hook readers and keep them hooked."

—Meg Gardiner, author of the UNSUB series

## DON'T LOOK DOWN

"A blackmail plot produces complications upon complications in a story of sex trafficking, class wars, and stolen identities. [A] satisfying page-turner."

—*Kirkus Reviews*

"Davidson keeps the reader guessing to the satisfying conclusion. Crime fiction fans will welcome this tale of family, secrets, resilience, and revenge."

—*Publishers Weekly*

"Davidson's wildly intense murder mystery grabs the listener from the beginning . . . The age-old themes of survival, class, ambition, greed, revenge, love, and deceit all come into play."

—*Library Journal* (starred review)

"*Don't Look Down* will keep the reader guessing. Davidson has created some truly memorable characters . . . This is the type of creative finesse that makes a reader keep coming back for more."

—New York Journal of Books

"*Don't Look Down*, by Hilary Davidson, is a fast-paced, twisty, classic city crime thriller that leaves one fully satisfied."

—Criminal Element

"*Don't Look Down*, the second novel in a series featuring NYPD police Sheryn Sterling and Rafael Mendoza, is a stunning trip through the Big Apple. It's also a deftly plotted mystery that begins with blackmail and revenge. An excellent book with good characters and a fantastic plot, but what I loved were Davidson's descriptions of New York."

—*The Globe and Mail*

# ONE SMALL SACRIFICE

"Fans of Karin Slaughter, Tana French, and Lisa Gardner will devour this new police procedural, which boasts a strong female detective and an intriguing antagonist. Sheryn will draw in readers, and Davidson's complex storytelling will keep them wanting more."

—*Library Journal* (starred review)

"A thoughtfully plotted and skillfully characterized procedural mystery . . . It's easy to get drawn deeply into the various motives and secrets of each character because it's so perfectly human for all of us to keep things hidden, even from those we love."

—*Kirkus Reviews*

"[A] taut series launch . . . Davidson's ability to maintain the suspense bodes well for future installments."

—*Publishers Weekly*

"The story line veers between alternate points of view . . . [while] perspectives on the same information provide different results. Writing the novel in this fashion amps up the suspense while also giving the narrative a complex and compelling flair. In addition, Davidson does an admirable job of making a complicated issue such as PTSD relatable. With an unpredictable ending and evidence that this is the start of a series, *One Small Sacrifice* is a book you should definitely check out."

—Associated Press

"*One Small Sacrifice* is a complex and engaging psychological thriller with fully realized characters. The plot throws light on the darker areas of human nature, of the fallibility of memory, and leaves the reader guessing until the very end."

—Authorlink

"A thriller, of the filled-with-dread-but-I-have-to-finish-it variety."
—New York Journal of Books

"In a story told from multiple points of view, Davidson has crafted a compelling police procedural."
—*Milwaukee Journal-Sentinel*

"This thriller, told from alternating points of view, will keep readers glued to their seats."
—*National Examiner*

"Davidson's stealthily plotted, rapidly deployed, multistranded mystery encompasses the most intimate of brutalities—including domestic abuse and postbattlefield PTSD, a solid handful of dodgy characters, and, in the most humane of touches, a dog named Sid."
—*Seattle Review of Books*

"Davidson's plotting is tight and complex, a slow build of twists and reversals that keeps characters and readers guessing until the final pages. The resolution is well supported and natural, while simultaneously surprising."
—*Quill & Quire*

"*One Small Sacrifice* is an intense page-turner with twists to the very end."
—*Ellery Queen Mystery Magazine* (5 stars)

"Davidson's latest novel is her best work yet. *One Small Sacrifice* is a fast-paced winner. Highly recommended."
—Harlan Coben, #1 *New York Times* bestselling author of *Run Away*

"Davidson has crafted a tightly woven mystery. Each thread of the intricate plot draws you toward one surprising revelation after another."
—Sandra Brown, #1 *New York Times* bestselling author of *Tailspin*

"Hilary Davidson's *One Small Sacrifice* is both a heart-pounding procedural and a rich, mesmerizing tale of the weight of trauma and the elusive nature of memory. Twisty, absorbing, and deeply humane, it's a thriller you won't want to miss."
—Megan Abbott, *New York Times* bestselling author of *Give Me Your Hand*

"Packed with secrets, lies, and surprises, *One Small Sacrifice* kept me guessing to the very end. A gritty kaleidoscope of a thriller."
—Riley Sager, *New York Times* bestselling author of *Final Girls*

"A taut, compelling narrative with a nerve-tingling climax. Davidson turns clichés of the contemporary novel on their heads to create a wholly believable cast of characters. I hope we'll see more of Detective Sheryn Sterling."
—Sara Paretsky, *New York Times* bestselling author of *Shell Game*

"*One Small Sacrifice* is a terrific thriller with a big heart. A smart, compelling examination of guilt, blame, and responsibility that will keep you turning the pages. Hilary Davidson is a rising star of suspense."
—Jeff Abbott, *New York Times* bestselling author of *The Three Beths*

"Hilary Davidson is one of the best crime writers on the planet. This novel is a dazzling work by a master operating at the height of her abilities. Dark, twisty, and psychologically complex, *One Small Sacrifice* kept me guessing and gasping until the final page. I couldn't put it down, even though I didn't want it to end."
—Chris Holm, Anthony Award–winning author of *The Killing Kind*

"*One Small Sacrifice* hooked me hard. Hilary Davidson has written a riveting and beautifully layered thriller that satisfies on every level. The characters surprise, the plot twists, and the pages turn themselves."

—Lou Berney, Edgar Award–winning author of *November Road*

"I tore through this book! Hilary Davidson is at the top of her game with this masterful and twisty new novel that's jam-packed with suspense. Filled with wonderfully diverse characters, breakneck pacing, and surprises at every turn, this modern mystery will thrill even the most old-school crime fiction lovers. This book satisfied me on so many levels."

—Jennifer Hillier, author of *Jar of Hearts*

# HER
# LAST
# BREATH

# OTHER TITLES BY HILARY DAVIDSON

# HER

# LAST

# BREATH

## HILARY DAVIDSON

 THOMAS & MERCER

Text copyright © 2021 by Hilary Davidson
All rights reserved.

Published by Thomas & Mercer, Seattle

www.apub.com

Amazon, the Amazon logo, and Thomas & Mercer are trademarks of Amazon.com, Inc., or its affiliates.

ISBN-13: 9781542028691 (hardcover)
ISBN-10: 1542028698 (hardcover)

ISBN-13: 9781542028707 (paperback)
ISBN-10: 1542028701 (paperback)

Cover design by Faceout Studio, Lindy Martin

Printed in the United States of America

First edition

*For Eli, Zoë, and Sage*
*With love always*

# PART ONE

Everyone sees what you appear to be, few really know what you are.

—Niccolò Machiavelli

# CHAPTER 1

## DEIRDRE

I didn't know what to wear to the funeral. Any other day, I would've called my sister for advice, because Caro always knew the right way to do things. But she was dead, and I'd never hear her soft, husky voice again.

After pulling every piece of clothing I owned—all of it black—out of the tiny alcove I used as a closet, I put on a tunic that could pass for a dress. Then I added tights and a cardigan that hid the tattoos on my arms. My feet went into a pair of expensive, impractical heels that could only have been a gift from my sister. Climbing the stairs out of my basement apartment in Queens, I felt queasy. But it wasn't until I took the subway into Manhattan and stood in front of the church that I felt like an imposter.

"Your name and invitation?" demanded a uniformed security guard.

"Deirdre Crawley. I'm Caroline Thraxton's sister."

The guard said something I didn't catch because I was staring at the facade of the church, awash in déjà vu. Catholic churches with elaborate stone scenes of the Resurrection or Judgment Day were a dime a dozen. This one had the Crucifixion front and center, rendered with a grim intensity that hollowed out my chest.

"St. Vincent Ferrer," I murmured. This was the church where my sister had gotten married four years earlier.

"What was the number on the back of your invitation?" the guard asked, clearly unsure whether he needed to be polite to me.

I blinked, trying to picture it. Some Thraxton minion had couriered the invitation over at six o'clock Monday evening. *Remembering Caroline Anne Thraxton,* it read, stark black type embossed on thick ivory stock. *Please join us for a memorial service and luncheon.* It had chilled me, the elegantly thorny black vines winding around her name, ready to choke it.

"It started with a seven." There had been six digits on the back, but only one came to mind. I'd thrown the invitation onto my bookcase and hadn't glanced at it again.

"You need that code," the guard said. "You can't get in without it."

At that moment, a switch flipped in my brain. I'd barely slept the night before; the truth was I'd barely slept since my sister had died. I'd made it to the church on autopilot, aware of my own steps as a zombie. But this callous creep was the first obstacle I'd encountered, and all my grief suddenly spiraled into rage.

"My sister is dead, and you're not keeping me out of her funeral." My voice was razor edged.

As if sensing that I wanted to hit him, the guard pulled his head back sharply. I pushed past him and stormed up the steps.

Inside, white roses bloomed like a pox on the dark wood of every pew. Guests in couture laughed and gossiped. There were white ribbons and tulle wrapped around towering bouquets at the end of every aisle. The church looked exactly as it had at Caro's wedding, and I felt as out of place as I had that day.

It would've made me cry if the guard hadn't been breathing down my neck.

"She doesn't have an invitation," he said to whoever was listening. "She doesn't belong here."

I tried to walk away, but he grabbed my wrist. I took a deep breath. *Caro, please forgive me for clocking a guy at your funeral.*

"She's aggressive. She shoved me out of the way," the guard was whining as I turned, balling up my right fist.

"Did she really?" answered a sly voice. "Consider yourself fired."

I unclenched my fist as if disposing of evidence. There was Juliet Thraxton, broad shouldered and big boned, in a curve-hugging black suit with a pair of diamond pins in one lapel. Her platinum-blonde hair was rolled up in a chignon and tucked under a feathered black hat with a short veil. It looked like a prop from an old movie, worn by a widow who'd paid some mope to shoot her husband.

Her plump scarlet mouth was still moving. "Do I look like I'm kidding?" she asked the guard. "I'm not. Get out."

His face was bright red. "But she—"

"Pushed you out of the way. I heard you." She flicked her hand at him as if he were a mosquito. "Thraxtons don't employ losers. Go."

He retreated, muttering furiously.

"Thanks," I said cautiously. Caro always said firing people gave her sister-in-law, Juliet, a purpose in life.

"Trust you to liven up a funeral." She gave me a thorough once-over and raised an eyebrow as if I'd failed to meet expectations again. Juliet was the queen of barbed quips, and for a moment I thought she was about to strike. Instead, she sighed. "You probably want to see Teddy," she said. "He's up front with his nanny."

"How's he doing?"

"He's having a tough time. Poor kid." She started to turn away. "Don't go looking for trouble. It finds you without any help," she added cryptically before gliding off.

I wasn't sure if that was a dig about the guard she'd fired, or a reference to my father. I scanned the crowd but couldn't spot him. He had to be lurking in the shadows with the other monsters. I felt conspicuous, parading up the center aisle of the church. People turned to glance at me, but I wasn't important enough to speak to. My sister's casket sat in front of the altar, but I wasn't ready for that. Instead, I looked for my nephew. Teddy was wearing the world's tiniest, sharpest black suit, complete with a white boutonniere. He stood on the pew to hug me.

"Auntie Dee," Teddy sighed into my neck.

What could I say to a three-and-a-half-year-old whose mother had died suddenly? Everyone who knew Caroline was still reeling from the shock. If it was hard for me to comprehend, it had to be impossible for her son. I had no idea what his father had told him.

"You're a tough guy, aren't you?" *Tough* was the biggest compliment my family offered. *Nice* was fine, *smart* was good, but *tough* was what we aimed for.

"Yep," he answered proudly.

Gloria Rivera, his nanny, got to her feet. She was anywhere between thirty and fifty—it was impossible to tell—petite and raven haired, her face round and her eyes brimming with sympathy. "I'm so sorry, Deirdre."

"Thanks." She was the only person in that church who'd said those words to me.

When Teddy finally let go, I drifted toward my sister's casket, pulled along by some invisible cord. The upper portion was open, so you could see Caro's perfect, unblemished face. My sister looked like nothing so much as Sleeping Beauty, golden blonde and rosy cheeked. I could almost imagine her sitting up suddenly, smiling as if this were all one big stunt to reunite our fractured family.

"I didn't know I could miss anyone this much," I whispered.

For a moment, in spite of the chattering crowd behind us, it felt like we were alone in that cavernous church. And then the spell was broken as a hand brandishing a gold claddagh ring touched down on the polished wood of the casket. I recognized my father before I saw his face. This was the moment I'd been dreading. My sister, in life, had run interference, keeping my father and me segregated in our respective corners on those rare occasions when we were forced into the same room—at Caro's own wedding, our mother's funeral, and Teddy's christening.

We stared at each other for a moment. His blue eyes were hard and cold. The air around us was poisoned. Nothing had changed. He opened his mouth to speak, but I turned and stepped away before he had the chance.

The minor chords of the pipe organ underscored the ugliness of the moment. I stumbled back down the aisle. Was it my imagination, or were people staring? At the wedding, I'd heard someone say, *Can you believe Theo married her?* There'd been no end of comments about what a lucky girl my sister was. One bejeweled, bouffant-haired guest even said to Caro, *You must feel like Cinderella.* My impossibly elegant sister couldn't come up with a better response than a shell-shocked smile. At her funeral, the mood wasn't any different, even if the lucky girl was now lying in a casket.

I needed fresh air. There was a lump in my throat I couldn't swallow. My mind tripped over what my mother would've thought of the scene. Her eldest daughter dead, her husband and younger daughter at daggers. My mother had always seemed sad when I was growing up—no matter what good thing was on the horizon, there was a dark shadow trailing behind it. If I was honest, she hadn't been wrong.

As I exited the church, the guards shot me a curious glance, but the one who'd hassled me was gone. I clattered down the steps. It was a sunny day, for April. I stayed upwind of a forlorn clump of smokers. On the sidewalk stood a creep with a camera, and he pointed the lens at me. I turned away, pulling out my phone. I needed a distraction before I exploded.

That was the moment I first saw the email. You have a private message from Caroline Crawley.

My sister had been Caroline Thraxton since her wedding day. The sight of her birth name made the message seem like something out of time, a digital relic of a person who'd vanished four years ago.

When I clicked on it, the screen turned parchment yellow. Osiris's Vault keeps all your data safe and secure, read the text at the top of the screen. Caroline Crawley wants you to read this letter.

There was an image of Osiris, the green-faced Egyptian god who was hacked to bits by his brother and reassembled by his sister. Mythology had been my thing as a kid, and I still loved it. Caro liked to tease me about the tattoo of an ankh—the Egyptian key of life—on my shoulder. Was this a sick joke? I scrolled down.

Written above a text box were the words Caroline's message to you. I took a breath.

Deirdre,

I keep thinking of Mom, and how you never believe you're going to end up like one of your parents, until you do.

If you're reading this, I'm already dead. No matter what it looks like, my death won't be an accident. Theo killed his first wife and got away with it. Bring him to justice, no matter what you have to do.

I love you, Dodo. Always.

Caro

# CHAPTER 2

## DEIRDRE

The words on the screen bled and swirled together. I shut my eyes, unsure what trick was being played on me. But when I looked again, Caro's message was still there. It was my head that was spinning.

"You're Caroline's sister, aren't you?"

The woman speaking was about the same age as me, but she wore a pink suit that looked expensive and matronly. She was skinny and coiffed like a weather girl, and she wore so much shiny makeup that her face glittered like a disco ball as the sun peeped out behind a cloud.

"It's Deirdre, right? Caroline's death must be such a terrible shock to your family." Her pink mouth moved fast.

"Yes."

"I'm Abby Morel, from the *Globe*. I knew your sister."

She oozed a sickly-sweet gardenia scent that made my dizziness intense. I wanted to get away from her but felt rooted in place. "Where from?"

"We used to freelance for some of the same outlets."

I weighed the likelihood of that. Caro had been a journalist before she turned to the dark side—that was how she referred to publicity.

"I know Caroline's death was a tragedy, but what do you think *happened* to your sister?"

"She had an undiagnosed heart condition," I said, repeating what a cop had told me.

"That never came up in her life? Nothing about it when you were growing up?"

"That's what *undiagnosed* means."

"Could drugs have been involved?"

I was too shattered to lock horns with her. Instead, I dashed up the steps of the church and sank into a pew at the back. The temperature inside the church had somehow dropped ten degrees, and I wrapped my arms around myself for warmth.

I couldn't see straight during the service. My brain shuffled back in time, replaying bits of conversation with my sister. I knew she wasn't in a happy marriage—the way Caro skittered off the topic whenever I asked about Theo told me everything she wouldn't say. But the idea her husband wanted her dead—and that he had killed before—seemed screwy. For a split second, I wondered if that shady reporter had a point—maybe Caro *had* popped a pill that delivered delusions? But that thought lasted for only a minute before guilt struck me with the force of a slap. I was ashamed of my disloyalty to my sister.

*Theo didn't kill her,* I told myself. *Caro had a condition no one knew about.*

She'd been out running early in the morning when her heart failed. It could've happened to anyone, the cop had told me. Plenty of people didn't know they had a condition.

*No matter what it looks like, my death won't be an accident.*

That jolted me, and I gasped so loudly even the priest glared at me. He was going through the motions with the martyred expression of a man used to dealing with heathens. I sat mutely while Caro's best friend, Jude Lazare, read a passage from the Book of Wisdom. "The souls of the righteous are in the hand of God, and no torment shall touch them.

In the sight of the unwise they seemed to die: and their departure is taken for misery, and their going from us to be utter destruction. But they are in peace."

I tried to dwell on that while Jude continued reading. *Caro's at peace,* I told myself. The cop said she died quickly. She wouldn't have felt pain.

*Bring him to justice, no matter what you have to do.*

I looked for Theo and found the back of his head. He was in the front pew with his family. It was where I should've been sitting— would've been, if I wasn't avoiding my father. Theo hadn't even been in New York when Caro died, I reminded myself. The cops had trouble locating him because he was on a plane. How could he be responsible for any of this?

When Theo stood to deliver the eulogy, my field of vision darkened to the point where we were the only two people in that cavernous church. I'd always kind of liked my brother-in-law. Caro and I had reconnected after years of silence when she started dating him. The first time she'd mentioned Theo, she'd compared him to Heathcliff, which made me hate him, sight unseen, because I loathed *Wuthering Heights.* But when I'd met him, I'd liked his seriousness, his inability to make small talk, and his sardonic sense of humor. Most people put their best face forward in public, but he'd been bracingly candid. *Caroline told me you left home and lived with your best friend's family when you were in high school,* he said within five minutes of meeting me. *I wish I'd done that. My father shipped me off to a boarding school I hated, but I was too cowardly to run away. Like an idiot, I did a lot of drugs instead.*

At that moment, sitting in the church, I wondered if I'd mistaken cold-bloodedness for honesty.

"Thank you all for coming today." Theo's voice was perfectly modulated. He had an accent Caro called *mid-Atlantic,* which made him sound like he'd been dredged up from the middle of a frigid ocean. The undercurrents hinted at wealth and good breeding, but they wrapped every word in chilly formality. "I can't tell you how much it means to me. I know Caroline would never have believed how well loved she was by so many people."

There was nothing wrong with the words. Theo's delivery was impeccable. He used no notes. He sounded good—and he looked good, with his wavy black hair and blue eyes, a muscular six one packed into an expensive suit. He wasn't tearful, but he got a pass on that, since the Crawleys weren't much for crying either. Cool reserve I understood. There was no hesitancy in his speech, but there was no emotion either. Every word was burnished, like a penny dropped into a fountain.

The funeral Mass was over in record time because most of the crowd followed the Thraxtons' lead, sitting woodenly in the pews while a few hardy souls wandered up for a blessing—Communion wasn't even being offered. Theo had asked me if I wanted to speak at the service, and I was glad I'd refused. I sat in a trance while Theo walked away from Caro's coffin. I needed to talk with him, but I didn't know what to say.

Before I could decide what to do, a tiny voice cried out sharply. "Don't touch me!" I couldn't see him, but it was Teddy. Theo changed course midstride, racing toward his son. When I got to my feet, Theo was beside Teddy, facing a tall, heavyset man holding a camera.

"I didn't lay a hand on him!"

"You did!" Teddy accused.

Theo grabbed the photographer's collar with one hand while he knocked the camera to the floor with the other. It made a cracking sound as it hit the floor, followed by a crunch as Theo stomped on it. "Stay away from my son!" His voice was low, but it carried through the church. He shoved the photographer and then picked Teddy up, turning to leave. The larger man came up behind him, clearly intending to tackle Theo. But his heavy footfalls gave him away, and Theo spun around and punched him in the face. The man dropped like a sack of bricks. Theo was still holding Teddy, and he marched out the side door with him.

I fled, stumbling my way out of the church in the foolish heels Caro had given me. Outside, I tripped on the flagstones, then caught myself on my hands, cursing. The vultures up front snapped photos, and I knew there would be some gossip sniping online that I was drunk at my sister's funeral, even though I didn't drink.

My mind was traveling in dark directions. I'd never seen Theo get violent. Watching that scene play out was an awful revelation. Caro and I had seen each other a couple of times a month, and we'd been in touch by phone or text every week. I felt like we were close, because she knew all about my problems. From my vantage point, she had very few of her own. It had never occurred to me that Theo was one of them.

# CHAPTER 3

## DEIRDRE

I hadn't wanted to attend the fancy luncheon before I got Caro's message, and I sure as hell wasn't going after I saw it. When I read it again, I noticed a link at the bottom that said, *Click for file access.* I did and a web page opened up—with the words *There are no files.* I was caught in a hell loop. I didn't know what to do, so I got back on the subway. Elmhurst, my neighborhood in Queens, was fifteen minutes from Manhattan by the express E train. I needed to be alone to think.

The train was mostly empty, and I flopped into a seat. My heart was racing, and my brain felt like it was spinning out of control. I took deep breaths from my diaphragm. It was funny—no one wanted to take the subway anymore, because they worried about inhaling germs—but there I was, sucking them all in to combat a panic attack. An old lady in a full plastic face shield gave me a death glare until I pulled on a paper mask. Face coverings weren't mandatory anymore, but some people were ready to fight if you didn't don a mask in close quarters.

I got off the train at Roosevelt and hopped on a local for two stops to Grand Avenue–Newtown. On a normal day, I would've walked, but on a normal day stilettos would not be tormenting my feet. I picked up a lychee drink at Kung Fu Tea and hobbled home.

Caro wasn't snobby about my neighborhood—it was close to where we'd grown up—but she didn't like me living in a basement. She'd offered to pay for a place in a building that, as she put it, would at least be a *legal* apartment. I was one of six tenants renting in a single-family home on Fifty-Fifth Avenue. I had a hot pot and minifridge instead of a kitchen, and there was a toilet and sink in my room, so it wasn't the worst place I'd ever lived. I'd never been easy about asking for help, and Caro's repeated offers always made me uncomfortable. *I have money now, and what's the point if I can't do anything good with it?* she liked to say. As I walked to the house, it hit me that my sister was the only person in the world who'd tried to make my life easier, and she was gone.

I held my breath when I unlocked the front door, praying my landlord wouldn't be home. Saira Mukherjee wasn't a bad person, but she was nosier about my comings and goings than my mother had ever been. There was a staircase from the basement to the backyard that I invariably used to exit the house away from Saira's prying eyes, but a tall gate that couldn't be opened from the street kept me from entering the house that way. She wasn't around, but I heard footsteps above me. I kicked off my shoes, picked them up, and rushed downstairs to my room. I unlocked the door and quickly shut it behind me.

My dungeon room—that was how I thought of it—was tiny and devoid of natural light. The walls were an unforgiving shade of green, as if an earlier occupant had decided to imagine life inside an unripe avocado. I wasn't allowed to paint over it, and I didn't really care. I didn't own much, just a futon and a folding table, a bookcase, and a lone chair for phantom guests I never actually had over. I disliked clutter, but the shelves were my secret shame, overflowing with books, photographs, and carvings. I had a bad habit of tossing mail on the bookcase. On top of a volume of Gustave Doré's drawings for Dante's *Divine Comedy*, I found what I was looking for: a large manila envelope with my name and address written in black ink in Caro's distinctive curlicued script.

*I was going to mail it if I didn't see you,* Caroline told me when she'd handed it over.

*What is it?*

*Remember when you said you wished you had some family photos? I finally got my act together and made you a few prints. There's more on the memory card.*

I'd glanced at a few shots when I'd come home that night, noticed one that included my father, and instantly tossed the envelope on my bookcase. Out of sight, out of mind.

I extracted the envelope and reached for a protein bar before taking a seat on the futon. Inside were new prints of old family photos. On top was one of Caro and me together, hugging in front of a Christmas tree when I was five and she was ten, both of us wearing red velvet dresses with flouncy hems that our mother had sewn for us. The next was one of us with our parents, taken two years later. That was the one I'd seen a couple of weeks back, the one that made me shove the photos back into the envelope. I'd hated it because it was a lie: in that moment, we looked like a happy family, which was something we'd never been. Now that Caro was dead, my heart thudded with longing as I stared at it.

I drank some of the lychee tea and braced myself. Caro must've gotten the photos from our father. The envelope held more than two dozen prints, a collection of four-by-sixes and five-by-sevens, with a pair of larger portraits mixed in. There were a couple of Teddy on his own, and one of Caro with her son playing on a golden beach, but most of the images were much older. She'd included a photo of our parents on their wedding day, standing in front of a Belfast church I couldn't remember the name of. Our mother looked beautiful, her face gentle and serene. Our father appeared smug, clearly proud of tricking this sweet woman into marrying him. I'd literally chopped him out of the one old photo I had, but I didn't have it in me to reach for the scissors after a funeral.

*I keep thinking of Mom, and how you never believe you're going to end up like one of your parents, until you do.*

There was a portrait of our mother as a teenager, and one of seven-year-old me in my first *gi* at the Higashi School of Karate. There were birthdays and Christmases, ending with the one when I was fifteen. After that, there were no photos of me. That was no surprise. For a stretch of almost four years, my mother was the only family member I spoke to—or more accurately, the only one who spoke to me. The surprise was that there was a lone shot of Caro that had to be from those years of radio silence. In it, she stood on a staircase wearing a short dress of pale-pink lace, her arm around a man who was clearly not her husband. He was tall and blond and ruggedly handsome. I would've guessed he was Caro's prom date, except he looked like he was in his thirties. On the back of that print, in my sister's elegant script, were the words *With Ben, at the Clarkson/Northcutt house in High Falls, New York.* There was no explanation, and I wondered if Caro had mixed it in by mistake.

After spreading all the photos on the futon, I realized Theo wasn't in any of them. It was as if Caro had written her husband out of her life. I knew he was away a lot for work, and Caro never seemed to care. But his absence suddenly felt all wrong.

*If you're reading this, I'm already dead.*

Caro's message twisted through my brain like a tornado. From the outside, her life looked charmed. She had married into a wealthy family, joined their business, and had an adorable son. It wasn't perfect—Caro's dislike of her sister-in-law was intense—but she loved Theo's father and stepmother, and I knew they spoiled her. I had no ambition to live on the Upper East Side, but even I was jealous of the town house they'd given Caro and Theo as a wedding present. With its gargoyle sentinels and stained-glass windows, it looked like something out of a gothic fairy tale, equal parts stunning and sinister.

*No matter what it looks like, my death won't be an accident.*

The last time I'd seen Caro was the Saturday before she died. She'd been distant and distracted, but my sister was always wound up tight when working on a big project. The Thraxton hotel chain had suffered in the pandemic, and a lot was riding on her public-relations campaign to revive the brand. Teddy had been running around, making me laugh, and keeping the conversation from getting too serious.

*Theo killed his first wife and got away with it.*

This was the one part of Caro's message that made me question whether it was real. *What* first wife? Theo hadn't been married before. Back when he and Caro were dating, I'd vetted him online. You couldn't hide a secret like that. Could you?

I turned every photo over again, reading Caro's notes. There was nothing about Theo's first wife. I grabbed my laptop, tried the file link from Osiris's Vault again, and came up empty. I inserted the memory card. There were 1,702 files on it. I clicked on the first few. A photo of Theo finally popped up; in it, he was standing over his father and son in front of a towering Christmas tree. His arms were crossed and his expression was inscrutable as he watched his father and son playing with a model train. They looked like they were having a good time; Theo did not.

*Bring him to justice, no matter what you have to do.*

I clicked through the first fifty files. Seeing so many photos of my sister in happier times brought tears to my eyes. Maybe there was a photo of Theo and his first wife, but I wasn't ready to deal with so much of my own family history to find it just then. I ejected the memory card and returned it to its plastic case. My screen switched to an article about my sister. I didn't know why I hadn't closed it. I noticed for the first time that the byline belonged to Abby Morel, the sparkling monster I'd encountered in front of the church.

The death of Caroline Thraxton has stunned New York.
The former journalist turned socialite died during an
early-morning run near the United Nations headquarters on First Avenue.

The facts of the case are still being established by the police. They believe Caroline Thraxton suffered cardiac arrest from an undisclosed heart condition at approximately six a.m. She fell on the Sharansky Steps above Ralph Bunche Park, injuring her head and arm. She was unconscious but still breathing when discovered by passersby but died en route to Tisch Hospital and was pronounced dead on arrival.

When asked whether drugs or foul play was involved in this sudden, shocking death—Mrs. Thraxton was a month shy of her 30th birthday—NYPD detective Luis Villaverde dismissed the idea. He called the incident an "unlucky accident," adding that the socialite was caught on multiple security cameras during her run and there was nothing suspicious. "Plenty of folks have heart conditions they don't know about," he added. Detective Villaverde refused to answer questions about any possible drug use by the victim.

Mrs. Thraxton was the wife of Theodore Thraxton II, heir to the Thraxton International hotel fortune. Caroline Thraxton was employed by the company as their director of public relations. Mr. Thraxton could not be reached for comment, but his sister, Juliet Thraxton, released a statement to the press on behalf of the family.

"We are devastated by Caroline's death," the statement says. "It is a tremendous shock to us all. We can't believe she's gone."

Caroline Thraxton is survived by her husband and her three-year-old son, Theodore Thraxton III, known to the family as Teddy.

My head buzzed and blood drummed inside my ears. It was like being a kid again, listening to the awful fighting going on in the next room, knowing I was powerless to fix it. There was a sharp pain in my chest, and I hunched over on the futon, hugging my knees, but that didn't help.

"You're not powerless," I reminded myself out loud. "You can't save your sister, but you can get justice for her. This is all on you."

That determination propelled me forward. I brushed my teeth and fixed my makeup, feeling like a warrior readying for combat. I needed a tough shell if I was going to do what I had to for my sister. I flipped through the prints one more time.

"Damn it, Caro, couldn't you have given me something solid, like the name of the first wife?" I muttered.

I tucked the photos and memory card back into the envelope. Then I pulled on a pair of tall black leather boots. I had one shot to round up some real evidence, and I wasn't going to miss it.

# CHAPTER 4

## THEO

*I don't want to be married to you anymore. Why is that so hard to understand, Theo? Get out of my house.*

When I stepped inside the church, I was surrounded by people, but all I could hear was my wife's voice taunting me. Guests came up in turn, telling me how sorry they were. None of them were as sorry as I was.

It was impossible to believe that a little over a week earlier, I'd been in Bangkok, meeting with government officials and representatives from Thailand's national museum about how to recover stolen artifacts. It had been oppressively hot and humid, to the point where the air seemed to shimmer at midday. I attempted to focus my mind in that direction.

It wasn't enough to stop my heart from thudding a fatal drumbeat.

*Get out of my house.*

Those were the last words Caroline said to me before she died.

All I wanted was to steel myself to deliver her eulogy. I ducked into a tiny alcove at the back of the church for a few moments of quiet. Instead, I found my father and sister, chatting away like magpies.

"You have to admit it's an impressive turnout," my father said. "I haven't seen this many people inside one building since the pandemic hit. Caroline was truly adored, wasn't she?"

"They're expecting a show, and they love a free lunch," Juliet answered drily. "Half of them don't know who Caroline was. The rest want to see what she looks like in the casket."

"Your jealousy is showing again," my father replied. "It's downright ugly, Juliet."

"Am I supposed to pretend I'm sorry she's dead?"

That was the moment they noticed me. My father was the first to recover.

"Theo. How are you holding up, son? You look exhausted. Are you sure you're up to delivering the eulogy? You don't have to, you know. I would be honored to speak about Caroline."

"I don't need your help." I was dreading the eulogy, but I'd be damned if anyone else delivered it.

"There it is, the old Thraxton charm," Juliet said. "Sweet as a viper and twice as deadly. What a lady-killer."

My sister was four years older than I was, and we despised each other. I felt bad about snapping at my father, because my sister was the one who deserved it.

"You look ridiculous," I said. "Thanks for providing the comic relief at a funeral."

It wasn't much, but Juliet was sensitive about any comment on her appearance. She flinched.

"Stop it, both of you," my father whispered, as if we were still children.

"Someone should greet the guests, instead of hiding back here," Juliet said. "I guess I'm stuck doing all the work, as usual." She strutted off, without a backward glance.

"I know it's a heartbreaking day for you, son." My father waved one hand, carelessly gesturing at the church. "I tried to make it something

Caroline would've enjoyed. The flowers. The music." He stared at the scene in front of us as if in a trance. "White roses and Mozart. She loved his Requiem." He chuckled softly. "Remember when she said she wished you could use it for your wedding? She thought it was romantic."

Caroline and I loved not only the music but also the legend of the anonymous man who commissioned the Requiem and the composer who'd attempted to steal it after Mozart's death. When we met, I discovered that underneath Caroline's sunny exterior beat a heart that loved all things dark and gothic. That wasn't anything I wanted to share with my father. "Thank you. I couldn't have managed it myself."

"Of course." My father's smile dimmed. "Did you tell the nanny she could sit in the family pew?"

"Yes. Teddy is closer to Gloria than he is to just about anyone else."

"It's bad optics, Theo. Imagine a reporter getting a photo of Teddy being comforted by the help during the service. That doesn't look good for any of us."

"You can't imagine how little I care about optics," I said.

"Well, I do. Why couldn't you leave Teddy with your sister?"

"I wouldn't entrust a tadpole to Juliet's care."

"That's not fair. She's great with animals." He grinned at me, as if he'd made a terrific joke.

"Where's Ursula?" I asked. Ursula was my stepmother, and the only person in my family whose company I enjoyed, even though I was well aware that her pleasant temperament was managed by a steady supply of wine and vodka.

"She had a little accident this morning," my father said.

"What happened?"

"She fell and hurt her wrist. Harris took her to the doctor in case it's fractured."

Harris was my father's assistant and bodyguard, all rolled up in one grim package. "She was drunk?"

My father glanced around, in case a pair of ears was too close, and nodded.

"I understand if you want to leave here to see her," I said.

"And reward her little stunt by missing Caroline's funeral?" My father shook his head. "Look at all these people. The biggest funeral our family ever had was my father's. But we didn't have all of these fine-feathered friends turning up for it. He was well off, but people looked down on him. The Motel King. This is like something you see on TV."

"Don't talk about Caroline's funeral as if it were a social occasion."

"A funeral *is* a social event. People loved Caroline. Some of those nasty little basement bloggers called her a 'climbing vine,' given her roots, but Caroline was a genuinely good person. She was kind and generous. Pair those traits up with money, and you have a recipe for social success. Even if her family came with more baggage than a Boeing Triple Seven bound for Disney World." He grimaced. "I should've sent Harris out to buy her father a suit. Did you see that shiny getup he's wearing? Looks like he made it out of a space blanket. I'd worry about photos, but the glare would blind anyone. Is he coming to lunch?"

"You will be respectful toward Caroline's family," I insisted, but my brain was stuck on something else he'd said. *Caroline was a genuinely good person.*

"I've never been anything *but* kind to Caroline's relatives, son." He frowned and walked away from me, shaking his head.

*I don't want to be married to you anymore. Why is that so hard to understand, Theo? Get out of my house.*

I hovered at the edge of the alcove, refusing to let my brain revisit what had happened next. It was impossible to get enough air into my lungs.

"Is it time?" the priest asked me.

"I need a few moments alone," I said. "Is there somewhere private?"

"Of course. Follow me." He led me through a small portal, then opened a door, revealing a private chapel. There were candles burning in front of a statue of a beautiful woman whose face was clouded with sorrow.

"Take your time," the priest added.

"Thank you."

He shut the door behind me. I stood stock still, waiting for the panic to subside. My body shuddered as if I'd walked into a freezer. How could I go through with the funeral, or anything else? This day would be endless, just as the day before had been, and the next one would be. I didn't know how I would ever explain Caroline's death to our son.

*Caroline was a genuinely good person,* my father claimed. No, she wasn't. She'd put up an amazing facade that fooled many people, but underneath was something hard and steely and vicious.

The quivering in my hands reverberated through my body. I approached the shrine, then collapsed on my knees—as if in prayer—but I had no words for a higher power. I hadn't been raised with any religion, and I wasn't even sure whom the statue represented. The Virgin Mary? Some dolorous saint with her eyes fixed on the next world because this one was too painful to bear? Instead, I gazed at the dozens of flickering candles, glimmering like beacons in a storm.

*I am full of hidden horrors,* whispered a voice in the back of my mind. That wasn't Caroline; this voice was in my head long before I met her.

There was nothing I wouldn't do to drown it out.

Stretching out my left hand, I set my palm atop a candle. As my flesh extinguished its flame, I felt a rush of pain that brought tears to my eyes. Its razor sharpness was fleeting, but the hot, throbbing sensation that came in its wake focused my thoughts in one clear, untroubled direction. I reached for another flame, and another, telling myself to stop but not being able to. When all the candles were out, and the air was singed with smoke and the oddly sweet smell of grease, I rose, nodding my head at the marble woman in a muted show of thanks. Then I made my exit, finally ready to deliver my wife's eulogy.

# CHAPTER 5

## DEIRDRE

I took a few diaphragm breaths before making the call. When my brother-in-law answered, I said, "Hey, Theo, this is Deirdre. Could you pick me up on your way to the cemetery?" The words made me queasy. I hated asking for favors. Any dummy could've hopped in a cab and made it to Green-Wood, but it was the only way I could think of to get time alone with Theo to talk.

"I just left the restaurant, but there's a car waiting there for you," Theo said. "I'll find out exactly where it is."

"I didn't go to lunch. I came home. Could you pick me up at Queens Plaza?"

"What happened? Are you ill?"

"I'm fine, Theo. I just need you to pick me up." This wasn't for me. It was for Caro. "I need to talk to you."

"Hold on." I heard a soft conversation in the background. "We'll head over the Queensboro Bridge. I'll text you when we're close to Queens Plaza."

He was good to his word. When he showed up, I leaped into the black town car. "Thanks for doing this," I muttered.

"Are you certain you're all right?" Theo asked. He looked genuinely worried. I recoiled under his gaze.

"No," I admitted. "The whole world feels like it's broken. I keep hoping this is a nightmare, and maybe I'll wake up. I still can't believe she's gone."

"Neither can I," Theo said. "I didn't sleep at all last night."

In the church, at a distance, my brother-in-law had looked like his usual self: impeccably dressed, ramrod posture, coldly attractive. Up close, he was worn out. There were purplish half-moons under his eyes, and his skin seemed sallow. His mouth was set in a firm line, and his jaw was so taut I could almost hear him grinding his teeth. My gaze slid down to his hands. One palm was raw and red and blistered.

"What the hell happened to your hand?" I asked.

He froze for a nanosecond before turning it over, out of view. "It must've happened when I hit that creep bothering Teddy."

In that moment, I knew Theo was lying to me. His knuckles were a little dinged up, but that didn't explain the scarlet wound on his palm. There was an uncomfortable moment when I couldn't help but stare, examining an old scar slithering under his French cuff. I could only catch the edge of it, but it was enough to remind me of the profile my sister had written about him. That was how they'd met in the first place. The article had a weird little anecdote in it about how Theo had been mauled by a zoo animal—a lion or a tiger—as a child. I made a mental note to look it up as soon as I could.

In the meantime, I had questions, but I didn't know where to start. "That was a good service this morning," I ventured.

"Really?" He frowned. "You thought so?"

"No, I hated it. But Caro would've appreciated it."

Theo sighed. "That was what my father thought. He planned every last detail."

"How was lunch?"

"It was like a circle of Dante's hell but with worse company. My father arranged for *religieuses au chocolat* for dessert," he said, referring to a tiered eclair that I couldn't imagine anyone but Caro liking. "Caroline's favorite. It was horrible."

"I'm glad I skipped it."

"It was surreal to sit there and watch a roomful of people having a wonderful time. This was just another party for them." He stared out the window.

"I don't know how Caro tolerated people like that." In that moment I remembered why I'd always liked Theo: we bonded over our shared misanthropy. "Was my father there?"

"He was." He turned his head toward me. "Was that why you didn't come?"

I shrugged. "Part of it."

"Even now, you two aren't speaking?" Theo asked.

I shook my head. "Nope."

"I haven't spoken to my father much in the past couple of years," Theo said. "But since Caroline died, I've been pulled back into his orbit."

"Why did you and your dad stop speaking?"

"He hasn't forgiven me for leaving the family business," Theo said. "He still calls it 'abandonment.' What about you?"

I really didn't want to get into it, especially right then. "My father and I never got along." That wasn't exactly the truth, but it would do for now.

"You didn't move out of your parents' house at fifteen because of that," Theo said. "It was his drinking, wasn't it?"

"Caro told you about that?"

"I know he was abusive," Theo said. "Not to you or Caroline—at least, not according to Caroline. But toward your mother."

I nodded, grateful that I didn't have to explain. My sister always had been our father's defender; it was the main reason we'd stopped speaking for several years. There was so much more to say, but nothing I wanted to add at that moment.

"Caroline said he'd had a problem with alcohol that made him abusive," Theo added. "But she also insisted that he's been sober for some time now. I'd never allow him near Teddy if he weren't."

"Sure, blame the alcohol," I muttered. It was typical of Caro—blame the drug and give the monster a pass. I cleared my throat. There were hard questions I had to ask. "Theo, a reporter at the funeral asked me if my sister was using drugs. I know that's crazy, but . . ."

"She was taking several prescriptions. It's unclear whether that affected her heart."

To my ears, he sounded defensive. My spine stiffened. "What exactly was she taking?"

"She went on an antidepressant after Teddy was born. I know she had prescriptions for anxiety and insomnia and headaches. Heartburn too."

I knew Caro had suffered from migraines and postpartum depression, but I had trouble believing the rest. My sister had always been a healthy person. "When did she start taking antianxiety meds?"

"I don't know. She never discussed it with me."

"What about illegal—"

He cut me off before I could finish my question. "I'm sure Caroline would never. As far as I know, red wine was her hardest vice."

"I didn't mean my sister. I meant you," I said, determined to rattle his calm front. "You used to be an addict, right? Have you taken anything illicit lately?"

"No, not in years." He looked genuinely surprised by the question, and I couldn't blame him. My father had regularly transformed into a monster under the influence of alcohol, and I couldn't help but wonder if Theo made a similar werewolf-like switch. I was still struggling to reconcile what I knew of Theo—a stand-up guy who worked for a nonprofit that repatriated stolen artifacts—with the man Caro had written about in her letter. "I had a double scotch at lunch," he added sheepishly. "I wasn't sure how to get through it otherwise."

He sounded honest, but I had to be skeptical. "I never saw a copy of the autopsy report. Would you be able to give me one?"

"There was no autopsy."

That jolted me. My sister's death was a terrible shock, and I'd been wallowing in grief instead of demanding answers. That had changed with my sister's message. Everything had changed. "Why not? Isn't that automatic when a person dies suddenly?"

"Only if there's evidence of foul play."

I swallowed hard. "What if there was, Theo?"

He stared at me blankly. "Was what?"

"Foul play." I leaned forward. "What if someone killed her?"

Theo and I stared at each other for a wary moment. He nonchalantly adjusted one gold cuff link. Again, I could see the edge of the scar on his wrist. Caro didn't confide much, but she'd told me he was covered in scars.

"You think the man she was seeing did . . . something to her?" Theo asked.

That answer was not on my bingo card. I'd expected him to downplay my suspicions, not invent a suspect. "What man?"

"Caroline wasn't just out for a jog the morning she died," Theo said. "We both know that, don't we? She was meeting someone."

His voice was quiet, but the words stabbed at my heart. He was actually accusing my dead sister of cheating on him.

"There was no other man," I snapped. "She would never do that."

"She wanted a divorce," Theo shot back. "Why would she ask for that if no one else was involved?"

It was my turn to stare dully at him. Finally, I croaked out, "Divorce?"

A shadow crossed his face. "I thought perhaps you knew." Theo turned his eyes to the window. "Caroline played everything close to the vest. She never really confided in anyone, did she?"

"When did this come up?"

"A couple of months ago," Theo said.

"Did you agree to it?"

Theo's answer was so quiet I almost missed it. "No."

The car gave a jolt, and I realized we had crossed the broad, grand gates of Brooklyn's Green-Wood Cemetery. *It's now or never,* I told myself. There was no graceful way to do this.

"Maybe Caro wanted a divorce because she found out about your first wife," I said.

"*What* did you say?"

"Is your first wife buried here in the Thraxton family plot?"

He glared at me without answering.

"You're not denying she exists, are you?" My voice was getting louder.

He glanced at his watch and looked out the window. I wanted to grab him by the lapels of his expensive suit and shake him until the truth rattled loose out of his skull.

"Where's your first wife buried, Theo?"

"How is that any of your business?"

The last shreds of any doubt fell away. My sister's message wasn't crazy. There had been a first Mrs. Theo Thraxton, even if that secret was lying in a cold grave.

"I don't know, Theo. Caro's dead. Your first wife is dead. Isn't that what police call a pattern?"

In a heartbeat, the air between us froze into ice. I knew he'd never speak to me again. But that didn't matter. He'd said enough.

When the car stopped, Theo got out and slammed the door behind him. I knew I should've been afraid of what he could do to me, what he could get away with, but I was powered by a cold rage of my own. He was responsible for my sister's death. Even if it killed me, I'd get justice for her.

# CHAPTER 6

## DEIRDRE

The gravesite felt like a minefield. There was a glowering Theo on one side and my father simmering on the other. I was glad when Theo's father came up to me.

"How are you holding up, Deirdre?" he asked. He was a dapper man—whenever I saw him, he was always fully suited up. He was shorter than his son, and his blue eyes were paler and his hair was iron gray instead of black, but the resemblance to Theo was still strong. It was the personalities that were polar opposites: Theo was as withdrawn as his father was gregarious.

"Not well," I admitted. It didn't seem right to tell him that his son was the reason why, at least not within Theo's earshot.

"Same here," he said. "When you feel up to it, I'd love for you to come over."

"Your son won't want to spend time around me."

He shot a glance Theo's way. "He doesn't get a vote. Anyway, he's not invited. I was thinking you, me, Teddy, and Ursula for dinner."

Ursula was Theo's stepmother. She had a serious drinking problem, which made me wary of her, but she'd always been nice enough.

"Sure. I'd like that." I looked around. "Teddy's not here, is he?"

"No. I thought it would be too much for him."

I nodded at that. It was almost too much for me.

The service started, led by the same priest who'd officiated at the church. I didn't want to think about my sister being lowered into the dank, wormy ground. Instead, I focused on Theo, whose eyes stayed fixed on the angel guarding the family plot. She was a graceful stone maiden with wings so finely carved you could make out the pattern of her feathers. Her face was obscured as she wept over a white marble block with **THRAXTON** carved in bold letters. The graves were subtly marked with small stone plaques.

After Caro's casket was lowered into the ground, the family was supposed to take handfuls of rose petals and sprinkle them into the yawning pit. No one wanted to do it. Theo stayed back, as did his father and mine. For the first time, I realized Juliet was absent; it seemed in character for her to refuse to set foot in Brooklyn. In the end, no one touched the rose petals but Caro's friend Jude Lazare and me. We threw in one handful after another. They were dark red against the burnished mahogany of the casket.

*Like blood,* I thought.

After the brief ceremony, my father stormed off. Watching him out of the corner of my eye, I noted that he didn't even speak to the priest, which showed how overcome he was by burying his eldest child. I looked around for anyone I wanted to talk to and spotted Jude. She was standing at the top of one of Green-Wood's rolling hills with another woman, and I walked up to join them. As I did, I noticed a man in the distance, watching us. He was tall and sandy haired, casually dressed in jeans and a gray shirt. He wore dark sunglasses, and I expected to see a camera in his hands, but they were jammed into his pockets. Caro wasn't a celebrity, but she was well-enough known in New York to garner tabloid interest.

For a split second, I wondered if I knew him. There was something vaguely familiar. But he was sly and picked up on my approach without looking directly at me. He turned his back and rushed off.

On instinct, I started after him. Theo's accusations were still reverberating in my head. No way had Caro been cheating on him. My sister wouldn't do that.

Jude's voice broke into my thoughts and stopped me in my tracks. "She was going crazy, and she needed help." Jude's back was to me, but the breeze carried her voice over clearly. "But not the kind of help you give."

The woman facing her was African American, tall and willowy, with graying braids coiled atop her head like a crown. But her voice was too soft for me to make out. All I heard were a few disjointed words, maybe catching every fifth one. "Don't . . . help . . . let . . . forget . . ." It was impossible to eavesdrop properly.

"That's not true, and you shouldn't have encouraged her."

I stepped closer and heard the tail end of the soft-voiced woman's retort: " . . . listened to her." But my movement caught Jude's attention, and her head swiveled my way.

"Deirdre," Jude said, moving toward me and pulling me into an awkward side hug. "How are you doing?"

"You're Caroline's sister?" The other woman turned to face me, her eyes warm and curious. "It's an honor to meet you. I know Caroline adored you."

That brought a lump to my throat. "Thanks."

"I'm Adinah Gerstein," she added, drawing her hands together as if she were praying and holding them over her heart. That had become a popular way of greeting people since the pandemic, and I liked it better than I ever had a handshake. "I have to tell you how sorry I am about Caroline. She was an amazing woman."

"I need to talk to Deirdre," Jude said. "Would you mind excusing us?"

"Of course." Adinah quietly backed away, giving us privacy.

"I'm sorry we didn't get to talk at the church," Jude said. Her brown eyes were red rimmed, but otherwise she looked beautiful. She wore a simple black dress and jacket, and her dark curly hair was pinned back in a restrained bun. She wore no jewelry except a small silver crucifix. She'd been born in Haiti but raised in Queens; she and Caro had been best friends since middle school. "Be honest—how are you holding up?"

"Who was that woman?" I asked.

"Adinah runs Diotima," Jude said. "Caroline gave them a lot of help from the time she was in college."

I recognized the name immediately—Caro was devoted to the Diotima Civic Society—but I had something else on my mind. "What were you saying about Caro going crazy?" I demanded.

"Oh, no, that wasn't . . . um, that wasn't about her. I'm sorry if it sounded that way, Dee."

"Oh." I felt foolish. My confrontation with Theo had left me paranoid.

"There is something else that's going to make you upset with me," Jude said. "Your father asked me to give you this, and I said I would."

She held out a small square box made of plain brown paper. It fit in the palm of her hand.

"Whatever it is, I don't want it," I said.

"Won't you even open it?"

"Nope." I didn't want anything from my father, ever, and I didn't plan to explain why. Even though they were close, I was pretty sure my sister had kept Jude in the dark about our father's true nature. Why else would she still speak with him? "But I need to ask you something. Did you know Theo was married before?"

"What are you talking about?"

"He had a first wife. Caro didn't mention that?"

Jude's face was stunned and intrigued all at once. "She never breathed a word to me. Theo's *divorced*?" She said the word with horror.

Jude was a devout Catholic, and that fact reared its head at the oddest times. I considered showing her Caroline's message. But we couldn't talk about it with Thraxton minions nearby.

"No, she's dead," I admitted. "I asked Theo about her, and he stormed off."

"To be fair to him, he's dealing with a terrible loss."

"I drove here with Theo, and he basically accused Caro of sleeping with another man."

"That's horrible," Jude whispered. "What exactly did he say?"

"That she was meeting with another guy the morning she died. Can you believe that? It's so obviously insane."

"Right." Jude blinked a couple of times. "Exactly. Insane."

Her reaction bothered me. It didn't seem like she thought the idea was that crazy. "*Was* Caro seeing someone else?"

Jude considered my question. "She never said that, but you know—aside from coparenting Teddy—they were basically living separate lives."

"Do you remember when that started?"

"Maybe a year after Teddy was born? Right around the time Theo left the family business."

"That's how I think of it too," I said. "Caro said Theo thought he was better than the rest of his family. But I remember thinking it was a lot cooler to be tracking down stolen idols like Indiana Jones instead of working for a hotel chain."

"He spends more time in boardrooms than ancient temples," Jude answered wryly. "Caroline felt like he was leaving her in the lurch."

"Because of her postpartum depression?"

"She struggled hard with it," Jude said. "Caroline told me her in-laws were really supportive of her, but Theo wasn't. He wanted her to travel with him. Just bring the baby and go. Oh, and he wanted her to quit her job at his family's company and become a journalist again. But Caroline needed help. Her in-laws stepped up. Theo didn't."

I recognized the truth of Jude's words. Theo's sister had never done much for her, but Theo's father and stepmother had. I knew Caro genuinely loved them.

"Do you think Theo would ever hurt Caroline?"

"Physically? No."

The ache to show her Caro's message was stronger than ever. *What's holding you back?* I asked myself. No matter what, I hated airing my family's dirty laundry.

"Did you know she wanted to divorce Theo?" I asked.

Jude was silent, pursing her lips. Her phone buzzed.

I was incredulous. "You knew?"

Jude touched my arm. "Caroline swore me to secrecy," she said. "Even though she's gone, I can't talk about it." She glanced at her phone. "I'm sorry, but I have to get going." Jude worked for the mayor, and she always had other places to be.

She tugged me into another awkward half-hug.

"You know you can call me if there's anything you need—at any time—right?" she asked. "Please take care of yourself, Dee."

Jude took off across the green grass with unusual speed for someone in heels. I shouldn't have been surprised that my sister had confided far more in her best friend than she had in me. Caro and Jude had been close all their lives. I was Caro's baby sister, and there was a long gap in our relationship that we'd papered over but never really resolved. I could pretend it didn't bother me, but the truth was the distance between us had always hurt like hell.

# CHAPTER 7

## Deirdre

Everyone else cleared out of the cemetery before I did. I watched grave-diggers from a distance, filling in the void around Caro's coffin, and I wanted to cry. I knew I should have shown my sister's message to Jude, but I hadn't been able to work up the nerve. It still felt unreal. I pulled out my phone and looked at the letter again.

The logical option was to go to the cops, but my experiences with the NYPD when I was a teenager made me never want to set foot in another police station. I knew they'd laugh at me if I went in armed only with that email. I needed more, and I had to dredge it up myself.

That meant starting with Osiris's Vault. Under Caro's words was some boilerplate legalese about privacy and opting out of future messages, which felt like a bad joke. But I kept scrolling and found the company's address in the Bronx. I walked to the nearest subway stop, passing businesses offering headstone engraving and other funeral services. They certainly hadn't vanished in the pandemic. I got on the R train and headed back into Manhattan, switching at Union Square for the 4 express train north.

The subway spat me out at Yankee Stadium. I'd heard that games would start up again, but the neighborhood was so desolate I wondered if a nuclear blast had gone unreported. The first couple of blocks east of the train were boarded up, some with restaurant signs forlornly hanging above. After I passed Walton Street, there were signs of life: people young and old in Joyce Kilmer Park, ringed around the fountain, and others congregating on the steps of the majestic Bronx courthouse. But after that it got eerily quiet again. Even the sidewalk was a mess, with broken concrete slabs and ringed with tall weeds. I turned left at Sheridan Avenue, which had fewer abandoned storefronts but more bail bondsman offices. It felt like a tumbleweed might blow by at any moment.

"This looks like a place where you'd find messages from dead people," I murmured aloud.

The front door was shut tight, of course. This was the kind of place where you'd lock down a bag of chips. Next to the door was a rusty buzzer with company names and suite numbers. It looked like it'd been updated around the time I'd been born, when some eager beaver got a label maker. Osiris's Vault wasn't on the list, but something called Joy Spa was. I pressed some buzzers until a garbled human voice came through the intercom.

She let me in.

Inside, the hallway was blindingly bright with yellow walls. The result was pathologically cheerful, like someone thought they could drag sunshine indoors against its will. I spotted Osiris's digs from down the hall, thanks to a blown-up image of their dead god—his skin a brighter green than his digital twin's—attached to the door. There was a keypad lock, and on impulse I tapped in 9-5-7, the code my employer used on an identical lock—the numbers formed a little triangle. At a soft click, I pushed the door open.

Inside the offices, it looked like someone had sprayed Martian blood on the walls. Beyond an open doorway were seven people at computers in a socially distant hive that could've easily seated twenty.

Images of Osiris were stenciled on the wall. Somebody really liked that graphic.

Nobody looked up when I invaded the hive, probably because they all had headphones on. I scanned the worker bees carefully. No tech company worth a damn handed out client information without a subpoena. I was looking for an ally, someone who'd help me out because of sympathy or sadness. I picked a woman with candy-pink hair and an impressively large silver ring lodged in her nasal septum.

"Hi," I said. "My name is Deirdre Crawley. I got a message from my sister through Osiris's Vault. Could you help me find out—"

"Noah!" the woman shouted, without even a glance at me. "We've got another one!"

A man's head popped up over a cubicle at the far end of the room. "Can I help you?"

"I got a message from my sister, Caroline Crawley Thraxton," I said, opting to use her maiden and married names, in case that might jog his memory. "She passed away last week."

"Condolences." He dispensed the word slowly, like it was honey in his mouth. "I'm Noah, manager for community relations." He slunk out from behind the cubicle wall, a scrawny man with spiky ginger hair cut flat across the top. Thanks to his pointy goatee, his head was a perfect triangle. He sported Buddy Holly glasses, an eyebrow ring, and a tattoo of a mandala on his forearm. A perfect hipster trifecta.

"Deirdre Crawley." I took a step closer.

"Whoa." Noah put up his hands, as if I'd pulled a knife on him. "Step back. More."

"Okay." People had been jittery about their personal space since the pandemic. A couple of worker bees had pulled off their headphones and were watching me. "Like I said, I'm here because of my sister. Today, at her funeral, I got a message saying that if she died, it was because her husband was going to kill her."

"Let me get you a form."

"Maybe I wasn't clear. My sister said her husband was going to kill her, and now she's dead." I gulped. I'd psyched myself up to tell the story in an unemotional way. I wasn't ready to fill out paperwork.

"Hold on," Noah said, ducking back toward his cubicle. He threw a bright-green sheet of paper at me. "This is what you need."

I caught it in midair. "My sister might have been murdered. In her message, she said—"

"Fill out the form." Noah's face was impassive.

"Her message said her husband, Theo Thraxton, killed his first wife. Until I read that, I didn't know he had a first wife. Nobody did. But it's true."

"Fill out the form."

All over my body, muscles were clenching in tight knots. I was desperate. "Can you at least tell me when her message was created?"

"We can't give information out about our clients. That would be a violation of confidentiality."

"But she's *dead*."

Noah shrugged.

"What will the form do for me?" I asked.

Noah sighed, as if I were being obtuse. "Then we'll check our records to see what information we can release."

I couldn't hide my disappointment, but I fished a pen out of my bag. The questions on the form were basic: my name and address, my sister's name and address, the reason for my inquiry. I filled it in, writing *My sister was murdered* as the reason for my query. Noah took back the form, holding it at arm's length between thumb and forefinger.

"Okay. Now you need to go. You'll hear from us in the next thirty days."

I choked. "Thirty days?"

"Look, we're a digital-storage service that promises our clients absolute confidentiality," Noah said. "We don't give information to anyone who walks in off the street."

"But the message said there were files."

"Then click through for them."

"There weren't any!"

"That means you're not authorized to see them," Noah said. "That's a dead end."

"I came here before talking to the cops," I said, desperate to spur him to action. "You want them to come in here?"

"They can fill out the form too." Noah shut the door behind me.

I braced myself against the wall, feeling physically ill. I'd been operating under a delusion, telling myself if people knew there was something suspicious about my sister's tragic death, they'd help me. If Noah was anything to go by, I was dead wrong. Worse, I'd had visions of myself finding a key piece of evidence, bringing it to the cops, and forcing them to investigate Theo. But I was closing in on a truth I wanted to avoid: I had no clue what the hell I was doing.

I left the building with my tail between my legs. Outside, on the cracked sidewalk, I kicked the side of the building. I did it again and again, until my foot hurt.

*Bring him to justice, no matter what you have to do,* Caro had written. My sister had faith in me, but it was misguided.

I lurched away from the building, my foot aching. I felt like an idiot. Moving slowly, I made my way south back toward 161st Street. After a block, I heard steps behind me. Turning, I spotted a heavyset guy hurrying toward me. "Hey!" he called, waving.

"Hey," I answered back. He'd been tucked into a cube in the office, though all I'd seen of him was a shaved head and a T-shirt with "Rough Trade" written across the top. As he came closer, I could make out the photo underneath. It looked like an album cover, with two androgynous figures, one in silhouette and the other in a white suit. When we were finally face-to-face, I realized the suited character was a curiously attractive woman.

He noticed me staring at it. "Carole Pope. She's an icon."

I didn't recognize the name, but I nodded. "Cool shirt."

"Noah sucks," the guy said, slightly out of breath. "He just called you a bitch and shredded your form."

"I regret not poking him in the eye. I should go back and take care of that."

"He gets away with shit on account of being the CEO's kid brother." The guy took a couple of breaths. "I really need to get out more. I'm Todd, by the way."

"Deirdre."

He handed me a folded sheet of paper. "I printed this for you."

I unfolded the page. *Caroline Crawley—account created April 3, 3:25 p.m.*

"That was two weeks before she died," I said. "What are the other dates on this page?"

"Most people create an account and log in a bunch of times to fine-tune their messages," Todd said. "Your sister logged in a lot on April third and fourth, checked in on the eleventh, then not again until the fifteenth."

I scanned them and almost stopped breathing at the last one. "April fifteenth, 5:17 a.m. That's the day she died." I stared at him. "You're telling me my sister wrote this message to me right before she died?"

"She started writing a message to you before that," Todd said. "I can't tell you about earlier versions. They're on a server somewhere, but you really will need a subpoena to get them."

"Why did I only get her message a week after she died?"

"That was the dead man's switch."

"The dead man's *what?*" My shock must've shown in my face, because Todd took a step back and put a hand up, like he was warding off evil.

"Don't freak out," he said. "You never heard that phrase? It's a security feature, basically a fail-safe. It's dormant so long as a person is checking in on it, but if they fail to log in within a certain time frame . . . boom. It goes off."

"The letter went out because my sister didn't check in?"

"Exactly. Her account was set for a week-long delay."

My eyes stung as if a thousand invisible hornets were attacking me. "Sorry." I wiped away a tear. "That's helpful."

"The bad news is the dead man's switch deleted all her files," Todd said.

"But the police can get that with a subpoena, right?"

He shook his head. "We're called Osiris's Vault for a reason. Our shit is locked down tight. Those files are gone for good. There's no way to recover them."

I felt so lost at that moment. My sister needed my help, and there wasn't a damned thing I could do for her.

"The other thing I can tell you is that your sister wrote messages to three people," Todd added.

I took a breath. If Caroline had written to me, she'd surely sent a message to our father as well. "Let me guess: Ryan Crawley?"

"Yeah. I didn't print that one out because I figured he's family, and he can show it to you. I don't need more trouble."

"Oh," I said, disappointed but unwilling to spill the truth, which was this: I was more likely to visit the moon than see any message Caro sent our father. She had always been close to him. When she'd had to choose between us, she'd taken his side. "Was the other one to Theo Thraxton?"

Todd shrugged. "Maybe? I don't know. In the name field, your sister put an *X*."

"Like *X* marks the spot?" I asked. *Heathcliff* was the only alias I remembered her using for Theo.

Todd shrugged. "I figured you'd know. I wrote down the email address for you." He handed me another piece of paper. "With the message."

My hands shook as I unfolded the page. There was Caroline's third message in black and white:

> If I fail, you have to do it. I am putting all of my faith
> and trust in you. My son's future depends on it.

"What the hell?" I asked aloud.

"It made the hair on the back of my neck stand up," Todd said. "It's spooky as fuck, right?"

It was, and it tightened the knot in the pit of my stomach. What had my sister been up to before she died?

# CHAPTER 8

## DEIRDRE

That evening, I had energy to burn, so I went to my dojo to punch and kick the heavy bag until it gave in. It was too late for a class, but Sensei Higashi kept the dojo open until eleven for students who wanted to train on their own. He was in a corner, jumping rope so fast you couldn't see the cord, though it cracked against the splintery wooden floor now and again. I was working on the bag when my best friend walked in. I caught sight of Reagan in the mirror.

"How'd you know I would be here?" I asked her.

"Where *else* would you be on the day of your sister's funeral?" she answered. "You're nothing if not predictable."

We were in the same rectangular room where we'd started studying karate together when we were seven. A mirrored wall ran along one side, with a framed photograph of Dr. Chitose, the founder of the Chito-ryu style of karate, hanging above it. The other walls were mangy gray, equal parts old paint and smoke from the pool hall that shared the hallway with the Higashi School of Karate. Around the dojo were black-lettered banners saying things like *Only those who have patience to do simple things perfectly can do difficult things easily.* At seven, I'd been a pocket-sized cynic who read that as a hackneyed cliché. That hadn't changed.

"You suiting up to spar?" I asked.

"Facing off against you in a mood? No, thanks." She set down the duffel bag she was holding. "Tiger Mom is worried you'll get rickets from living on protein bars. She cooked for you."

"She's the best," I said.

"You say that because you don't live with her anymore," Reagan said. "Last Saturday, I slept in until eight, and she lectured me about wasting my life. I told her I worked seventy hours last week and got a spiel on how hard she and my dad had to work when they were our age."

"I like that she's tough." Reagan's mom was named Vera, but I could only think of her as Mrs. Chen. She was incredibly kind, but also bracingly direct and opinionated. Now that Caro was gone, Reagan and her mom were the closest thing I had to family. When Reagan's dad had gotten sick with a brain tumor when we were ten, my best friend had practically moved in with my family. She stayed with us for the two years Mr. Chen suffered through before he died. Then Reagan and her mom had taken me in when I was a teenager who couldn't live in her parents' house anymore.

"She's kind of worried about you." Reagan crossed her arms. "She figured we'd hear from you after the funeral. I told her you'd be hiding out like a wounded wolf."

"It wasn't just the funeral. It was . . ." The words died on my lips. Reagan knew me well enough not to say anything. I took a few breaths from my diaphragm. That was one thing karate had taught me that I carried everywhere. "What would you say if I told you there's something suspicious about my sister's death?"

Reagan didn't flinch. "She died suddenly, and no one knew she had a heart condition. You *could* call that suspicious."

"More than that. Something else."

"Is this about a feeling you have, or evidence?" Reagan was a data analyst, and I had yet to meet anyone whose work matched their personality better than hers. She had a photographic memory and the ability to recall conversations perfectly. It could be annoying sometimes, because she questioned everything.

My phone was against the wall, charging. "I got a message from my sister today," I said, picking it up and scrolling through my email. When I found what I was looking for, I passed the phone to Reagan.

She stared at it for what felt like an hour. When she finally looked at me, she was frowning.

"It sounds like your sister," she said. "But are you a hundred percent sure it's real?"

I ticked the reasons off on my fingers. "She mentioned what our mom went through, and who else knows that? She called me Dodo, which was her nickname for me when I was a kid. I found out it's true that her husband was married before. What part doesn't ring true?"

"That first line—*I keep thinking of Mom, and how you never believe you're going to end up like one of your parents, until you do*—I can literally hear Caroline's voice in my head saying that," Reagan said. "But the part where she says to bring her husband to justice? What does she expect you to do?"

I had been wondering about that myself. "Maybe she meant I should go to the police. Or maybe she wanted me to do to Theo what I did to my father."

"Absolutely not." Reagan's voice was sharp. "Your sister cared about you. She wouldn't ask you to do something that would land you in jail, Dee. Stop thinking like that."

I sighed. She was right.

"Caro wrote it because she knew she was in danger," I said. "She was expecting something awful to happen."

"That makes sense," Reagan said. "But here's another thing that doesn't sound like Caroline: she knew Theo killed his first wife, and she *stayed* with him? No. She wouldn't do that."

Reagan was right about that too. She was good with puzzles, and she was sliding bits of information into place, creating a picture I could barely grasp the edges of. Maybe I wasn't ready to look at it.

"When I confronted Theo, he was shocked I knew about the first wife. Maybe Caro just found out about her? That could be what put her in danger."

"Back up," Reagan said. "What's this about you *confronting* Theo?"

"I was in the car with him on the way to Green-Wood. I felt like . . . like it was now or never. I had to find out if what Caro wrote was true."

"One day, you'll pass the marshmallow test, Dee. But today is not that day. You just lost the element of surprise."

"I don't care."

"Dee, if this guy killed his wife, what do you think he'll do to you?"

"I don't care," I repeated.

Reagan set the duffel bag on the floor and retrieved the medicine ball. It was a misshapen leather sphere weighed down, we suspected, with lead. Gyms had them, too, but the dojo's was unique. It looked like Dr. Chitose himself might've sent it over from Kumamoto, back in the day. It was no longer spherical, if you wanted to be picky about it, and it was crisscrossed with dozens of Frankenstein-worthy seams that were probably sewn with fishing wire. It had been in the dojo as long as I could remember.

She threw it at me. There was no way to catch it without absorbing some of the blow with my body.

"Okay, you've got some sense of self-preservation," Reagan observed.

I tossed it back. Reagan was five four, but she had a lot of muscle, and she caught the ball easily. "My sister trusted me," I said. "She sent me this message asking for help."

"Caroline could've sent your father a message too. Have you talked with him?"

I almost dropped the ball. Sometimes Reagan seemed to have ESP. There was no point hiding any detail from her, because she'd drag it out of me. "I went to the company that forwarded the message. They were assholes, but one guy tried to help me. Caro sent a message to our father, but I don't know what it said."

"You could ask him, you know."

"Ha ha. And there was a third message."

"To her friend Jude?" Reagan guessed.

I set the ball on the floor. I'd guessed Theo, but I'd been wrong. Jude was a much better guess.

"I don't know," I admitted, retrieving the page from my bag. "There's no name, just an *X*. This was the message."

Reagan took it in quickly, and her eyebrows shot up. "This is nuts. Is that Jude's email? It looks like a random string of numbers and letters."

"It's not the one I have for her."

"This is getting crazier by the minute. Who else was your sister tight with?"

I shrugged. "I can't think of anyone."

"Maybe the police can figure that part out."

"I don't have a lot of faith in cops."

"Fair enough, based on your experience," Reagan said. "Promise me one thing. You *will* go to the police. You *will not* try to get revenge on Theo by yourself."

"You think I can't take him?"

"Dee, listen to me. You can't do this alone," Reagan said. "If we're going to get justice for your sister, we need the police to be involved."

"We?"

"Yes. We," Reagan said. "Dummy."

There was a hard lump in my throat. "Okay. I'll talk to the cops before work tomorrow."

# CHAPTER 9

## DEIRDRE

I lay awake for a long time that night, staring at the ceiling in the dark and listening to the rumbling of my landlord's washing machine. Saira prowled around the house at night, sometimes vacuuming or mopping or scrubbing the walls until two or three in the morning. Wilson, the tenant in the room next to mine, was half my size but snored like a foghorn, and I caught every blast through the paper-thin drywall. Finally, I gave up pretending to sleep and reached for my computer.

There were two messages I needed to send. The first was to the mysterious X, and I typed the email address Todd had given me into a new message. Hi, I'm Deirdre Crawley, I wrote. I'm Caroline Thraxton's sister. I know she sent you a message to read after she died, and I want to talk to you about it. Can you message me back? Or call? Thanks. I added my phone number and pressed send.

One down. The next one would be harder to write.

I turned on the light and reached for the photos my sister had given me. Flipping through them, I found the one of Caro and the man I didn't know. *With Ben, at the Clarkson/Northcutt house in High Falls, New York.* I studied his face. He was handsome in a bland way—clean-cut hair, well-tanned white skin, chiseled features, perfect teeth—and

I found myself squinting at his image, trying to picture him in black shades like the man who'd been watching Caro's funeral from afar at Green-Wood. It could've been him, but that was just a guess. There was a lot about Ben Northcutt online. He was the definition of Intrepid Reporter, having been a finalist for the Pulitzer Prize. He'd written three books on politics, drugs, and terrorism in South America, focusing on the years he spent living in Colombia and Argentina. His website linked to articles he wrote for *Esquire* and *GQ* and the *New York Times* and the *Guardian*, and I devoured one after another. There were plenty about political corruption and the drug trade, but the ones that stayed with me were haunting, especially a series about human trafficking for slave labor in the mines of Venezuela and Colombia. Others were about the rehabilitation of child soldiers who still struggled with PTSD, gangs in Bogotá who used zombifying drugs on their victims, and the excavation of a World War II–era Nazi hideout in the middle of Argentina.

The bottom line was that Ben seemed like a badass. Even his author photo—unsmiling and serious, next to a pile of human skulls—was kind of thrilling. I took a deep breath and tapped out the world's dullest email—Hey Ben, this is Deirdre, Caroline Crawley's sister, I really need to talk to you—and gave him my phone number. There was nothing I could do but wait.

It was tempting to read more of Ben's work, but I remembered I meant to look up Caro's. When she'd graduated from SUNY's journalism school in New Paltz, we weren't speaking—I was seventeen then and living with Reagan and her mom—but I'd kept track of Caro online, reading some of her articles for women's magazines and travel sites and mocking them. It had been another two years before we'd spoken to each other, and right around that time she'd published a profile of Theo Thraxton in a glossy magazine I couldn't recall the name of. It came up quickly online. The title was "Thraxton Heir or Modern-Day Indiana Jones?," which was objectively terrible by any measure. It was part of a

"30 under 30" article, and it was short. But I remembered it was filled with curious nuggets that didn't usually turn up in puff pieces. I clicked on it and found a photo of Theo in a full-body neoprene wet suit, standing next to a broken stone head with seaweed on it. I started reading.

The Thraxton name is synonymous with luxury. With a hotel empire that operates in 38 countries, you would imagine that Theodore R. Thraxton Junior—or Theo, as he prefers to be called—has his hands full as the company's vice president and CEO of global operations. But Thraxton, 27, has an unusual side hustle, repatriating stolen antiquities to their home countries.

"The truth is, I never wanted to be in the hotel business," Thraxton admits. "That was my father's dream for me, and I failed on my first try when I was studying in Berlin." But Thraxton went on to enroll in Harvard's ambitious MBA/JD program, where he graduated near the top of his class.

"My intent wasn't to practice law," Thraxton says. "But I grew up seeing how people manipulate the law to get what they want. It's not a level playing field. I wanted to understand how to navigate the system." His first success happened last year, when he helped the Thai government recover several pieces of Ban Chiang pottery—believed to be at least 2,000 years old—from an American museum that would prefer not to be named.

"Museums tend to be careful about the provenance of pieces today, but that wasn't always true," Thraxton says. "It's part of the legacy of colonialism, holding on to other people's heritage."

Perhaps it's not surprising that Thraxton is such a high achiever at a young age—his mother, Penelope Archer, a legend of the London stage, won her first Laurence Olivier Award when she was eighteen for her starring role in *Romeo and Juliet*, and his father, Theodore Senior, famously bought his first luxury hotel with cash he won at a roulette table in Monte Carlo. "I come from a dramatic family," Theo admits. Asked about his own drama, he demurs. "The most dramatic episode of my life was when I was three years old and fell into the tiger enclosure at the Berlin Zoo," he says. "I'm lucky to be alive, even with all the scars. Drama, I can do without. I'd just like to do some good in the world."

I read the piece over twice. Other articles mentioned Theo, but they were boring business stories about Thraxton International's global expansion. More recently, pieces quoted him on issues like the campaign to return the Elgin Marbles to Greece. None of it was personal. I found a *New York Times* "Vows" column about Caro and Theo's wedding, but I couldn't bring myself to click on it just then. There were a couple of tabloid photos of the two of them together at charity balls, and then several of Caro splendidly dressed, but always alone. "Socialite Caroline Thraxton Chairs First Annual Gala for Domestic Violence Charity" popped up, and I noticed the byline belonged to Abby Morel, the reporter who'd tackled me at the church. I scanned it, but it was mostly pictures of rich people in fancy clothes. The charity in question was the Diotima Civic Society. It had come up the last time I'd argued with Caro—maybe a year ago—about how she'd become a corporate drone.

*You always wanted to be a journalist,* I'd said. *So why are you stuck doing publicity for a hotel chain?*

*I was a journalist for a while, and it was terrible,* Caro had answered. *I got to write puff pieces under my own byline, or work like hell for someone else's byline and let them take credit. In both cases, I worked for peanuts.*

*But journalism was your dream.*

*It was, but a lot's changed since then.* Caro didn't make a direct reference to the years we'd lost touch, but that floated between us uneasily. *I'm doing more good now than I ever did as a journalist. Diotima wouldn't be able to do their amazing work without funding.*

*That's great for now,* I'd snarked, *but the hotel chain probably won't survive the pandemic.*

Caro had smiled at that. *You'd be surprised how well it's doing.*

I closed my laptop and turned off the light. My heart squeezed so tight remembering my sister that it physically ached. I'd been roughed up in and out of the dojo plenty of times, but no other pain ever hurt that much.

# CHAPTER 10

## THEO

My sister-in-law's words haunted me at the gravesite. *Caro's dead. Your first wife is dead. Isn't that what police call a pattern?* It had come out of the blue, her rage so sudden and swift that I couldn't even process it.

She had caught me off guard. I wouldn't allow that to happen again.

But her words followed me for the rest of the day. Even in my bedroom that evening, they echoed in my mind. I found myself staring at the framed photographs that covered one wall. There was one in particular I couldn't take my eyes off: Caroline and me together on a boat. In the background was the sparkling deep sapphire of the Mediterranean and a cloudless azure sky. Caroline wore a mint-green bathing suit with a matching cover-up, disguising any hint of her pregnancy. I was barefoot but encased in a blue neoprene wet suit. We were both grinning, drunk on the blissful freedom of our honeymoon. Everything was perfect for a time.

Then it all changed.

I stared at that hopeful image, wondering where we had gone wrong. It had happened slowly and then very quickly, like a boulder picking up speed as it crashed downhill. When I ran our time together through my mind like an old newsreel, I could pinpoint the moments of crisis and bad decisions. I didn't want to think about the ones I'd made; it was so much easier to be angry at Caroline for the harm she'd done.

The wall of photographs was the one element that distinguished my room from a trendy hotel, and I attempted to distract myself with them. There was one of a newborn Teddy, and another of my son building a sandcastle on a beach. One was of my mother in costume for a West End production of *Antigone*, her black hair coiled in ancient Greek style and held back by a gold diadem; even in a black-and-white photo, her eyes were piercing. There should've been photographs of us together before she divorced my father, but I'd never found them. Instead, my childhood was represented by a lone shot of my sister and me on skis, when I was five and she was nine, and another of us around the same time with my father and stepmother at their wedding. In both shots, Juliet scowled at the camera, while I looked dazed. There was a blank space where there had been a photograph of Caroline and me on our wedding day. I'd cut my right hand when I'd smashed the glass and broken the frame.

That reminded me of what I'd done to my left hand in the church that morning. The wound was wrapped in a beige bandage now, but the pain underneath was sharp. How could I have been so stupid and selfish? My son needed me. I didn't have the luxury of wallowing in pain and self-harm as I had as a student. I could never do that again.

I crept down the hall to Teddy's room. Since I'd put my son to bed, he'd already summoned me back three times. In the last instance, he'd been upset to the point of tears that he couldn't find his floppy-eared stuffed rabbit, who had fallen on the carpet. Since his mother's death, every loss—however temporary—hit him frighteningly hard. I cracked the door open and felt tremendous relief at the sight of my son, asleep, hugging Bunny tightly. Reassured, I closed the door and made my way back to my room. As I did, I heard a crash and a shriek from the kitchen.

I hurried down the stairs to the first floor and headed to the back of the house. There was a stained-glass window with a red flower over the kitchen door, illuminated by the light inside. Opening the door, I found my stepmother kneeling on the floor, picking up the remains of a shattered wine bottle with her bare hands. Guilt surged through me; I should have checked on her that afternoon, but I'd forgotten to. An elastic bandage was wrapped around her wrist.

"Ursula, are you all right?"

"Theo! How are you keeping?" she asked with a bright smile, as if we were having a social visit. Her diamond drop earrings glittered in the bright artificial light, and there was red lipstick smeared on her teeth. She was wearing a somber black dress as if she were finally ready for the funeral.

"What happened?"

"I dropped a bottle, dear. Don't make a big deal of it."

I heard footsteps behind me, and Theo's nanny, Gloria, appeared, wrapped in a fluffy pink robe. "Oh, no! Are you okay, Mrs. Thraxton?"

"I'm fine, fine. Just *ungeschickt*, as my husband always reminds me." Ursula meant *clumsy*. Her accented English was so fluent people usually assumed she was British, but German words popped out of her mouth when she was dead drunk, as she very clearly was at that moment.

"I can clean up," Gloria offered.

"No, I'll do it," I said. "Thank you for everything today, Gloria. I can't tell you how much I appreciate it."

Gloria leaned closer. "She's been coming over all the time," she whispered. "I think your father is cutting off her supply earlier and earlier." She gave Ursula a concerned glance and retreated from the room.

The wine was still spreading over the Italian tile floor. I looked for a mop and bucket and couldn't find either.

"There's a dustpan in that closet," Ursula said, as if she were the one who lived in the house.

I retrieved it and cleaned up the mess as best I could. As I did, Ursula removed another bottle from the wine fridge. She carefully extracted the cork and poured a glass for herself.

"How's your wrist?" I asked. "Father said you had an accident this morning."

"I tripped and fell," Ursula said. "It's only a sprain. Your father likely told you I was drunk, but I wasn't. Not very drunk, anyway. I was upset about Caroline."

"I'm glad it was just a sprain. You need to be careful."

"I wanted to ask how you are feeling, dear," Ursula said, then took a long gulp of chablis.

My stepmother had never been subtle. I suspected that my father, after his marriage to my mother—a volatile stage actress everyone described as *complicated*—was glad to be married to a woman who was straightforward in her wants. Ursula liked money, jewelry, and alcohol, though not necessarily in that order.

"It's been a very long day," I said.

"A long day, a long week, a long year," Ursula said. "It never ends, does it?"

Without asking, she reached in the cupboard for a tumbler and poured some wine for me. "No, thanks."

"You're going to want it," Ursula said. "What did you do to your hand?"

She was right; I took a long drink. It never ceased to amaze me that—no matter how inebriated she was—Ursula was the most meticulous person I'd ever met. No detail went past her unnoticed.

"Did my father send you over?"

"Absolutely not. Nor do I report to him."

"I used to think you were reporting to Klaus." Ursula was the younger sister of Klaus von Strohm, my father's business partner. Where my father was jocular and outgoing, Klaus was saturnine and stern.

"My brother the *Arschgesicht*?" Ursula raised an eyebrow as she elegantly cursed him out. "I'm certain he hoped I would report back to him when I married your father. Men always think women exist for their service. They can fuck themselves." She took a long drink. "Your hand, dear?"

"I burned my hand on a candle in the church today."

"Only one candle?"

"A few."

She finished her glass and set it on the counter. "I thought you stopped doing that years ago."

"I did. Today was the first time in a very long time." This was the truth; I hadn't sliced or burned my skin since Teddy was born. In the past couple of years—ever since I'd left the family business—I hadn't even thought about it.

"Are you taking drugs again?"

"No. I haven't since I went through rehab."

"I'm glad to hear it." Ursula poured more wine into her glass. "Because that was a nightmarish time for us all."

"I know," I said softly. We were silent for a minute. "I need to ask you something, Ursula. Did Caroline ever ask you about my first wife?"

My stepmother nodded sadly. "She did. It was almost three months ago. She was a little bit sneaky about it."

"What do you mean?" I asked, my brain doing the arithmetic. Caroline had first mentioned divorce two months ago, but she'd never explained why she suddenly wanted one.

"She came to your father's house several times, looking for photographs." Ursula took another drink. She and my father lived in a tremendous town house directly across the street from ours, but my stepmother only ever referred to it as *your father's house*. The smaller town house Caroline and I shared had been a wedding gift from them. "One day, when no one else was around, she said to me, 'Is there a photo album from Theo's first wedding?'"

60

I inhaled sharply. "How did she . . . ?"

Ursula put up a hand. "I have no idea—I am simply telling you what I know, dear. Caroline caught me by surprise with that, but she was too clever for her own good. I said, 'What photo album?' Of course, I should have said, 'What wedding?' But it didn't really matter. Caroline said, 'Wasn't Theo married before?' and I said of course not. She persisted. 'Isn't that why he dropped out of university in Berlin?' Ah, pardon me, she said *college*, not *university*. I asked who told her this baffling thing."

"What did she say?"

"She tried to pretend you—yes, you yourself, Theo—had made some oblique reference." Ursula rolled her eyes. "I grew up with a father and brother in the Stasi. This pretty little girl thought she could trick me?"

I didn't say it was likely because Ursula was drunk when Caroline tried to ambush her, but the thought crossed my mind. My stepmother could read me, though.

"You are thinking it is because of the wine." She lifted her glass and drank defiantly. "I have been keeping secrets for the Thraxton family ever since my brother placed me in your father's house. I am a vault. I do not slip up. I did not spill a word about your . . . mistakes."

I closed my eyes for a moment, and Mirelle's face appeared, as if conjured from the back of my mind. There had been a time when I'd thought about nothing except her death, but I'd finally realized I had to keep moving forward, in spite of what I'd done. I could still do good in the world. I could spend the rest of my life making up for my mistakes. *I am full of hidden horrors,* whispered a voice, and I shuddered. There had been so much blood when Mirelle died . . .

"It was a terrible time for you, Theo," Ursula went on. "But it was an awful time for all of us. We thought we were going to lose you. Your father was terrified. You were like a wraith, so close to death . . ."

"Can we not talk about that?" I said.

"I'm sorry," Ursula said. "I know it's hard for you. Of course you feel guilty. But that woman was the devil. She deserved what she got." Ursula drained her glass and cocked her head at what was left in the bottle. After a nanosecond's hesitation, she refilled her glass. "I loved Caroline," she said quietly. Her pale-blue eyes were watery. That was a side effect of too much wine, but I knew she was sincere. "My loyalty is to you, and your father, of course, but I tried to help Caroline in my own way."

"Of course you did, Ursula."

"It would have been better if she'd married into a different family," she said. "Marriage to a Thraxton is sheer misery."

I took that as a comment on my father, but it could just as easily have applied to me. "Did you tell Caroline that?"

"I believe the words passed my lips."

Even my stepmother, who'd raised me as her own child, thought I was a monster. I couldn't blame her. She knew everything about me and what I'd done.

"There is only one person I can think of who hates you enough to open up the Pandora's box of your past," Ursula added. "She would laugh to see your marriage crumble."

I understood what she meant immediately. There were any number of people who wouldn't mind watching my life fall apart, but only one who would actively try to destroy it.

# CHAPTER 11

## THEO

I walked Ursula home, even though it was only across the street. Then I went back to morosely contemplating photographs on the wall of my bedroom. Had there ever been any photographs of Mirelle and me together? In this digital age, when people chronicled every mediocre meal, it seemed impossible that there weren't any. But we'd met at a particularly dark period in my life, and I'd only spiraled further down afterward. I'd started using drugs like ketamine and midazolam when I was a teenager to block whispered words and violent images from my mind. Adding heroin to that mix had dragged me into hell.

*I am full of hidden horrors,* whispered the worst of the voices.

I picked up my phone. It was after ten o'clock, but Dr. Haven kept unusual hours. She answered on the third ring.

"I'm sorry to bother you so late. This is Theo Archer"—my best attempt at an alias was using my mother's maiden name—"but I was really hoping to make an appointment with you."

"We can talk right now if you're in crisis," she said. "Are you okay, Theo?"

"I'm fine," I lied. The truth was, I never felt like I had any privacy in a building owned by my family. The town house had been a wedding gift to us, but my father's name was still on the ownership papers. He wasn't the relative I was worried about at that moment; that honor went to my sister, who had always been ready to stab me through the heart. When Ursula said there was only one person who hated me enough to reveal my past to Caroline, Juliet was who she meant. "But if you have any open appointments tomorrow . . ."

"You could come by at eleven, but I only have half an hour," she said.

"I'll take it. Thank you."

I'd seen various psychologists and psychiatrists at my father's insistence when I was young, but I quickly realized they all reported back to my family. My sister delighted in mocking me, emailing therapy suggestions to help me over what she described as my pathological fear of animals. I hadn't set foot in a zoo since I was three, and unfortunately my son was obsessed with them. I'd found Dr. Haven on my own, and she was my secret. But the therapy I was working on with her was not at all what Juliet was suggesting.

I heard a dull thud, and I leaped up. The sound had come from Teddy's room. I hurried up the hall and opened the door.

My heart skipped a beat, because Teddy wasn't in bed.

I turned on the light, and there was a squawk from the other side of his room. Teddy and his accomplice, Bunny, were sitting in front of his bookcase.

"What are you doing?" I asked. "You're supposed to be in bed."

Teddy pulled Bunny closer. "Nothing."

He had several large storybooks pulled out and strewn around the floor. He was holding something in his hand but shielding it from my sight.

"Teddy, what are you doing?"

"Nothing," he repeated.

"It doesn't look like nothing. What are you holding there?"

"Can't tell you," he said.

"Why not?"

"Mama said it's secret."

I came closer. "That's changed now, Teddy. Mama's gone, so you can tell me everything."

Teddy's eyes were big as quarters, and he gazed at me pleadingly. "But when she comes back?"

I sat on the rug beside him. "I wish she would. But she's not going to, Teddy. It's just us now."

He was hugging something to his chest.

"Can I see that?" I asked.

He allowed me to take it from him. It was a heart-shaped gold locket. Inside was an adorable childhood photograph of Caroline and her sister.

"It's a picture of Mama," he said softly. "With Auntie Dee. They're just little."

"It's beautiful," I said. "You took it from Mama's room?"

"No! Mama left it here." He pointed at his bookcase.

"Why would she do that?"

"She said gremlins move things around. It's safe here."

Caroline had been making bizarre accusations over the past several months, accusing me of invading her privacy.

"Can we go to the zoo tomorrow?" Teddy asked me, his tone brightening.

"Maybe you can go with Gloria?"

"You *never* go with me." He hugged Bunny tightly. "Mama will take me."

My son sounded so determined when he spoke, as if the past week had simply been a bad dream. It broke my heart. "You know Mama isn't coming back, don't you, Teddy?"

"You *said* you can still see her." His voice was shrill with the piercing logic of a young child. It was my fault for not knowing how to explain to him that his mother was dead. When he cried, I tried to console him with the idea that you can hold someone you love in your heart, even though you can't touch them. It was foolish of me to hope that a boy who wasn't yet four could grasp that concept; I couldn't manage it myself.

"The service at the church was for her, Teddy," I said gently.

"Uh-huh."

"You need to get back into bed," I said.

"I'm not tired."

"What about Bunny? He looks sleepy, doesn't he?"

Teddy considered his friend seriously. "You *are* tired, Bunny," he said, sounding slightly surprised, as if the stuffed animal had spoken.

I tucked them both into bed and got Teddy some water. "No more adventures tonight," I said. "Sweet dreams."

"Where's Mama now?" Teddy asked.

My heart skipped a beat. "She's in a better place, Teddy." Until that moment, I'd never understood why people offered platitudes like that to children. But I had nothing else to give him.

# CHAPTER 12

## DEIRDRE

At eight in the morning, I was at the Seventeenth Precinct on East Fifty-First Street waiting to talk to Luis Villaverde, the detective quoted in the article about Caro's death. I hadn't had any contact with the police after they'd told me she was dead. Someone else—Theo was the obvious suspect—had dealt with the identification and formalities.

Villaverde gave me a toothy grin. He was in his midthirties, olive skinned and dark eyed. He wasn't tall but he was muscular, with dents on his nose and scars on his face that made him look like a washed-up boxer. "How are you holding up?" he asked.

"We had the funeral yesterday," I said. "It was hard."

"Sudden deaths are always tough to square. Especially when someone's as young as your sister. What can I do for you?"

"I need to talk to you about the case."

"The case?" He eyed me skeptically.

"Could we talk somewhere private?"

We ended up in an interview room, sitting in metal chairs across from each other over a metal table. "I guess this makes it hard for people to leave graffiti," I said, thinking of the wooden table I'd been questioned at when I was fifteen. There had been dozens of sets of initials carved into it, plus choice insults for the cops.

"Mostly it's because of bedbugs," Villaverde answered. "What did you want to talk about?"

"What's going on with the investigation?"

"We don't have an open investigation." He looked bemused. "Your sister died of a heart attack, to put it in the simplest terms. Unfortunately, she had an underlying heart condition from her pregnancy."

"What are you talking about?" Even though I was confused, a memory zipped through my brain. "Wait, is this about Caro having hypertension when she was pregnant with Teddy? Because that stopped after he was born."

The cop flipped through some notes on a yellow pad. "According to her doctor, she had an arrhythmia that became an ongoing issue. Your sister didn't tell anyone, far as we can tell. Her husband didn't know. Your dad didn't know."

No one had explained Caro's heart issue to me before. "I can't believe it was serious enough to kill her. She never said anything."

"She might've lived if she hadn't hit her head," Villaverde said. "People think a concussion only harms your brain, but it affects your heart. It constricts how it beats. It's a tragedy, what happened to her, but as soon as we establish that there was no foul play involved, it's not our department anymore."

"How do you know there was no foul play?" I demanded. "Why was there no autopsy?"

"Look, a lot of people think an autopsy is automatic," Villaverde said. "But that's only true if the person was a victim of violence. Otherwise, it's largely up to the family. We asked in this case, and her husband said no."

Of course Theo had refused. Whatever he'd done to Caro had been careful and quiet.

I found the printout of Caro's email. "I got a message from my sister yesterday. She wrote it just before she died. You need to read it." I slid it across the table so that he could.

"You got this *yesterday*?" Villaverde raised a dubious eyebrow. "She died over a week ago."

"Caro set the message up to go out if she died."

"How do we know this is legit? Anybody could set something up online."

"My sister is the only person in the world who'd make these references to our family."

He gave it a quick once-over. "She called you *Dodo* in it. That's your nickname?"

"It was when I was in kindergarten. She was Caro and I was Dodo. That's what our parents called us." I didn't understand why he was zeroing in on the least interesting part of the message. "There's more to it than that. *I keep thinking of Mom, and how you never believe you're going to end up like one of your parents, until you do.*" I took a breath. "That's a reference to a letter my mother wrote a long time ago. It's the real reason I know this email is from my sister. Literally no one else knows these details about my family."

"What details?"

At that moment, it would've been easier to strip down to my underwear and hurl myself out a window than tell him the truth. But what choice did I have? "My father used to hit my mother. They argued all the time, and it would get physical. Especially when he was drinking, which was pretty often back then."

"Were the police ever called?"

I started to laugh, before I caught myself. "We were supposed to act like it didn't happen. In my family, it was a bigger crime to tell an outsider about private stuff than it was for my father to hit my mom in the first place." My parents were immigrants from Northern Ireland; nothing was more sacred to them than their code of silence.

"Did your father hit you or your sister?"

"No. We were girls, so it was our mother's job to discipline us."

"Did your mother hit you?"

"That's none of your business." The words burst out of my chest. I wasn't there to talk about my mother. She had died of cancer just before Teddy was born. We'd disagreed on a lot of things, but I'd always loved her.

He frowned, but he let that slide. "How bad did it get with your father?"

"When I was fifteen, I found a letter my mom had written, in case anything ever happened to her. She put it in the family Bible." My chin sank toward my chest, as if I were in confession. The contents of her message were seared into my brain. *Ryan Crawley is not a terrible man, but he's capable of terrible things. If I am beaten to a bloody pulp, or die suddenly in an "accidental" fall, know that my husband is responsible. He'll be contrite, but it will be too late. Please take care of my girls. I love them.*

The memory made me shiver, even all these years later. Caro was away at college then, and I'd called her in a panic to tell her what I'd found. She'd been bizarrely calm. *Put it back,* she'd told me. *Pretend you never laid eyes on it.*

*How can I do that?* I'd cried. *He's going to kill her one day.*

*Stop being so dramatic,* Caro had said. *This is just what they do. Ignore it. Focus on your own life.*

The cop cracked his knuckles, snapping me back to reality. "Okay," Villaverde said, returning to the printout of Caroline's message; I'd gotten up before the crack of dawn that morning so my landlord wouldn't catch me using her printer. *"If you're reading this, I'm already dead. No matter what it looks like, my death won't be an accident. Theo killed his first wife and got away with it. Bring him to justice, no matter what you have to do."* He cleared his throat. "Who was this first wife?"

"I didn't know she existed until yesterday," I said. "But I confronted Theo about it. He didn't tell me her name, but he admitted he was married before."

"He give you any details?"

"I asked if she was buried in the family plot Caroline was being buried in. Theo said no."

"That's it?"

Even I had to admit it sounded weak. "He was angry. He couldn't believe I knew. I can get more out of him. He ran off, and because we were at the gravesite, I couldn't corner him again. But I'll—"

"You don't need to do anything."

"But I can—"

"This is our job, Deirdre. Just leave it with us."

"What are you going to do?"

"We'll check out this tip about the first wife," Villaverde said. "If there's anything relevant, we'll reopen the case."

"There's nothing about her," I said. "I was up all night searching for everything I could find about the Thraxton family. There's no mention of Theo being married before."

"If he was, we'll find out. There's always a paper trail."

It was agony, hearing him say *if*. I sat straighter in my chair. I knew I was someone he'd laugh about later with his partner.

"What was Theo's alibi?"

"His what?"

"His alibi," I repeated. "What was it?"

"He was on a business trip to Thailand," Villaverde said. "But we never followed up on alibis in the case of your sister's death, because we have it on security camera."

I remembered a line from an article I'd read: *the socialite was caught on multiple security cameras during her run and there was nothing suspicious.* But that only meant no one had *seen* anyone harm her. What if her heart condition wasn't just from arrhythmia? I tried to think of a way to say that without sounding like a nut.

"We have your sister on tape for most of her run that morning," he added. "On a bunch of different cams from block to block. Do you want to see it?"

*NO,* my brain screamed. I didn't want to watch my sister die. I couldn't imagine anything worse.

But I said, "Okay."

I was in a trance as Villaverde led me to his desk, which held a huge computer screen. Before I knew it, I was watching grainy black-and-white footage of Caro. She wore a fitted dark top and leggings, and her blonde mane was pulled back in a ponytail. I watched her jog up to an empty intersection and pause, pressing her hand against the center of her chest.

It was like a horror movie, only I knew exactly how this one ended.

"The one thing that was a little funny was that your sister went running down to the United Nations," Villaverde said. "Her nanny said she liked to run in Central Park. Any idea why she went south instead?"

"No," I whispered, my eyes transfixed by the screen.

I watched Caro run, her calm face oddly pained. Had she known she was going to die?

"This is the bad part, at the Isaiah Wall," Villaverde said.

Caro clutched her chest and paused, but she slowly made her way up the steps, then vanished.

I stared, barely blinking, waiting for more.

"Where did she go?"

"The steps curve up. There's a blind spot after that landing," Villaverde said. "She'll be on screen again in a sec. I can fast-forward . . ."

"No." I wanted him to leave it. As the seconds ticked by, sweat dribbled down the back of my neck. There was Caro, straightening up at the top of the stairs, rolling her neck from side to side. She took four steps and vanished again. The next camera that caught her was farther away. My sister stepped through a waist-high gate and disappeared.

"Where did she go?" I demanded.

"Into the park. There are no cameras in there. But no one else goes in or comes out while she's there." He fast-forwarded. "There's five minutes of nothing. Then this."

Finally my sister reappeared, only she was moving very slowly, hunched over like she'd aged seventy years. Her left hand was on her chest, and her right was touching the back of her head. She faded off camera again and materialized at the top of the steps beside the Isaiah Wall. Suddenly, both hands went to her heart, and she convulsed. Her body made a graceful little quarter-turn and she dropped, disappearing from the camera's view until her body fell onto the stone landing. Even though there was no sound on the video, I could hear a sickening thud.

"You saw her clutching her chest?" Villaverde asked. "She was already in cardiac arrest then. That's why she fell."

"Why was she touching her head?"

"Dizziness from her heart, probably."

"Did she have a head wound?"

"I told you she got a concussion," he said. "You saw her fall. She hit those steps hard."

He had an answer for everything, but we were drawing different conclusions from the video. I was absolutely certain about one thing: there was a reason Caro had run a mile south to the United Nations area that morning, and no one had bothered to find out why.

"There's more to this story," I said. "Why did she even go into that park?"

"Being completely honest, I think she was meeting someone there," Villaverde said.

I gulped for air. "Why?"

"Here's the list of what she had on her when she died." He pulled out a folder. My eyes felt bleary, but I could make out a list: *Watch (Cartier). Diamond wedding band. Diamond stud earrings. Memory card.*

"Memory card?" I said. "She was out jogging. She wasn't carrying anything."

"There was a little zipped pocket in the waistband of her leggings," he said. "You could fit a house key there, maybe a credit card. But all your sister had was this little memory card."

"Where is it now?"

"With her husband," he said. "Theo Thraxton took possession of everything."

# CHAPTER 13

## Deirdre

It was stupid to walk from the police station to the spot where my sister had collapsed. I knew that. Caro had died over a week ago. What could I possibly find? But I had to see it for myself.

The iconic United Nations building with the international flags flying in front was a little to the north. The UN headquarters was directly across, a mirrored-glass skyscraper that looked like a lonely domino on the empty landscape by the East River. Caro had dropped in front of Ralph Bunche Park, a tiny green oasis named for the first African American to win the Nobel Peace Prize. The curving Isaiah Wall was on my right, brushing against a spiral staircase that led one story up. There was a Bible verse on it:

*They shall beat their swords into plowshares, and their spears into pruning-hooks: nation shall not lift up sword against nation, neither shall they learn war any more.*

I appreciated the antiwar sentiment, but I was ready to pick up a sword for my sister. The cops weren't going to listen to me. *Bring him to justice, no matter what you have to do,* my sister had written about her husband. But I couldn't see a way to do that. It wasn't even clear if Theo had been involved in her death. What had made my sister write that panicked message in the early-dawn hours the day she died?

I wanted to head home and study the memory card she'd given me. There had to be something important on it I'd missed. But my phone buzzed at nine a.m. sharp, reminding me I had to work. I'd taken an unpaid day off when Caro died, then another for the funeral, and I couldn't afford to lose more money. I worked for a company called Snapp, an app that allowed New Yorkers who couldn't make time to buy toilet paper outsource their shopping and domestic chores. Plenty of other services did that, too, but Snapp's edge was in giving clients a warm body to organize all the stuff they bought. That was where I came in. In Snapp parlance, I was a curator. It was an exalted title for someone who spent her days opening toothpaste and soapboxes, cleaning the contents, and then arranging them in Olympic-sized bathrooms scented with candles that cost more than what I spent on food in a week. To most of the clients, I was like a friendly ghost. They never met me, and that was by design. The app's tagline was *Snapp and it's done.* Normally, I communicated with clients by text or email. Some of them never got in touch at all.

The text was from my boss, an angry Gen Xer whose hair was always greasy and who had weirdly short arms, which had led to the predictable nickname T-Rex. He hated everyone he managed on Snapp's payroll, and the feeling was mutual. This was his message to me: WTF, D? What are you doing at Tudor City?

I gritted my teeth. One of the worst things about Snapp was that bosses liked to spy on my location. Had to talk to the police about my sister, I texted back.

T-Rex's reply popped up ten seconds later. You took yesterday off for your sister's funeral.

I could feel my face flush.

The police are investigating her death, I texted back. This is serious. And I'm on my way to work anyway.

I was hurrying north as I typed. I was a little over half a mile from the Sutton Place apartment where I needed to be.

Irresponsibility has consequences, T-Rex typed back.

His veiled threat made me ball my fists. He was a creep who knew how to push my buttons.

I'd started at Snapp as a marathoner—that was the person who ferried heavy bags between shops and apartments—but I'd been promoted during the pandemic, because clients only allowed workers with proven antibodies to enter their homes. I'd gotten sick early on, and my monthly tests had made people think I was a safe bet, so clients paid a premium for my work. Of course, Snapp didn't lower those rates after most people had gotten vaccinated. It was a weird fit, because I was a minimalist who disliked extra stuff, and I was organizing kitchens for people who kept a dozen types of salt on hand.

My first client of the day was an older lady I liked, even though I'd never laid eyes on her. She always tipped well, and more of her purchases were for her three schnauzers than for herself, which seemed weirdly sweet. I worked at her place for two hours, walked six blocks to the next one, which was a little more chaotic—that home had three kids, who were way more destructive than dogs. The doorman had the bags the marathoner had dropped off. Afterward I ate a protein bar and checked my email. There was nothing from the mysterious X, and I emailed the address again. There was a sweet message from Jude. Just wanted to check in, she'd written. How are you doing? Sending hugs.

I flinched slightly. I wasn't good with hugs, even virtual ones.

I kept moving, because I was on the clock and there were no breaks.

Things went well until the middle of the afternoon. My work had a kind of mindless drone quality to it that I hated, but it also left me alone with my thoughts. I didn't have much contact with humans, which was fine with me. But when I saw the address on my next client—Beekman Street, barely three blocks downtown off City Hall Park, I texted T-Rex.

I was direct: I'm not going there.

As was he: You are. Consider it penance.

Not happening. Last time ASB tried to rub up against me.

There was a tiny pause in our exchange. I thought you were able to take care of yourself, T-Rex shot back. It was like waving a red flag in front of a bull.

ASB was Aubrey Sutton-Braithwaite, widely considered by Snapp employees as the world's worst human. He was twenty-nine years old and had never worked a day in his life, thanks to his hedge-fund-manager father. But that didn't mean Aubrey didn't have his own colorful career. He'd been a suspect in a series of arsons in the Hamptons. He'd been arrested for DUIs on multiple occasions. At least two women had restraining orders against him. Of course he'd never spent a day in jail. Aubrey was like a free-floating cancer cell, wreaking havoc wherever he landed, but suffering no ill consequences himself. He was *always* home when I went to his apartment. That day was no exception.

"Deirdre." He looked me over from head to toe when he answered the door. Aubrey's eyes were small and close-set, which made him appear shifty. Whenever the reboot of *America's Most Wanted* launched, there'd be an episode devoted entirely to his exploits. "Nice boots. You come here from your dominatrix job?"

"Fuck off, Aubrey." Snapp had already cycled through a dozen female curators who'd quit instead of setting foot in Aubrey's lair again. The world's worst human wouldn't allow Snapp to send him a male curator, and the company pretended it wasn't enabling sexual harassment. It was all about the customer's happiness, after all. Instead of responsibly cutting all ties with Aubrey, my boss sent me when he could. I tolerated it because I made triple my usual pay, plus I knew I could kick Aubrey's ass if I had to. *Just don't turn your back on him* was T-Rex's advice, as if I were dealing with a wild animal.

I stormed into the apartment, dumping the four bags the marathoner had dropped off on the Italian marble floor of the kitchen. Aubrey's place was a cautionary tale. You could take a gorgeous apartment with towering ceilings, fluted columns, and crown moldings, and slap up some very pricey artwork—a Rothko hung in the living room, giving the city view serious competition for eyeballs—but all it took was the stale smell of sweat, week-old pizza, and pot to give it that overpowering *eau de frat house*. It didn't help that dirty towels, old gym clothes, and sporting gear sprouted like toadstools from every flat surface.

"Your cleaning lady quit again?" I asked.

He grunted in response. That was as good as our exchanges ever got. As much as I wanted to run out of there, I had to work. Aubrey stood four feet away from me, arms crossed, trying to make his stringy biceps pop. He was lean and lanky, with the kind of body you might get from being a mildly ambitious gym rat who sampled illegal performance enhancers.

"You got the condoms?" he asked.

"If you ordered them, they're here."

"You better not have brought the regular ones. I need the extralarge magnums. Bet you'd love to see why."

"You just lost *that* bet."

"My girlfriends say I'm amazing."

"I didn't know inflatable dolls could talk."

"Bitch," he muttered.

I slid the fancy gold box of condoms across the countertop. "One box of balloon animals, coming up."

"Take them out of the box and organize them on my night table."

"I'm not your condom curator."

"You're supposed to do whatever I say." Aubrey pouted.

"Not even close. I'm here because your mommy and daddy know they screwed up raising you." I carefully lined up kombucha bottles in his Meneghini fridge. Until I'd started this job, I didn't know there were refrigerators that cost as much as an average American made in a year. "They know you're a useless baby."

"Ha ha. Your parents screwed you up, Deirdre, for you to keep working in a dead-end job like this."

"Yeah, it's my fault for failing to be born rich," I shot back. "Go back to playing *Call of Duty* or whatever it is you do all day." I piled a couple of fancy cheeses in the fridge. I swear, this creep ordered random things to keep me captive longer. I was probably his only human contact of the week.

"You're in a shitty mood today," he observed. "Who died?"

I put down a six-pack of Sapporo's Space Barley and stared at him. There was no way Aubrey knew about my sister. He didn't even know my last name. It would be wrong to lash out at him. *He's just a loser living on an allowance from his father,* I reminded myself. *He's nothing.*

"Oh, that's right," he added. "Your sister died. I read all about it."

"You can read?" I said, but I felt chilled to the bone. Clients were supposed to be given curators' first names only. But I should've known that rules were just for drones like me.

I tried to work more quickly.

"Are you sad about it?" Aubrey asked.

I didn't answer.

"I wouldn't be sad if my sister died," he went on. "She's a bitch. Was your sister a bitch like you?"

Tuning him out was the only option. In my haste, I dropped a bottle of tequila on the tile floor. I stared at the flood of dark-red liquid and glass shards in despair. That was Clase Azul Extra Anejo, worth more than I made in two weeks, tips included.

"Shit!" shouted an excited Aubrey, zooming in closer. "You're in trouble now."

I was stuck in place, mentally calculating what I would have to do to make up the cash. It was impossible. There was no way to do it.

"You better hope I don't tell your boss."

I glanced up. Aubrey's beady convict eyes were open as wide as I'd ever seen them, and their usual flat, dead aspect had been replaced with something shadier. Without meaning to, I'd misplaced the hard shell I wore like armor. Aubrey had been waiting for this moment. While my brain was processing those facts, he pounced, shoving me back against the stainless-steel fridge, grabbing my breast, and shoving his thick, sour tongue into my mouth.

In a split second, I shifted from anguish to rage. Revolted as I was, there was something akin to joy in the knowledge I had a legit target for my fury. First, I jabbed my fist into his Adam's apple. When he flinched back, I swung my arm around, striking him in the face with my elbow. He yowled and hunched over in pain, turning away from me. I kicked the back of his kneecap, and he fell onto the fancy tile floor with the soft squish a bag of wet dirt would make.

"I know you tried to pull some creepy shit on the other girls who came here," I told him. "You're not going to do that to me."

I kicked him in the stomach for good measure. He retched like he was about to cough up a hairball and curled into a fetal position.

"Noooo," he whimpered. His eyes were squeezed shut, but his face was wet with a gross combination of tears and snot that I didn't look too closely at.

"I'll let myself out now," I said. "Word of advice: next time you feel like grabbing a girl, remind yourself she feels like killing you."

I started out of the kitchen, and thought better of it. I went back to kick Aubrey in the kidneys. Then I left without a backward glance.

# CHAPTER 14

## Deirdre

Leaving Aubrey's apartment, I felt nothing but shame. No one had ever deserved an ass kicking like that guy, and the look of surprise on his face when he realized he wasn't going to overpower me was intoxicating. But underneath was a bitter awareness that if I'd been on top of my game, it never would've come to that.

I hurried along Beekman Street, unsure where to go next. There was no way I could call T-Rex and tell him what happened. Even in a best-case scenario, with him agreeing that I'd never have to go back to Aubrey's apartment, I'd be on the hook for a two-thousand-dollar bottle of tequila.

When I saw City Hall Park, I felt a moment of relief. Jude's office was steps away. It was just after five; there was no doubt she'd still be at her desk. I messaged her and got a response immediately. She was waiting for me at the security post in front of city hall.

"What's wrong?" she whispered to me after my bag was x-rayed and I was waved through.

"A creep just pounced on me."

"Someone you know?"

"Yeah. A Snapp client."

"Did he rip your shirt?"

I glanced down. I was wearing a black shirt over a black tank top, and I hadn't even noticed it lost a few buttons when Aubrey grabbed me. It didn't look indecent, but Jude knew me well enough to realize it wasn't a style choice. "Yeah, he did."

"We can talk to the police here," Jude said. "I'll have an officer come to my office."

"No, thanks. I already talked to the cops this morning. That's enough for one day."

"What happened this morning?"

We were at Jude's cubbyhole of an office. She ushered me in and closed the door behind me. On the wall behind her was a framed degree from Georgetown University with *Judeline Esther Lazare* in black calligraphic script. There were a few photographs of Jude with boldface names in politics and entertainment. I spotted a framed coat of arms—the Haitian palmiste, with a lone palm tree and spears and cannons and anchors—and a lone hibiscus plant on her desk with a single flower in bloom. Everywhere, there were books.

"I went to the cops because . . . sorry, I should've told you this before." My mouth was dry. It was hard to get the words out.

"Told me what?"

"I got a message from Caro when I was at her funeral yesterday."

Jude's expression was sheer astonishment. "How is that even possible?"

"It was an email she set up in advance." The cop, Villaverde, had kept the printout I'd given him, so I found the message on my phone. Jude stared at it for a long time, frowning deeply. "I can forward it to you," I offered.

"I'd say yes, but even my private emails can be subpoenaed." She handed my phone back. "I can't believe it. Why wouldn't Caroline tell me she was in danger?"

"She didn't say anything to me either."

83

"It's my own fault," Jude said, wiping her eyes.

"How could it be?"

"I wouldn't listen to her." Jude grabbed a tissue and blew her nose. "She told me things—things she swore me to secrecy about—but I . . ." Her voice trailed off as I stared into space. "I didn't understand how bad it was."

"What did Caro say?"

"Months ago, we had lunch, and she told me she wanted a divorce from Theo," Jude said. "I asked why, and she wouldn't give me a direct answer. Of course, they were apart for much of the pandemic—you remember, right?"

"Sure, Theo stayed in Europe for months."

"Right, but those were unusual circumstances. I asked Caroline, 'Is he a good father to Teddy?' She said he was. I asked if Theo ever hit her . . ." Her eyes teared up again, and she grabbed another tissue.

"What did she say?" I leaned forward. This was important.

"She said no, but that wasn't the point. Then she asked what would I do if I found out someone I loved had committed a terrible crime?"

"What crime?"

"I don't know. I told her my faith would guide me, that if a person truly had remorse, that if they had truly changed, I would forgive."

"You're a better person than I am, Jude. I'm an eye for an eye."

"Violence begets more violence," she said. "But if a person has no remorse . . ." She swallowed hard. "Caroline told me Theo had been lying to her as long as she'd known him."

"About what?"

"I can't say what. It would embarrass her." Jude rubbed her temples. "It wasn't a crime, though. She never told me what *that* was supposed to be."

"She found out Theo killed his first wife." I put it together in a heartbeat. Growing apart was one thing—Caro was a fairly devout person, and she wasn't going to get a divorce unless there was a reason—but discovering her husband was a killer would've been the end of everything.

"I brought up practical things to her," Jude said. "I said she wouldn't want to give up her beautiful town house in a divorce. She told me she wouldn't have to."

"Why not?"

"She said her in-laws were on her side. Her father-in-law owns the house . . ."

"I thought he gave it to them as a wedding gift?"

"He didn't sign it over, apparently," Jude said. "He controls the purse strings. He told Caroline that the house was hers and Teddy's, and Theo could go back to living at one of the hotels."

I hadn't stopped to think about what Theo's motive might be for killing Caroline. His family was the one with money, but that big cushion of cash wasn't actually his.

"What about Teddy?" I asked. "Who'd get custody?"

"Caroline wanted full custody, but Theo said he'd fight her for it. He told her . . . he said she was an unfit mother."

In that moment, every nerve ending in my body was electrified. I wanted to kill Theo with my bare hands.

"I kept something from you yesterday," Jude said. "I didn't want to upset you."

"What?"

"That woman you overheard me talking to, Adinah Gerstein? We were discussing Caroline."

"So you *did* call her crazy."

"I didn't mean it that way." Jude's expression was horrified. "But Caroline was struggling, there's no doubt of that."

"Struggling how?"

"She'd suffered from depression for a long time. It wasn't just post-partum. That only brought things to a head." Jude's shoulders drooped. "Did she mention the gremlins to you?"

"The . . . gremlins?"

"The ones who put her shoes in different boxes and moved her jewelry around," Jude said. "They rearranged the books on her shelf. She must've told you some of this stuff."

I thought about that. A few months back, I'd noticed that Caro had fired most of her staff, including the cleaning people. Her Upper East Side town house had been growing increasingly musty. When I'd mentioned it to her, Caro said the staff couldn't be trusted. It had struck me as weird, but I'd never had a staff of any kind, so what did I know?

"Maybe something about the staff moving things around. She was so organized she'd notice the littlest thing."

"Caroline was seeing things that weren't there," Jude said. "The last time I talked with her, she told me she was going to fire her son's nanny."

"Gloria? Why?"

"She said Gloria was reporting on her to Theo."

I wondered if that was true. Gloria had always been terrific with Teddy, but who knew where her allegiances were? "That's bizarre."

Jude nodded and glanced at her phone, lying faceup on the desk. "I should probably get back to work soon."

"There's one other thing I need to show you." I wasn't carrying the printout the guy at Osiris's Vault had given me, but I'd photographed it with my phone. "Caro sent three messages. One to me, one to our father, and one to someone listed as X. Here's that last one."

"'If I fail, you have to do it. I am putting all of my faith and trust in you. My son's future depends on it,'" Jude read aloud. "Who did this go to?"

"I wondered if Caro sent it to you."

"Definitely not. Did you reach out to this email address?"

"Yeah," I said. "Nothing back yet. Do you know who the email belongs to?"

"No," Jude said. "The letters and numbers make it look like spam."

Jude's phone rang, and I glanced at the screen. The name on it was Ben Northcutt.

"Wait, isn't that—"

"Caroline's boyfriend?" Jude sighed. "Unfortunately, yes."

# CHAPTER 15

## THEO

"I'll be damned. Look what the cat dragged in," my sister said when she found me in her office, a corner suite at the Thraxton International headquarters in Midtown Manhattan. Tall and broad shouldered, Juliet entered the room with the aggressive grace of a well-fed predator. She'd lost her hat but was wearing a navy suit that could've passed for a twin of her funeral attire. "You're the last person I'd expect to find here. Security still allows you in?"

"I had to check my conscience at the door," I said.

"As if you had one in the first place." Juliet smirked. "But please, continue your self-righteous routine. Just don't scare the axolotls."

I was standing beside an aquarium that housed a pair of pale ghosts, who were resting at the bottom of the tank. Each was six inches long, with gills and tails like a fish, yet they also had four lizard-like legs. Their broad, rounded faces had eyes so far apart they were on opposite sides of their heads, the hallmark of a beast of prey. "What are they?"

"They're a type of spooky salamander," Juliet said. "Meet Dewey and Louie."

"Where's Huey?"

"Those two ganged up and ate him," Juliet said. "Siblings are the worst."

I stepped away from the glass. "You missed the service at Green-Wood."

"I went to the church, Theo. And the luncheon. I don't have the luxury of spending all day at a funeral." Juliet sat down behind her desk. "Besides, there was more than enough drama at the church. Between you punching out that tabloid sleaze and Deirdre getting into it with a security guard, people really got their price of admission."

"What happened with Deirdre?"

"A new hire got aggressive about demanding her invitation." She shook her head. "Security was shown photos of every family member. It's not like Deirdre isn't distinctive looking. He had no excuse."

"You fired him?" It wasn't really a question. Firing staff was Juliet's hobby.

"Of course I did."

That exhausted our limited supply of small talk. "I need to talk to you about something important."

"I knew you weren't here just to check out my amphibious office mates." She eyed me with the careful attention of a crocodile sizing up its lunch. "Go ahead, ask me *anything*."

"Did you tell Caroline about my first wife?"

Juliet stared at me in what appeared to be unfeigned astonishment. Then she started to laugh. Her face flushed and her shoulders shook.

"What's so funny?"

"Nothing." Juliet wiped her eyes. "I just realized what a great conversation starter it would be: 'You know, this reminds me of the night Theo murdered his first bride . . . ' Think of all the situations it could work in."

"You're not funny."

"Did you mention Mirelle to Caroline?"

"I can promise you, I never uttered Mirelle's name to her."

I turned to leave Juliet's office, then stopped dead. The ancient Egyptians believed in a female demon named Ammut, who was equal parts lion, hippopotamus, and crocodile. Ammut wasn't worshipped, but she was feared. After death, in the Hall of Two Truths, she devoured impure hearts, preventing those souls from ever resting. Whenever I encountered Juliet, I speculated on the possibility of a demon from antiquity being reincarnated as a sadistic socialite with a penchant for gold jewelry, strappy sandals, and sashimi.

"You never uttered Mirelle's name," I said slowly. "But you told Caroline *something* about her."

Juliet's eyes brightened. "You are getting good at this game, Theo. All right, you win. I may have dropped a sly little reference into a conversation I had with Caroline."

"What did you say?"

"Nothing much. It was ages ago."

"You have an excellent memory," I said. "What happened?"

"Caroline was planning some postpandemic European travel—Paris, Barcelona, blah blah blah—and it just came up. I asked if Berlin was on her itinerary, and she said she'd always wanted to go. I said that I supposed you never took her there because it would bring back *tragic* memories. Caroline thought I meant when you were a drug addict who flunked out of college, but I told her that I meant it because of your first wife."

The room felt like it was spinning. I sucked in my breath. "What did she say?"

"She was upset. I said, 'Didn't Theo ever tell you about his first wife?' She said no, never. I told her the family never talked about it, because it was such a dreadful story, what with her being murdered and all. She begged me for details, but I wouldn't give them to her."

"Did you tell her anything else?"

"Not a word. It drove her crazy." Juliet smiled. "She kept asking me, and all I'd say was, 'It's too tragic.'"

"Why would you do that?"

Juliet shrugged. "Caroline was always so smug. It was hateful. She had just spent an hour bragging to Father about some stupid award she was getting for philanthropy. You know how lavish she was with throwing Thraxton money around. Father thought it was *wonderful* news, of course. I couldn't resist popping her bubble of perfection."

"You were jealous of her." I heard the echo of my father in my voice; he'd accused Juliet of jealousy at the church.

"What was there to be jealous of?" Juliet shot back. "Caroline was an anxious little mouse who didn't fit in anywhere. She obsessed about every stupid little detail, whether it was a press release no one would read or what toothpaste to use. Am I the only person not surprised she had a heart problem? I'm amazed it didn't give out earlier."

Before I could respond, the phone on Juliet's desk rang. She answered it.

"Yes, he's right here," Juliet said. "I'll send him up." She set the receiver down. "Father will see you now."

I frowned. "I didn't come here for him. I wanted to talk to you."

"Well, he knows you're in the building and wants to see you, which is more than I can say for myself. I have work to do, Theo. Go away."

She pretended to look at something on her computer, but when I didn't move, she slid her gaze in my direction again.

"Did you enjoy it?" I asked her.

"Enjoy what?"

"Being cruel to Caroline."

Juliet propped her head on her hands as if she were considering the question. "Everyone should have a hobby."

My sister mocked everything, but I wasn't letting her shunt this off to the side.

"Before we married, you gave Caroline an etiquette guide," I said. "You told her she would need it."

"I remember. She actually seemed excited about it."

"She was," I said. "She read it cover to cover. But then you gave her another etiquette book, and another. She was willing to give you the benefit of the doubt, but you simply had to prove what a horrible person you were, didn't you?"

"If you're hosting charity galas, you have a responsibility to know what a fish fork is."

"You were hateful to her, and you made her life miserable."

Juliet leaned back in her chair, smiling. "Let me get this straight. I'm a bad person for schooling a climbing vine from Queens? Okay, fine. What does that make *you* for keeping so many dirty little secrets from her?"

"What's past is past."

Juliet laughed. "Our father's famous words. How convenient for you, Theo. It lets you off the hook, doesn't it? You didn't tell your new wife that you'd killed your first wife because that's in the past." She leaned forward. "Let me tell you something. The fact you butchered a woman is the first thing I think about when your pathetic face crosses my mind." She picked up the phone on her desk. "Now get out of my office before I call security."

# CHAPTER 16

## DEIRDRE

I blinked at Jude. "You mean *ex*-boyfriend, right?" I said, thinking of the old photo I'd thought Caro sent me by mistake.

"I don't know." She tapped a button to decline the call.

"You're saying my sister was seeing this guy?" I was incredulous. Caro had never hinted at anything like that to me. "I don't believe it."

"I'm not a hundred percent sure," Jude said. "They were extremely close, and then Caroline broke up with him and they never saw each other again. Until he popped up a few months ago."

"Caro gave me a bunch of photos, and there was one of her with Ben. I couldn't understand why. It was from a house in High Falls . . ."

"From when they lived together."

"They what?" I couldn't hide my astonishment.

"They lived in High Falls for about a year. It was back when you two weren't speaking," Jude said.

"But my mom and I never stopped talking. She didn't tell me Caro lived with anyone!" Even more than I was shocked, I was hurt. When I'd stopped living with my family, it wasn't exactly voluntary—I'd ended up in the not-so-tender care of the juvenile detention system at fifteen. After months of legal drama and multiple psychiatric evaluations, I'd been released to my parents' care. But I couldn't live with them again, which is how I wound up, like a stray animal, at Reagan's house. I talked with my mom every week—and saw her every month—but she was the only family member I had a relationship with. It wasn't until my mom was diagnosed with cancer that my sister came back into my life. There had been four long years of silence between us, and while we picked up where we left off—sort of—we never addressed what had happened. I was nineteen then and Caro twenty-four, and we were both immature enough to pretend it was water under the bridge.

"I don't know anything about Ben," I said, thinking of how he hadn't answered my email. "Caro was already dating Theo when we reconnected. Tell me about him."

"They met in journalism school," Jude said.

"They graduated together?"

Jude laughed. "No. He was a guest speaker. He'd graduated a decade earlier."

"Oh."

"They were close, but he wasn't really The One," Jude said. "He was this fearless reporter who would drop everything to fly to Bogotá just to talk with a source. Caroline said once that she wasn't sure if she was in love with him, or if she wanted to *be* him."

"Caro was a hearts-and-flowers kind of person. You're making her sound cynical."

"She was," Jude said. "I mean, Theo definitely swept her off her feet, but that was the first time I ever knew her to be head over heels about someone. And it didn't last."

I thought about that and realized Jude was right. Caro had always regarded relationships with a jaundiced eye. More fallout from our parents' disastrous marriage, even if she'd refused to admit it.

"Did Caro tell you she was seeing Ben again?"

"She told me when they reconnected. That was six months ago. But until . . ." She stopped speaking for a moment. "Three weeks ago,

Caroline wanted to drop off my birthday gift. I told her I was going to bed, but she said she was practically in my neighborhood already. You know I live by the Midtown Tunnel, right? When she came over, she said she'd been at Ben's. He's living in his parents' old pied-à-terre in Tudor City."

Theo's voice was echoing inside my skull. *Caroline wasn't just out for a jog the morning she died. We both know that, don't we? She was meeting someone.* The news reports about Caro had mentioned her dying across from the United Nations. I'd stood in the spot that morning, at the foot of that grand stone staircase. It had led up to Tudor City.

"That doesn't mean anything," I said defensively.

"She told me Teddy liked him. They bonded over zoos and exotic animals."

I was quiet for a minute, processing that. You didn't introduce someone to your kid unless you were serious. I bit my lip. "Why is he calling you?"

"It started the day after Caroline died," Jude said. "He thinks Theo was involved."

"I hope you have Ben's address," I said. "Because I'm going to need it."

# CHAPTER 17

## THEO

My father's office was a floor above Juliet's, at the south end of the building. Standing guard in front of it was his man Harris.

When I was a boy, I thought Harris was a brooding giant. He was a solid six foot four and broadly built, with tree-trunk limbs and a bald head that shone like a bronze bullet. When he spoke, which was seldom, it was with clipped vowels and an accent that was hard to place. He was from Bermuda, but he'd served in the British military at some point before he'd come into my father's service. He'd never been married and had no children. He was solitary as a stone castle, with the cold, predatory eyes of a reptile guarding a moat.

He ignored me as I stepped inside. My father's longtime secretary, Olga, was probably the only person in that building who was glad to see me. She got up and embraced me. "I'm so sorry about your wife, Theo. The service was beautiful. Caroline would have loved it. She was such a good girl."

I opened the door that led into my father's domain. It was a corner office, of course, with a spectacular panorama of the broad tree-lined boulevard that was Park Avenue. Angels would weep at a view like his. But my father had black screens installed over the glass walls, which permitted one to see the outline of the buildings but allowed no sunlight in. It was permanently twilight in his world. In his youth, my father's obsession had been with visiting archaeological sites in sun-drenched climes. He'd paid for that passion with two bouts of skin cancer. The world had once been his oyster, but my father had been forced to retreat into a dark shell.

It was a grand place for a man who'd inherited a motel chain that stretched across America and turned it into a global luxury hotel brand. At one end was a dark wood desk as immobile as a bank vault, elaborately carved with lion heads and claws and intertwined flowers. The desk chair was carved wood as well, but lacquered and gilded so the winged goddesses that formed the armrests looked ready to take flight. Still, they couldn't match the grandeur of the pair of ancient terra-cotta rams guarding a cabinet by the window; they were at least thirty-five hundred years old and obviously belonged behind glass in a museum.

"You haven't set foot in this office in a year," my father grumbled. "And when you stop by, you go see your sister but not me? What has Juliet ever done for you?"

"She's made me completely miserable," I admitted. "But I needed to talk to her about Caroline."

"Juliet's the last person I'd ask about her. She was like a scorpion with a kitten."

"She told Caroline about Mirelle," I said quietly.

I expected him to be furious. My father had a strict code about family secrets, and Juliet had violated his cardinal rule. But he appeared deflated, resting his elbows on the desk and cradling his head in his hands for a moment. "I knew it had to be either Juliet or Ursula."

"You knew?" I asked, stepping closer. "Why didn't you tell me?"

"I'm sorry, son. I was hoping things would work out between you and Caroline. I didn't want to meddle." He sighed. "Caroline asked me about your first wife. She was upset, but she wouldn't tell me how she found out."

"What did you say?"

"That it was a mistake, that it wasn't a legal marriage. I thought that was what she was upset about. I was wrong. She asked me how the girl died."

I felt as if I were trapped in a vat of acid; I was burning up, inside and out. "You told her?"

"I said drugs were involved, that you were high when it happened. I tried to be vague about details." His head drooped, as if his neck had just decided to quit its job. "Don't hate me. I ended up giving her a version of the truth, because I didn't know what else to do."

"What version?"

"I told her you'd gone through a terrible time when you were a student in Berlin. She already knew about the drugs. I think she knew you used to self-harm." He glanced at me, as if for confirmation; I nodded. "I told her you got involved with a terrible woman who made everything worse. And that one night, you were playing some kind of . . . uh, game . . . together, and she died."

No wonder Caroline had wanted to divorce me. Not only had she discovered a dead woman in my past, but my father had implied that it was from a sex game gone wrong. "I don't know how Mirelle died," I said.

"Bloodily," my father answered. "Juliet took photos of you."

My sister hadn't mentioned that part, but I had no doubt she'd shown Caroline whatever she'd snapped.

"Caroline wanted to know why you hadn't gone to jail, or even been charged," my father added. "She was persistent, and I cracked. I admitted that I had you whisked away to a rehab facility in another country. That I covered things up as best I could." He stared into the distance. "I felt like she didn't look at me the same way again after that. We were always so close, and she was as sweet as ever, but there was a gulf between us."

"You admitted you covered up a crime," I said. "What reaction were you expecting?"

"I hoped she would understand. A man can do a bad thing without actually being bad himself."

It was the ends-justify-the-means argument I'd heard my father make all my life. It didn't seem to apply here. "Juliet just attacked me for never telling Caroline about Mirelle. But how could I? She would have hated me. Anyone would."

"Juliet is a snake, and you shouldn't listen to anything she says. I wish you'd come back and work for the family business, Theo. You're away on your own too much, and it's affecting you. What's past is—"

"Don't say it." I felt light-headed, almost sick. "Why did you summon me here?"

"We need to talk, son. About your alibi."

"My alibi? For what?"

"For Caroline's death," he said.

I stared at my father, barely able to breathe. "You've lost your mind."

My father waved his hand in the air dismissively. He was a large man with a face creased like ancient parchment, a look that was emphasized when his brows were tightly knit together, as they were at that moment. "Please don't lie to me, Theo. It's disrespectful."

"Are you accusing me of killing my wife?" My voice was tight and strained. "I wasn't even in New York when it happened."

"I know that's not true, Theo."

I froze. How could he possibly know that?

He stared at me balefully before getting up and making his way to the bar trolley. He poured himself a scotch. "Drink?" he asked me.

"No, and you don't need one either. You're talking nonsense."

It was a challenge to read his expression in the dusky light of his office. His face was crowded with shadows that crept through its hollows and peaks.

"Son, you seem to be unaware of several cold, hard facts," he said at long last. "I know you lied to the police. You pretended you weren't in New York, when I know you were." He took a drink and carried his tumbler of scotch back to his desk.

"Look, Caroline had a heart condition. The police said there was nothing suspicious about her death. I don't even know what you're trying to accuse me of."

"I'm not saying you did anything to Caroline." He took a drink. "But you lied to the police, and I fear that will come back to haunt us. You told them you were flying back from Bangkok, but they can check on facts like that."

I stood there, breathing hard. He was right. It had been stupid of me to lie to the police about something so basic.

"Look, Caroline was like a daughter to me. But you're my flesh and blood. I want to help you if I can. Just tell me the truth. Were you seeing another woman? No judgments, son. I just think it's better if I know what we're dealing with."

There was menace swimming under his words, circling like a shark. I *had* seen another woman, but not in the salacious way my father meant.

"I don't need help," I said.

"Maybe you don't. But I'm here for you, son. I hope you know that."

He said it so kindly. If anyone had been listening, they would've given him a father-of-the-year medal. But I'd accepted his help before, and I knew that he always expected an exponential return on whatever he gave. If he had his way, I'd quit my work and rejoin him at the company; he'd made it clear, many times, that was his dream for me. I'd tried to work in the family business and had only proven to myself that I didn't want to be involved.

"I should go," I said.

"Theo, I saw your hand."

I glanced at my left hand, which I'd thrust into candle flames at the church. The palm was red and blistered, but I wasn't in any mood to explain.

"I noticed it the day Caroline died," my father added. That got my attention. He wasn't talking about the burn, but the cut on my right hand. It hadn't been a deliberate injury.

"What about it?" I asked. It was mostly healed up, though still discolored.

"There was broken wood and glass at your house," he said. "Don't worry, I cleaned it up. But Theo . . . there was some blood."

I wasn't about to tell him the truth about what had happened. "I've been having nightmares again," I said quickly.

"Oh, no." His face changed in that moment; his affable self vanished and left behind a blinking husk who looked as if he had swallowed pure vinegar. "About the attack?"

I nodded. I wasn't lying, exactly; I was having nightmares, but they didn't explain the glass and blood my father had mentioned. "Teddy's roughly the same age I was then. Perhaps that's why."

"I know you tire of me saying the past is past, but it really is, son," he said. "You can't go back. You can't change it; you can't fix it. All you can do is leave it behind."

I assumed my father had regrets. No one who'd lived the life he had—affairs, divorces, shady business practices—could avoid them. But the way he talked, one could deposit those feelings in trash bags and bury them. For me, that was impossible. "I've tried."

"Try harder. Put it in a lockbox in your brain and push it into a dark corner forever." He sighed long and hard, an orchestra of parental helplessness. "Do you think the dreams started again for a reason?"

I didn't have the heart to tell him the nightmare had never really stopped, that it had always lurked in the background. In it, a tiger loomed over me, pinning me down with its body as it swiped at my torso and arms. It wasn't frantic about it; it was almost calm. The claws were dripping blood, but when I looked closely, they didn't look like claws at all, but gleaming knives.

I'd stopped talking about it years ago because my father had sent me to a variety of behavioral therapists, all of whom tried to cordon off my brain from the trauma I'd suffered when I was three and a half.

"Teddy is always asking to go to the zoo," I said cautiously.

"You don't need to be fearful for Teddy. He's not going to get into any animal's cage these days."

My father usually avoided talking about my accident; I jumped at the opportunity to discuss it more directly. "Do you remember exactly how it happened to me at the Berlin Zoo?"

"It was your mother's fault," he answered quickly. "I wasn't even there that day. When I saw you, it was at the hospital. It was awful. I should never have let your mother take you to the zoo. She was deranged. She probably put you in there to bond with the tiger."

I heard a terrible echo in my head at that moment. My father had said similar words about my mother many times. It was as if he didn't realize that would make me wonder if I'd inherited some mental defect from her.

There was an uneasy silence between us. "I should go," I said finally.

"Shall we have dinner together later?" he suggested, as if we were one big, happy family. "We need to spend more time together, now that Caroline's gone."

"I have work to do."

I didn't add that I didn't want to spend time with him because I knew he was lying to me. Juliet lied too; so did Ursula. I'd thought I could trust Caroline, but I'd been wrong. In my entire family, there was no one I could count on to tell me the truth.

# CHAPTER 18

## Deirdre

Jude's city hall office was only two express stops away from Grand Central. I took the 4 train north and exited the subway, heading east on Forty-Second Street. A massive sign with the words **TUDOR CITY** in bold letters sat in the sky near First Avenue. Almost twenty-five years in New York—my entire existence—and I couldn't understand how I'd missed it before.

I found a stone staircase on the block between Second and First Avenues, and I headed up. The development hovered a block above the rest of Midtown, and while that didn't sound like much distance, it felt serene when I clambered to the top. There was a small park to my left and another to my right, across the viaduct that bridged Forty-Second Street. Ben's building was right in front of me, its towering beauty hidden by massive scaffolding. The top floors were visible, with white stonework dramatically edging the red brick. It was clearly a stunner. On my way in I checked out the stained glass around the arched doorway and the polished suit of armor lurking just inside. Tudor City was committed to its theme; I had to give it that.

"I'm visiting Ben Northcutt in 13G," I told the uniformed doorman. He was wearing a surgical mask, which wasn't that common anymore in Manhattan, though you still saw a lot of them in Queens and the Bronx.

"Your name?"

"Deirdre Crawley."

I waited while he called upstairs, muttering my name into the receiver. "Yes, sir, I'll tell her." He hung up. "Mr. Northcutt isn't available right now."

"Excuse me?" I'd rushed over, desperate to talk to Ben. I hadn't expected to find the door slammed in my face.

"Sorry, miss, he's busy."

I wandered outside, unsure what to do next. Reagan often joked about my failure to pass the marshmallow test, but she wasn't wrong. I was an impatient person who would happily take one marshmallow that instant instead of two in twenty minutes' time. I crossed the street and stood in front of the little park. I tried leaning against its wrought-iron fence, but that was uncomfortable. I checked my messages and waited. I had no guarantee that Ben would appear, but I had literally nothing better to do.

Half an hour later, his sandy head popped out the front door. He really did look like his author photo.

"Ben!" I called.

His head swiveled in my direction. He frowned.

"I'm Deirdre," I said. "Caroline's sister. I wanted to meet you."

"Hey," he said, coming toward me. "I was going to reach out later tonight. I wish we could talk now, but I've got to meet with someone." He glanced at his watch. "Could we talk tomorrow?"

"Sure. I just—"

"Great. I'll text you." He started moving away, down the steps. I realized he didn't even have my number. He was blowing me off.

"Was Caro meeting you the morning she died?" I yelled after him.

He stopped suddenly and turned. "Don't."

"I need to know. Was that why she came here? Because she was seeing you?"

He trotted up the steps so we were face-to-face again, glancing to either side, even though the street was empty. "Keep your voice down."

"I talked to the police this morning. They need to know Caro was coming here to meet you."

"How does that matter?" He sounded exasperated.

I lowered my voice. "My sister sent me a message saying her husband was going to kill her. She wrote it before she went out, the morning she died. On the day of her funeral, I confronted Theo, and he told me Caro was seeing someone else. Clearly, he meant you." We stared at each other. "You need to tell the police about it. It changes things. It gives Theo a motive to hurt Caro."

"I know Theo's responsible for her death," Ben said. "But it's not that simple. I can't talk to the police."

"Why not?" I demanded.

"How much did Caroline tell you about what she was doing?"

I didn't understand the question. "Meaning what?"

Ben shook his head. "I know your sister loved you, but I don't think she told you what was really going on. I don't need a loose cannon blowing shit up."

"You can either tell me what you mean, or you can tell the police. I'm not keeping secrets about the affair you two were having. If that's why Theo killed her, the cops need to know."

Ben leaned forward, so close I could smell spearmint on his breath. "What Caroline was doing was illegal. You want to make that fact public and burn down your sister's reputation? Go ahead. But that's on you. You should think about what *she* wanted, not what you want."

He turned and rushed down the steps, leaving me speechless. I didn't know what he was talking about. I was afraid to find out.

# CHAPTER 19

## THEO

When I walked out of my father's suite, I thought I was done with my visit to Thraxton International. But an invisible cord pulled me toward Caroline's office.

I hadn't been there since I'd left the company, more than two years earlier. Caroline's domain hadn't changed. The walls were a calming blue, and the furnishings were nineteenth-century vintage and in perfect condition. The desk was elaborately carved mahogany with snarling lion faces and clawed feet; it had a dozen drawers, each marked with a different carved flower. There was an elaborate teak cabinet and a glass-fronted bookcase, and a curious Victorian sofa, reupholstered in white satin, with two plush seats facing away from each other. It felt like a perfect metaphor for my wife: everything under lock and key, and nothing ever confronted directly.

I was staring at photographs when I heard a sound from the doorway. I turned and saw Hugo Laraya watching me. He was the first friend I'd made in law school and still the best. My father, always swift to appraise a person's value, snapped Hugo up immediately when he graduated, placing him at the white-shoe New York firm that Thraxton

International kept on retainer. I couldn't blame Hugo for taking the job, but it had put up a wall between us, especially after I left the company.

"They told me you were skulking around in here," Hugo said.

"I'm sure my family has every security camera in the building trained on me."

"C'mon, Theo. You wouldn't believe how often your dad says he wishes you'd come back to work here."

Hugo leaned against the doorframe with the insouciance of an otter who'd been hired to shoot a Dolce & Gabbana advertisement. The top of his dark mop of hair rose just above my shoulder, though he usually wore a hat, carefully styling his silhouette to appear taller. He was of Filipino descent, but he embodied an impeccable, Waspy elegance that graduated into dandyism. That day, he was decked out in a gray Saville Row suit with a pale-olive fedora and patterned pocket square. We were the same age, but he always seemed older. It was probably the hats.

"I always wondered how Caroline managed to accomplish so much with such a pristine desk," Hugo said. "This room looks more like a stage set than an office."

"How have you been?"

"Fine," Hugo said. "You know what? I'm going to grab a coffee. I'll be right back."

He set a large ivory envelope embossed with the name of his firm—Casper Peters McNally—on Caroline's desk and left the room.

The invitation was too enticing to pass up. I knew Hugo was an excellent lawyer, so this wasn't a slip-up. There was a reason he'd left the room, even if he was legally barred from telling me what it was. I slid the pages out of the envelope.

The first document was a request for a restraining order to prevent me from taking my son out of New York.

I flipped through the rest quickly. I didn't have time to read much, but the gist of it was clear: my sister was launching a legal case stating that I was too unstable to parent my own child.

---

Dr. Haven's office was in Elizabeth, New Jersey, and I'd chosen her partly because my father didn't believe "real" therapists existed beyond Manhattan's borders. She had written extensively about guided mental imagery therapy—also known as Katathym imaginative therapy—which intrigued me because my own memories were knotted up in terror. As a child, I'd had endless nightmares about tigers pulling me apart as their claws turned to knives. There were long, blank spaces from my childhood when I remembered nothing, bookended by indelible images.

As a teenager, I'd found drugs and cutting my own skin effective ways to push back the memories that haunted me. I'd started seeing Dr. Haven a couple of years earlier, though the pandemic had disrupted that. But that day, I needed a different kind of help.

"I'm sorry I only have a half hour," she said when I walked in. "But we can—"

"My wife is dead, and my sister is attempting to steal my son," I said.

The room was quiet for a moment except for the ticking of the grandfather clock in the corner.

"I'm not saying you don't need therapy," Dr. Haven answered. "But you need to be in a lawyer's office right now."

I was too agitated to sit, so I paced across the well-worn wool rug.

"I came to you because I realized that my family has lied to me about . . . a lot of things," I said.

"What you've described to me is like a hall of mirrors. Your family made you feel like you couldn't trust anyone. Even yourself."

"They're going to do the same thing to Teddy if they get the chance," I said. "That's why I wanted custody if Caroline and I divorced. But I think my sister is intending to blackmail me."

"Did you talk to her?"

"No. I wasn't supposed to see the documents I saw. It was putting me on notice about her legal maneuvering."

"Why would she want custody of your son?"

"She doesn't," I said. "She wants control of the family business."

"But you told me she already runs the business."

"She does the work, but it's still my father's. He's very—" It was on the tip of my tongue to say *old fashioned*, but I knew that was a euphemism. "He's sexist. He wants an heir. That's why he gave me his name and begged my wife and me to use the same name for our son. When Teddy was born, my father said that one day, my son would inherit everything. He wasn't joking; he meant it. Juliet is well aware. This is her power play."

"She would blackmail you? However many details you're comfortable sharing, you know you can speak confidentially here."

"Yes." I'd told Dr. Haven a great deal, more than I'd ever revealed to anyone else. But I'd never mentioned Mirelle in any of our sessions. Perhaps it was time. "You know that I was a drug addict. I met a woman when I was in my second year of school in Berlin. We fell in love. She was the first person who seemed to understand me, to understand what I needed . . ." I gulped for air. "We were only together for three months, but it was the happiest, most carefree time of my life."

"What happened?"

"We got married in a small church in the French countryside near Colmar," I said. "Technically, it wasn't a legal marriage—I didn't know until later that you needed to have a civil ceremony in France to be married." My father had pointed that out to me months after Mirelle's death, after I'd gone through rehab. The way he'd relayed that information implied that it wasn't supposed to matter that Mirelle was dead. She hadn't *really* been my wife, after all. "A few days later, I woke up, and Mirelle was dead. She had been stabbed. There was blood everywhere."

Dr. Haven stared at me, her expression rapt. "What happened then?"

"I called my father. He was away on a trip, but he sent . . ." I closed my eyes. Who had he sent besides Juliet? I couldn't remember. *It couldn't have just been her,* I thought. But that was stupid and sexist; Juliet was as physically strong as I was. "My sister got me onto a plane and took me to rehab. My father eventually showed up there. I was in the facility for close to a year."

"What about your wife?"

I appreciated her referring to Mirelle that way. "My father told me he'd taken care of everything. He told me to forget it, to pretend it never happened. Juliet wouldn't even talk to me for years after that. She started calling me 'lady-killer.' She still does, as a matter of fact. But now she's trying to use it to take custody of Teddy."

Dr. Haven steepled her fingers. "How much do you remember of that night?"

"I just told you."

"No, you explained what your father and sister told you," she pointed out. "What do *you* actually remember?"

There were only two moments that I was certain of. One was surfacing from an opioid haze in my apartment and seeing Mirelle on the floor next to me, her eyes open, her chest and neck covered in blood. The second was being on a private plane with Juliet. *You ruined my week in Paris, you stupid piece of shit,* she'd said. *I wish you were dead.*

"I was a mess," I said softly. "I don't know what I did."

"It sounds like you've spent your adult life running away from it," Dr. Haven said. "Did you never think about exploring what happened, finding out what led to this woman's death?"

"No," I admitted. "I only ever wanted to bury that night." The image of Mirelle soaked in blood haunted me; the truth was, I deserved so much worse. It had occurred to me—many times—that I belonged in jail.

"Did your father disapprove of your relationship with this woman?" Dr. Haven asked.

"He was horrified by it."

"We've been focusing our therapy on your childhood memories, but I have to be honest. I think nothing is more important than recalling *these* memories. Have you ever tried to stimulate your recall of that night?"

"Never."

"What about retracing your steps from those days?"

"I haven't set foot in Berlin since that time. Or Germany, for that matter."

"Theo," she said. "You have to face this. You need to know what you did."

She was as nonjudgmental as a person could be, but her urgency was unmistakable. "I know."

"You're aware from the therapy we've done that there's nothing more important than triggering your sensory memory. You need to visit Berlin to do that. I'm not saying it will all come back, but that would be essential to unknotting this."

"I can't go away right now. My son needs me."

"Your son needs a father who can nurture him," Dr. Haven said. "If you're determined to distance yourself from reality, you won't be able to do that. Take a couple of days for yourself. It really is that important."

"I can't leave Teddy," I said.

"Are you able to be there for him now, or are you dealing with too many of your own issues?" she asked.

I couldn't argue with that.

"Theo, do you remember when you first came to see me?" she added. "You told me your family had lied to you throughout your life, but for the first time, you had proof."

"Yes." I could never forget. That proof—a letter I'd received three years ago—was with me at all times.

"You wanted to know why your family would do that to you. I told you I couldn't answer that—only you could. But you can't hide from the truth, no matter how ugly it is. You need to face it."

She was right. I had no choice. I pulled out my phone and booked the first flight I could get to Berlin.

# CHAPTER 20

## Deirdre

I went home to pick up the memory card, but I was too keyed up to stay in my dungeon room, and too exhausted to hit the dojo. I ended up at my neighborhood library. It looked like a middle school, three stories of beige-brown brick with a pair of fancy glass cubes some bougie architect dreamed up later. **Queens Library** was spelled out in shiny metal letters over the entrance. It was only when you got inside that the **Queens Public Library at Elmhurst** sign was visible. It always sounded funny to me, like Elmhurst was a destination. My working-class neighborhood was best known for its horrifically high death rate in the pandemic.

Technically, you weren't allowed to eat, but I'd learned you could quietly scarf down a protein bar just about anywhere. I decided to work my Ben Northcutt search harder. Reading about his work on a sleepless night had made him seem like a badass. Encountering him in the flesh made it clear he was a jackass. I had questions about Caro and her taste in men. She'd teased me about my aversion to relationships, but none of my hookups had tried to kill me or called me a criminal.

All I found was more of the same. Ben was a Big Deal in journalism, and aside from his career there was nothing interesting about him.

As far as I could tell, he'd never been married and had no kids. Maybe he was a cipher, but he was a boring one.

After the clock ran out on my half-hour slot, I moved to a table and put the memory card in my laptop. All 1,702 photographs came up. But I opened the card's settings and realized it was set to only show images. I changed it to show all files, and suddenly there were 1,798.

A shiver went down my spine.

That intense feeling lasted ten seconds, until I realized all the unseen files were spreadsheets. I skimmed each one, figuring a clue would jump out at me any second. Nothing did.

There was exactly one person I knew who loved spreadsheets. I texted Reagan, asking how late she was working.

**Eight,** she texted back. **But no dojo tonight. Want to come over for dinner?**

As a matter of fact, I did.

I had no other messages, not even from Snapp. I'd sent a text to T-Rex about Aubrey pouncing on me like a jackal, but there had only been radio silence. I didn't mind being yelled at, but the quiet was unnerving.

At twenty to eight, I headed over to Reagan's, stopping on the way for a bodega bouquet. Reagan and her mom lived in a cozy two-story house with gingerbread trim. It looked like it had popped out of a storybook. Mrs. Chen hugged me when I came in, and I didn't even mind. It felt like home.

"You have not been eating," Mrs. Chen said. "I can tell. You are too skinny, Dee."

"She's still living on protein bars," Reagan said, ratting me out.

"They're full of vitamins," I argued, aware I sounded lame.

Mrs. Chen shook her head. "You can't beat people up if you don't eat!"

She knew me *so* well.

That evening, I cared about food a lot. Mrs. Chen made a spicy pork stir-fry with carrots and peppers and peanuts. After dinner, she hurried off to video chat with her sister in Guangzhou. I pulled the memory card out. "Remember when I told you Caro gave me a zillion photos? There are spreadsheets too."

"And you want me to explain them? Fine. But only if I get to see some snaps of mini-Dee."

I handed the card over, and she put it into her laptop, a shiny new model that put my bashed-in one to shame. The first picture opened, and she started to heckle me mercilessly.

"I can't believe your mom was able to wrangle you into dresses. And pink ones, at that."

"Be careful. There are shots of you on there. That awesome haircut you gave yourself when you were twelve has been documented for the ages."

"Aw, hell," Reagan muttered. "That's blackmail material." She started opening up the spreadsheets. "How did you finish work so early today? Mom wanted to ask you over for dinner, but you don't get home till after ten on Thursdays."

"T-Rex sent me to Aubrey's apartment."

"Shit. Did that creep try anything this time?"

"He went for full molestation today. Groping *and* kissing."

"Tell me you tore his limbs from his body," Reagan said.

"Close enough. He was on the floor when I left. He wasn't getting up anytime soon."

"You need a different job. One that doesn't put you in mortal danger." Reagan's attention shifted to the screen. "Hello, financials. My happy place."

I gazed at the screen. It was some kind of operational budget, but unlike my best friend, I zoned out when looking at numbers.

"Okay, this spreadsheet is telling us a sad story," Reagan said. "I know you hate math, but this is pretty simple. See this number? That's the operating budget for the Thraxton hotels in Europe last year. That's a big number. And see this number?" She pointed at the screen. "That's gross income, and it needs a couple more zeroes to break even."

"You're saying the chain is losing money?"

"They're hemorrhaging money," Reagan clarified. "Maybe this is a bad year from the pandemic. If it's not, the company won't be in business much longer."

Reagan opened up more files, but they were more of the same.

"Why would your sister give you this?"

I thought about what Ben had hissed at me. *What Caroline was doing was illegal. You want to make that fact public and burn down your sister's reputation?* "I don't know."

"Your sister was the public relations director," Reagan said. "There's no reason for her to even . . . oh, wait. Hello there."

"What is it?"

"Take a look." Reagan angled the screen so I could see it better. "The operating costs are lower, which is good news, but look at the cash they're raking in."

I peered at it. "More zeroes."

"Lots more! Which would be great if this spreadsheet was for a different continent or time period. But it's not."

"What are you saying?"

"If this is real, Thraxton International is keeping two sets of books."

I gulped. "For what? Tax fraud?"

"Maybe." Reagan scanned it over. "Or it could be to raise capital. No one's lending them money with that first balance sheet, but the second one looks like a good bet."

"I don't understand why Caro would give this to me. Or why she'd even have it in the first place."

"Maybe it's leverage over Theo."

"Maybe," I agreed. But I knew Theo had left his family's business. Maybe the tax fraud stretched back years and implicated him—he was the family member with the fancy degrees. But it seemed like this information would mostly hurt the in-laws Caro loved rather than the husband she loathed.

# PART TWO

No evil dooms us hopelessly except the evil we love, and desire to continue in, and make no effort to escape from.

—George Eliot

# CHAPTER 21

## Deirdre

On Friday, I woke up at five a.m. to a text from Ben Northcutt. I feel like we got off on the wrong foot, he wrote. Want to get coffee today?

I wanted to ask how he'd gotten my number—because I sure hadn't given it to him—but I was exhausted and fell back into a fitful sleep.

When I woke up at seven, a text from T-Rex had just come in: You're fired.

I was furious, but I wasn't surprised. There was a numbness that had settled into my bones whenever I contemplated my job and the many things I hated about it. But seeing this two-word text highlighted its awfulness. I switched to another app and checked my bank account. It was anemic. I got paid every two weeks, but normally Aubrey danger pay went into my account within twelve hours. It wasn't there.

I shot back, Is this a joke? even though I knew it wasn't.

T-Rex's response came through in a minute. You know what you did.

He could only have meant Aubrey. Nothing else had gone wrong with any of my clients.

You owe me money, I wrote back.

There was no response.

I had exactly two protein bars, and as I studied them, I considered my employment prospects. They were not good. There was always a market for able-bodied worker bees, and I figured I could snag another job like that quickly. I also knew I'd hate it just as much as I'd hated working at Snapp.

I took the subway in to Manhattan, switching at Grand Central and heading north on a 6 train to the East Fifty-First Street Station. There was a Thraxton property on Park, a landmark of blue glass and studded steel that was supposed to look stylishly intimidating but mostly resembled a goth fishbowl. Two floors were corporate HQ, and the rest was a hotel. Caro had given me an employee pass years ago, and I stopped by on a semiregular basis—sometimes to say hi to my sister but always to stock up on food in the employee pantry. I wondered if the pass would be deactivated now that Caro was gone, but it still worked. I took the stairs up to the third floor. I was steps away from the pantry when I changed my mind and took another path, following the plush red carpet to Caro's office.

The door was closed, but it wasn't locked. I stepped inside but couldn't seem to take a step beyond that. Caro's office was painted in an azure blue that made it feel suspended in the sky, even though we were barely off the ground by New York City standards. The furniture was glamorous, of course. On one wall was a silver plaque from the Diotima Civic Society, surrounded by framed photographs of Caro with international dignitaries, interspersed with images of Teddy. My sister always looked perfect, never a hair out of place, at ease with presidents and royalty. I don't know how she did it.

"It's not the same without her, is it, Deirdre?" said a deep voice behind me.

I turned. Caro's father-in-law, Theodore, was there, dressed in a black suit. His gray hair was neatly combed, and there was a baby-blue square in his chest pocket. Still, he had an unmistakable air of misery around him.

"I find myself walking by, or picking up the phone, and I'm surprised that she's not here," he added. "I have a funny voice message she left me, and I've played it a dozen times, just to hear her voice."

I nodded. I wasn't used to the idea that she was gone. I wondered if I ever would be.

"She sent me a bunch of family photographs recently," I said. "Hundreds of them on a memory card." I gulped and closed my mouth, remembering what else was on that memory card.

"Anything special?"

"Small things I'd forgotten. Shots of us in matching outfits that Caro probably wanted to burn."

"Sometimes being reminded of little moments like that is the greatest gift. Caroline was a person who made every day seem special. It's an unusual talent."

"She made everyone feel special, whether or not they deserved to."

He smiled. "Well put. You have a similar sense of humor, you know. Caroline was very careful about what she said, but if you knew her well, she was a riot."

That was true. Caroline was decorous to the point of dullness in public, but she was sharply observant and could be sarcastic in private.

"What brought you here today?" he asked.

I didn't want to tell him about my plan to raid the pantry. "I don't have anywhere else to be right now. I just got fired from my job."

"Fired?" His brow knit in concern. "Why? What happened?"

"Honestly? I kicked the shit out of a slimeball who groped me."

"Deirdre!" He was clearly shocked. At first, I thought it was my choice of words, but I was wrong. "Are you going to sue? Do you have a lawyer?"

"No." I didn't want to add the obvious, that I was never going to be able to afford one.

"You do now." He extracted a case from his pocket. I assumed it was a wallet, but when he opened it, there were only business cards inside. He removed one and handed it to me. "This is one of mine. He's young

121

but he is brilliant. Don't hold it against him, but he was a classmate of my son's. You should call him."

I glanced at the name embossed on the front. *Hugo Laraya, Attorney at Law, Casper Peters McNally.* "I can't afford him."

"You don't need to pay him a dime. He's on retainer here."

"Thanks." I stuck the card in my pocket.

"Do you need money? I'd be happy to help."

I could feel my face flush. I wasn't used to taking charity, and the spreadsheets on Caro's memory card made me wonder if his finances were on the up-and-up.

"I'm fine."

"I don't want to intrude if you'd prefer solitude," he said. "Theo was in here yesterday. He's already flown off to Germany. Berlin, I believe."

That made my head swivel. "He left already? Did he take Teddy?"

"No," Theodore said. "Teddy has had enough upheaval. I won't permit someone as unstable as my son to disturb his life." There was steel undergirding his words.

"Why would Theo take off like that? Why Berlin?" I'd never been outside the US, but the city was synonymous with decadence in my head. In fairness, that was from watching *Cabaret* and *Babylon Berlin.*

"I know he's my son, but I find it impossible to understand him or the choices he makes. Theo is used to doing whatever he wants," his father said quietly. "I can only blame myself for that."

Mentally, I flipped a coin. Tell Theodore what I knew? I decided yes and took a deep diaphragm breath.

"Caroline told me Theo killed his first wife." It came out abruptly, more brutally than I intended.

The old man winced, as if I'd kicked him. "I knew she'd found out. We talked about it." He sighed. "Do you mind if we sit down? It's hard going over this territory."

I moved to take a seat in Caro's chair behind her desk. Her father-in-law sat down in the cushioned chair in front.

"I can tell you what I know and what I believe," Theodore said. "There was a period in his life—early on in college—when Theo was using drugs and engaging in . . . destructive behaviors, let's call them that. First, you should know that the woman's death wasn't intentional. I truly believe that. Theo and she were participating in some kind of, ah, game . . . while they were high. That was how she died."

He clearly meant a sex game, and I was torn between wanting details and needing to vomit. "What was her name?"

"She went by Mirelle and Marianne and a couple of other aliases. I never knew her last name. She was a gold digger who got her hooks into Theo. But then she died."

I couldn't exactly blame him for taking his son's side, but the cold way he dismissed the woman as a *gold digger* set my teeth on edge. "What happened afterward?"

"I put him into rehab."

"What about the dead woman?"

"What about her?"

He sounded surprised, and I stared at him in horror. His son had killed someone—accidentally or not—and the life of the dead woman was irrelevant to him. He didn't even think about it.

"What happened to her body?" I asked. "People must've wondered about her. About where she went, and if she was okay."

"I don't really know," Theodore said. "I believe the police looked at it as a break-in. My son had cash and drugs in the apartment . . ." He heaved out a long sigh. "I put Theo in rehab hundreds of miles away. I'm ashamed of that now. I helped Theo evade responsibility for that girl."

"Do you want to do that now?"

Theodore's eyes caught on mine. Neither of us could look away.

"If Theo had something to do with my sister's death, would you help him get away with it?"

"No," Theodore said firmly. "I thought he'd settled down when he married Caroline. I hoped he had. I believe he did, for a certain time. Then he reverted to form."

"Caro wasn't killed in a game," I said. "Do you think Theo did something to her?"

"It doesn't seem possible, but . . ." He closed his eyes. "Caroline wanted a divorce. I understood why. Theo wanted custody of Teddy. That's why . . ." His voice trailed off.

"What?"

"I haven't told anyone this," Theodore said. "But I saw Theo at their house before Caroline died."

"Wasn't he out of town?"

"He wants people to think that," Theodore said. "I confronted him about it yesterday. He denied being there, but I know he was lying to me. He was at the house."

"Are you positive it was him?"

"Absolutely. I was awake at five in the morning. Theo came by and went into the house. He was only there for a few minutes. I got a very good look at him on his way out. It was him."

"You need to tell the police," I said.

"Tell them what? That Theo went to his house at five in the morning? Caroline was still alive when he left." Theodore shook his head sadly. "I've had paranoid thoughts about his visit. What if he did something to one of Caroline's medications? I have no proof at all. Only fears."

"What about security cameras? He must be on them."

"The security system had been disabled," he said. "Obviously both Caroline and Theo had the codes."

"Do you think Theo was involved in my sister's death?"

"I don't want to think that." He rubbed his eyes. "When I confronted him, I thought he'd give me an explanation for being there. It could have been anything. But Theo lied about it. I can't think of any innocent reason why he would do that."

# CHAPTER 22

## THEO

My flight over the Atlantic was miserable. Awake, I obsessed about what Teddy had said to me when I told him I had to go away for a couple of days. *You're leaving again? Okay. Bye.* Asleep, Caroline's face floated through my mind. *I don't want to be married to you anymore. Why is that so hard to understand, Theo? Get out of my house.*

All of my options were awful ones.

More than once, I pulled the letter I always carried out of my pocket. Reading it over always made me question my sanity.

Dear Theo Thraxton,

I am writing with reference to an article about you published in Verve Magazine. In it, you are quoted as saying, "The most dramatic episode of my life was when I was three years old and fell into the tiger enclosure at the Berlin Zoo." As I hope you know, Zoo Berlin (as we call ourselves) has some 20,000 species of animals spread over 33 hectares. At the moment, we have no large felines as our Predator House is under major renovation, and those animals were rehomed to other zoological gardens. However, I felt it necessary to investigate your claim, as it would be unfair to rehome without warning an animal that had attacked a child. At that point, I learned that no such attack ever occurred here.

I am unsure what motives a person would have to fabricate such an attack, but I hope that you will retract this claim. Zoo Berlin has always made the safety of our animal residents and our human visitors a top concern. There are people who believe zoos are inherently unsafe and unfounded claims such as yours give them fuel for their fire.

Thank you for your attention to this matter.

Sincerely,

Ute Neumann

I had never bothered to contact the letter writer, but her message had turned my life upside down. I remembered the day of the attack— at least, I recalled walking through the zoo with my mother, hand in hand. Some pieces were fuzzy—my mother had purchased a stuffed tiger, the most macabre souvenir in the world, for me—but others were clear as day. The sharpest moment was falling into the enclosure. Somehow, I had clambered to the top of it and dangled over the edge for what seemed like forever, to my mind. Finally I fell, and the tiger pounced on me in an instant, ripping into my flesh.

That tiger stalked me in my sleep.

The letter was a shock, but I set it aside at first, thinking my family had simply made a mistake in the telling of the story. Perhaps it had been a different zoo, and I'd confused it because my tiger's collar was marked "Zoo Berlin." When I started poking at the story, I'd found no zoo with an incident that matched my memory. What I'd discovered were various tales of tigers owned by wealthy families attacking a guest. None of them fit my recollection, and that made me realize what my family had told me was a lie.

It wasn't the reason I left Thraxton International, but when the time came to choose the path I wanted to follow, that made it easier. My mistake was in thinking that Caroline would want to leave with me.

———

My flight arrived in the middle of the morning. I checked myself into the first hotel that came up in the app I checked. It was called the AC Hotel Humboldthain, named for the rustic park immediately to its south. It was technically in Mitte—the central district of Berlin—yet in Gesundbrunnen, an area that was traditionally working class and not terribly touristy. The remains of the infamous wall and Checkpoint Charlie were a world away. It wasn't an area I knew, but it had a transit hub that could get me almost anywhere in Berlin.

My room had a knotted-pine floor, moody black-and-white portraits, and stark black furnishings with crisp white linens. First thing, I took a long, hot shower. Afterward, I caught sight of myself in the bathroom's mirrored walls. I stared at my largest scar. It was strangely compelling, this red welt that ran from the hollow of my throat straight down to my navel. As a student in Berlin, I'd gotten a tattoo—three lines of text penned by Christopher Marlowe, divided by that sinister red line:

> Hell hath no limits / nor is circumscribed
> In one self place / for where we are is hell,
> And where hell is / must we ever be.

I had other scars on my body, jagged gashes on my torso from the animal attack. Ironically, the long, straight scar was what had saved my life—it was the surgical scar from when doctors had operated on me. Away at boarding school in England, I had been part of a group of boys who dared each other to do frightening things, cutting deep into skin or exposing flesh to flame. There was bluster in it, a determination to broadcast how tough we were. Only the pain, for me, meant something more. It tamed the dark side of my brain, the one that whispered, *I am full of hidden horrors,* the beastly demigod demanding a sacrifice. Even in that disturbed band of miscreants, I stood out. Everyone was fascinated by the scar that bisected me as if I were a lab specimen. It was a comment on the powers of childhood imagination that when I told other boys an Aztec cult had tried to sacrifice me to a tiger, this seemed like a reasonable explanation.

Dressing quickly, I pushed the scar out of my mind. I'd given myself two days to revisit the past. I was all too aware that my leaving New York—and my son—would only provide fodder for my sister's case against me. For the briefest of moments, it occurred to me that Dr. Haven could be setting me up. After all, she had encouraged me to leave New York, which was a boon to Juliet's plotting. *Stop being paranoid,* I warned myself. But paranoia was my only defense against my family.

I took the U-Bahn south to the Brandenburg Gate, as if I were a normal tourist. As a student, I'd only seen it at night, when the eighteenth-century colonnade was wrapped in golden lights. During the day, I found myself staring at the very top, with the four-horse chariot driven by the goddess of victory. I'd spent eighteen months in Berlin, and I'd never managed to visit the Reichstag, a block to the north, nor the Memorial to the Murdered Jews of Europe, a block to the south. I had, however, spent a decent amount of time in the Tiergarten, Berlin's answer to Central Park.

I stayed on the major boulevard that bisected the park—the Strasse des 17 Juni, named for the East Berlin uprising. If I wanted to re-create my time in Berlin, I would have to follow the park's rambles, past fountains and stone works of art. But I'd often been high when I'd wasted days in the park. The Soviet War Memorial was on the boulevard, and I had a far clearer memory of it, because that was where my father's business partner, Klaus von Strohm, liked to meet. *Your father wants me to check up on you, but I promise not to do that too much,* he'd said just after I'd started at the university. *What is the point of living in Berlin if not to be a bit decadent?*

I wasn't sure how Klaus defined *decadent,* but I went off the deep end. At boarding school, I'd smoked marijuana and taken mushrooms; in university, I'd quieted my nightmares and the voices in my head with ketamine and midazolam and opiates. It was a steep crash.

The Victory Column—with its golden idol to military might— loomed in the distance, gradually becoming more prominent as I walked west. Zoo Berlin lay just a little to the southwest of it. As a teenager, I'd felt bold, returning to the city where I'd almost died as a child. But I'd never set foot inside its grounds again. I told myself this would be the trip when I changed that.

But my priority was remembering my time in Berlin with Mirelle.

Just beyond the western edge of Tiergarten was my university, built around Ernst Reuter Platz. After the first couple of months, I'd spent little time in its classrooms. They barely registered in my memory.

I headed south, following Knesebeckstrasse to the boulevard of Kanstrasse, where signs pointed east to the zoo, a couple of blocks away. I didn't know what I was thinking, choosing that area as my new home when I was eighteen. At that age, I'd firmly blocked out the past. Maybe I'd done it so successfully with drugs that the zoo didn't register anymore.

My apartment had been somewhere south of the boulevard. I couldn't remember the name of the street until I came upon the sign for Niebuhrstrasse, which was filled with elegant buildings. It didn't take me long to find it after that.

I could still remember the day Mirelle had knocked at my door. Dark haired and pale, with rose-red lips, she looked like a fairy-tale princess come to life. *Sorry to bother you,* she'd said in French-accented English. *I just moved here, and I lost my phone. Could I make a call?*

I remembered staring at her neck, which was encircled by a black choker with silver studs, much like the girls at the fetish clubs I was visiting. What caught my attention was a glass vial hanging on a longer silver chain. It was filled with something red. Mirelle had noticed my gaze.

*I'm secretly a vampire,* she'd said with a coy smile.

I could feel my heart pounding just from staring at the building, remembering it all. I had met her in October, near the start of my second year at the university. By the end of January, Mirelle was dead. I'd spent years pushing every memory of her away. But it occurred to me for the first time how odd it was that this beautiful woman had simply landed on my doorstep one day. There was another detail that I recalled as I stared at my former home. I had told Dr. Haven that I'd come to inside my apartment, but that wasn't true. I lived on the fourth floor, and I never closed the blinds at night, because I loved catching glimpses of the stars. But Mirelle's apartment was on the first floor, and she kept the blinds closed for privacy. When I'd opened my eyes, the lights were on. I'd seen the blinds first, before my head turned and Mirelle came into focus.

I wanted to step inside the building, but no one answered when I rang the office bell; the building never had a live-in superintendent when I lived there, so that wasn't a surprise. I peered into the window of the room that had been Mirelle's, afraid the police would come by at any moment and arrest me as a Peeping Tom. The lights were off, but I could see the floor was blond wood, not the dark that I remembered. Of course they'd replaced it.

I remembered shouting Mirelle's name. I'd reached for her, and realized the knife was in my hand. When I tried to move, it felt like I was weighted down. That could have been the drugs. But for the first time, I was sure that someone else had been in the room with us.

# CHAPTER 23

## DEIRDRE

I had mixed emotions leaving the Thraxton International offices. Caro's father-in-law hadn't been anything other than kind to me, and I appreciated him telling me about Theo. But his casual dismissal of the woman Theo had killed—accidentally or not—left me unsettled. He regarded her like a piece of furniture. I knew he didn't think of Caro that way, but he would only be an ally to a point. No matter what he claimed, he'd help his son out of a jam.

I texted Ben, asking if he could meet me. He answered immediately, suggesting the café at Pershing Square. I walked down Park and through Grand Central Terminal, exiting at Forty-Second Street. Even before I crossed the street, I spotted Ben. He was sprawling in one of the café's metal chairs, casually dressed in torn jeans, a green button-down shirt, and scruffy leather boots. As I got closer, I saw he was reading Ernest Hemingway. Clearly he had a manual on macho male journalist tropes.

"Deirdre." He smiled at me and waved, setting the paperback aside.

"Hi," I said, sitting down.

"I thought this would be convenient for you, since you're coming in on the 7 train."

There was an awkward silence between us while I mentally filed through our minimal exchanges. "How do you know I live in Queens? And how did you get my number?"

"Caroline told me." He said it as if it were obvious.

"Why would she?"

"Because she figured we'd be natural allies, I guess," Ben said.

"Then why didn't she give me your contact info?" As I asked the question, I thought of the photo she'd sent me. Aside from letting me know Ben existed, it hadn't given me much.

"I bet she meant to. Caroline had a lot to deal with."

"My sister never mentioned you to me. What was going on between you two?"

There was a startled silence. "Wow. Your sister always said you were direct," Ben said. "She wasn't kidding."

I stared at him, refusing to fill the silence. He caved first, sort of.

"Just because someone asks you a question doesn't mean you have to answer it." Ben smiled at me, and it felt like he was used to getting his way with that grin. "Not that I'd want my interview subjects to realize that."

"I know Caro and Theo were living separate lives. I'm not judging you."

"Thanks for your permission."

I'd been putting down Ben's reaction the day before to the fact I'd surprised him at his building, but I was starting to think he was just an asshole. At that moment, a waiter homed in. Ben ordered black coffee—predictably—and I asked for water. I should've specified "tap" because the waiter returned quickly with a small bottle of Pellegrino.

"I wanted to meet you because I need information," I said. "Did Caro send you a letter to read after she died?"

"I can't talk about that."

I pulled up the image of the message and held it up. *If I fail, you have to do it. I am putting all of my faith and trust in you. My son's future depends on it.*

The color drained out of his face. He wasn't so cocky now. "Where did she send that?"

"It's to this random-sounding account. Is that you?"

He stared at it blankly. "Yeah. I have a bunch of burner accounts for sources."

"But you hadn't seen the message?"

He shook his head. "I don't check them that often. But that message was for me."

X, she had called him. I guess that meant *ex*, which I wasn't even sure was accurate. "What does it mean? What did Caro want you to do?"

"I can't share that."

"You can tell me or you can tell the cops." I didn't know when I'd become a cheerleader for the NYPD, first asking Theo's father to talk to them and now offering to sic them on Ben. I just didn't have anything else to threaten him with.

"Look, Deirdre, I would love to be able to confide in you," Ben said. "But I don't know whose side you're on."

"I'm on Caro's side," I said. "I don't care about anything else."

"Show me the message she sent you."

It was my turn to be affronted. "Excuse me?"

"If she sent me a message, she sent one to you," Ben said. "I need to see it."

Reluctantly, I pulled it up on my phone. He read it silently, nodding to himself.

"So she did tell you," he said. "That's good. Otherwise, you wouldn't believe me about Theo."

"What did Caro tell you?"

Ben raised an eyebrow. "She never described the torture her husband put her through? The shit that was happening at her house?"

"Like what?"

"Did she ever mention how she had no privacy? How things would move from room to room, how her private possessions would be rearranged?"

"I only heard a little about it."

"Caroline was afraid to tell anyone," Ben said. "It made her sound crazy. Claiming that someone moved your shoes to the wrong shoebox makes you sound psycho. But that's by design."

"By design?" I repeated. "I don't get it."

"It's psychological warfare," Ben said. "It's like death by a thousand cuts. It was a tactic perfected by the Stasi—the secret police—in East Germany. They sent officers to move things around in dissidents' homes when they weren't there. It was meant to disorient them, and it was a perfect way to distance them from people they cared about. Because when they told people close to them, it was dismissed as lunacy and paranoia."

"Let me get this straight. They just *moved* stuff? They didn't take things?"

"Right. Taking things gives you a legitimate crime to report. Saying a ring is missing doesn't make you cuckoo. But saying someone came into your home and rearranged your jewelry box . . . well, how would you tell anybody that with a straight face?"

"They'd think you did it yourself and forgot." There was an ugly logic to what he was saying.

"I think she was embarrassed to tell people what was happening," Ben said. "It felt like the ground beneath her feet wasn't steady."

"Was Caro meeting you the morning she died?"

"Yes. She was supposed to drop something off for me."

"A memory card?"

"How the hell did you know that?"

"When I went to the police, they showed me a list of what was on my sister when she died," I said. "There was a memory card zipped into the pocket of her leggings."

"I was supposed to pick it up from her," Ben said. "But Theo came to the house early that morning and freaked Caroline out. He overheard her talking to me on the phone—I don't know how much he heard, but Caroline was terrified. He wasn't supposed to get back from his trip for another day. She texted me that she'd come down to my building, even though she wasn't feeling well. She'd been having heart palpitations. That bastard killed her."

"You were going to her house?"

"A couple of blocks away. Caroline didn't want the in-laws knowing." Ben stared into the distance, his jaw tight. "Theo showing up changed everything."

"What was on the memory card?"

"Evidence," Ben said.

I could feel my own heart rattling the cage of my chest. "Evidence of what?"

"Theo is a criminal," Ben said. "The entire Thraxton family is a criminal organization. Caroline wanted me to be able to prove it."

# CHAPTER 24

## DEIRDRE

Ben stared at me, clearly eager for my reaction. I took a sip of water. "Is this about them keeping two sets of books?" I asked.

His jaw dropped in open astonishment. "Caroline said she only told Jude and me. How do you know about it?"

"Jude knows?" I countered. My heart dropped to the concrete floor of the outdoor café and bounced back, bruised.

"How do *you* know?" he repeated.

"Caro sent me a memory card with hundreds of photos. Last night, I discovered there were spreadsheets on it too."

"I guess that was her insurance policy," Ben mused.

"I don't understand why the Thraxtons have two sets of books."

"They're money launderers," Ben said. "They have a long history with crime. That story about Theodore Senior winning his first big hotel in a poker game is bullshit. He was involved with criminals, and they needed a fresh face to run their scam."

"Was that what you meant last night? When you said what my sister was up to was illegal?"

He nodded. "She knew what the Thraxtons were doing, and she didn't leave."

I wanted to defend Caro. She was an honest person, and I knew she devoted herself to helping people. Jude had mentioned all the money my sister had given Diotima, and it wasn't the only charity. But I felt bile rise in my throat as I contemplated Caro's awareness of her in-laws' criminal ventures. I could hear her voice when I'd called her in a panic about the letter our mother had written. *Ignore it. Focus on your own life.* Maybe it wasn't fair of me to think about that—Caro had been all of twenty when she'd said those words to me—but I knew my sister was willing to turn a blind eye to issues that didn't concern her.

I took a drink. "I don't understand the scam."

"Hotels are a shady business," Ben said. "Their clients can be from anywhere in the world, and you can't prove they exist. They play it like every room is full, and everyone's ordering room service and flowers and getting massages. You can launder millions through one hotel that way."

I swallowed hard. Going over the spreadsheets with Reagan, we'd assumed the lowball number was fake and that the Thraxtons were hiding money from the tax man. It hadn't occurred to us that they'd fake the profits.

"How long have they been doing this?"

"Years. When I expose them, Theo's going to jail."

"But Theo's the one who left the family business," I pointed out. "How's he responsible?"

Ben's mouth tightened in a snarl, like he was ready to curse me out. "Are you on his side?"

"Of course not. But I don't understand how this implicates Theo. It's the rest of his family who'd go to jail."

"Fuck the Thraxtons," Ben said, spitting out their name contemptuously. "They think they're better than everyone else, but they're just a bunch of crooks."

I sat there, trying to make sense of it. "Ben, my sister wrote me a message saying that her husband had murdered someone else. She was afraid he'd do the same thing to her."

"He did."

"Then why are you obsessing about the business? Because that doesn't touch Theo."

"What's your big idea?" He kicked at a pigeon, who stood its ground and gave him a dirty look.

"Theo killed a woman—girlfriend, wife, whatever you want to call her—in Berlin when he was a student there. His father admitted it to me."

"Caroline told me about it. She couldn't even get the woman's name. It's a dead end."

"No, it's not," I insisted. "His father told me enough details. The woman used different names, including Mirelle and Marianne. She was stabbed to death in their apartment in Berlin. Theo was young at the time—he was in college. His father whisked him out of the country and into rehab, and the police thought the woman died in a break-in over drugs and cash."

"You call that enough details? I can see why you're not a journalist."

"And I can see why you pull this lone-wolf act. No one could stand working with you for more than five minutes. But for Caro's sake, I'm going to try. You're supposed to be a journalist. Dig into the story of this dead woman."

Ben shook his head. "Caroline couldn't believe the old man covered everything up for his son."

"Why does no one ever focus on the woman who died?" I asked. "Everyone acts like she's this nonentity, that her death doesn't matter except for what it did to Theo."

"Then *you* look into it."

"I don't even know where to start!"

"Do what you're doing now. Ask questions. Shake some trees and see what falls out." He shrugged. "People think journalism is about writing. It's not. It's about being persistent."

I didn't speak German or have the option of flying off to Berlin. I didn't even have a passport. The idea that I was going to solve this cold case from my dungeon room in Queens seemed insane. "What are you going to do?"

"I'm going to keep researching the story Caroline wanted me to work on," he said. "If you want to help, give me the memory card."

"I'll email you the spreadsheets," I said grudgingly.

The waiter brought our bill, and Ben paid it. I didn't object because I couldn't pay for my Pellegrino with protein bars.

"You said before that Theo killed Caro," I said. "But I don't understand what he did, besides showing up at the house."

"He was terrorizing her."

"Caro ran down to your neighborhood," I said, thinking out loud.

"All she had to do was give the memory card to my doorman," Ben said.

"But she didn't. She still had it." Caro had gone into the park instead of Ben's building. Why? What had drawn her there?

"Right." Ben was stock still, as if frozen. "What are you saying?"

"Don't you think that's weird?" I asked. "I mean, she ran all the way south, over a mile, and then something keeps her from going a couple more yards to give you the card?"

"What are you trying to say?"

There had to be a reason Caro detoured into the park. "What if someone followed her?"

"Theo *had* been at the house," Ben mused. "He could've waited for her."

Another thought had crossed my mind. Caro's father-in-law had watched Theo going into and out of the house. That meant he could've seen my sister leave for her run. Theodore's involvement was an unlikely possibility. But if Caro was giving a journalist information about his company's ongoing fraud, who knew what he'd do?

"It didn't have to be Theo," I said. "Her phone wasn't on her when she died. If someone else saw her messages or call log, they'd figure out she was meeting you."

"No one knew," Ben said, standing. He picked up his book.

"Anyone who has access to her phone knows."

"Caroline used a burner," Ben said. "She knew enough to do that."

He strode off before I could ask him anything else. My rule-following good-girl sister used burner phones? How would she even know where to get one? The feisty pigeon hopped up on the chair Ben had vacated.

"Did any of that make sense to you?" I asked it. "Because I am very confused."

# CHAPTER 25

## Theo

The Thraxton hotel in Berlin was on Museum Island, a small patch of land sitting in the middle of the river Spree. It was as far east from the Brandenburg Gate as the Tiergarten's Victory Column was west, and I took a taxi to get there quickly. That provided an accidental sightseeing tour of the grand boulevard of Unter den Linden, with its neoclassical opera house and the imposing Humboldt University. This was a deviation from my plan to walk the streets I'd known as a student in Berlin, because I'd rarely visited this area in those days. But as I'd stared at my old apartment building, the certainty that another person had been in the room had only grown. I didn't think it was my sister; I couldn't remember seeing Juliet until I was carried onto the private plane that took me to rehab. Someone else had carried me onto the plane; Juliet was already there. I'd gotten a decent look at the man's face as he'd strapped me into a seat. It hadn't been Klaus, with his distinctive shock of white hair and huge belly. It was a man I couldn't remember ever seeing before.

The taxi deposited me beside the Lustgarten—a name I'd snickered at as a student; it translated as "Pleasure Garden"—which was across from the cathedral. If I'd been in the city as a tourist, I would've loved nothing more than to head north. That way lay the Pergamon Museum with its Babylonian, Assyrian, and Roman treasures; the Neues—or New—Museum, with its bounty from Egypt and Troy; and the smaller Bode Museum, with its Byzantine art and assortment of curious collections. But I took a deep breath and headed south.

The Thraxton International property was a grand fantasy of a building that had its own moat, as if it were a castle. It was largely glass and metal—like all of my family's hotels—but with baroque touches that included steel gargoyles with gleaming fangs.

Inside, I asked at the desk for the manager. It was a happy surprise when Pierre Dorval appeared, dressed in a sharp navy suit, and kissed me on the cheek. He was in his midforties and one of the most casually elegant humans I knew, with a mane of curly chestnut hair that fanned out like a halo. "I'm sorry, I know people hate that since the pandemic. But I am—what do you Americans call it—a hugger!"

"It's good to see you," I said, meaning it. "I had no idea you were in Berlin now." Pierre had been managing the Thraxton hotel in Paris when I'd left the company.

"The opportunity came up a year ago, and I grabbed it," Pierre said. "My husband is from Copenhagen, so he was thrilled. I am—what do you call it—'living the dream.' What brings you to Berlin?" He clapped his hand over his mouth. "Oh, Theo, I just remembered Caroline. I am so very sorry. She was the most wonderful person. The news does not feel real yet."

"It's been an awful time."

"How is your little boy? He must be four now?"

"Almost. It's been hardest of all for him." I shifted gears quickly. "That's why I'm here, actually. I was a student in Berlin twelve years ago. I wanted to reconnect with some people I knew then, people who worked here. I'm embarrassed to say I can't remember their names. Could I see the personnel files?"

"Of course!" Pierre answered. He turned and spoke in rapid-fire German to the desk staff. I couldn't follow what he was saying very well, except that some files were digitized and some were on paper. One of the desk staff headed to the back.

"Have you eaten?" Pierre asked me.

"No." I'd forgotten about food. The last meal I'd had was the boxed breakfast on the plane. "But I'm in a hurry."

"Of course you are. Americans are always in a hurry. It is the land of the White Rabbit—'I'm late, I'm late, for an important date!'" Pierre shook his head. "The dining room is amazing. You have to eat here. The files will take a little bit of time. Let's wait for them in style."

The dining room *was* amazing, capped with a Byzantine dome that rivaled that of the Bode Museum's entryway. The floor was inlaid blue mosaic tiles that shimmered like waves; as I gazed outside, directly onto the river, it felt as close to walking on water as I'd ever get.

"Your sister gets all the credit for this," Pierre said when we were seated at a table by the window. "The renovation happened before I arrived, but I was told it was Juliet's vision."

I glanced around again, spotting her handiwork in the clean-lined, modern steel furniture paired with gilded mosaics. "Juliet takes every detail seriously."

"She took over the global portfolio after you left," Pierre said. "Frankly, I miss working with you. Why did you leave, Theo? I never understood."

Pierre worked for my family—and only on the legitimate side of the business—so there was only so much I could say. Still, I wanted to be as truthful as I could. "When I was growing up, I would see these amazing works of art—Babylonian lions, Egyptian funeral art, great paintings—coming through my father's hotels. Sometimes they'd go on display; sometimes they'd end up being sold. But I'd see them and think, 'That belongs in a museum.'"

143

"I understand. When I was a kid, my family vacationed in the South of France," Pierre said. "One time, we went to a museum that had been an artist's house. There were a pair of ancient Egyptian statues there—tremendous things, taller than me." He gestured with his hands. "I couldn't believe they had ended up in a private home. They clearly belonged in a museum."

"There's always been a gray market for pieces like that," I said. "A lot of institutions won't take pieces anymore if they don't know their provenance, but private collectors will. I told my father that if he wanted me to work with him in the hotel business, he had to stop taking part in it."

"But he did, yes? Honestly, there's nothing like that being moved through here. There wasn't in Paris either."

I took a breath. "My father is clever about technicalities. He feels like he's honored our agreement, but he was skirting the edges of it. That's why I quit."

That was as much as I could tell Pierre. The truth was, as far as I knew, my father had stopped trafficking in stolen antiquities. However, he'd embarked on a different illegal venture with some new partners. That was it for me. I'd told Caroline exactly what he was up to. She hadn't cared. *What does it matter, when there's so much good you can do with the money?* she'd asked me. We were, from that moment on, an ocean apart, figuratively and literally.

"That is why you do what you do now?" Pierre said appraisingly. "Please do not tell me that you are here to take our Nefertiti away. Germany acquired it from Egypt legally."

The bust he referred to was on permanent display at the Neues Museum, just north of where we were sitting. "The German team that found it had a license from Egypt, but Egypt was under Ottoman rule, and the British were dominating Egypt," I said. "It's all part of the legacy of colonialism."

"Do you think, if all their artifacts were returned, they could care for all of them?" he asked. "You've been to Istanbul. Think of the national museum. They have so much Roman art they are drowning in it. It lies outdoors, getting rained on, with cats crawling all over it."

We spent the next hour discussing art and politics, which was a welcome distraction. Afterward, we went to his office, where a series of files was laid out on his desk. Thraxton International had a photograph of every staff member, so if the man I remembered had worked at the hotel, I knew I'd find him. It didn't take me long. The thirteenth file I picked up belonged to a man named Mehmet Badem. As I stared at his photo, time seemed to stop. That was the man who had carried me onto the plane.

"Does he still work for you?" I asked, holding up the photo.

"I don't know him." Pierre peered at the file. "He left work here on permanent disability five years ago. Some kind of accident, but it doesn't say what happened. How odd." He flipped through the pages, then went to his computer. "He does receive a pension."

"You have his address?" It was hard to contain my eagerness.

While Pierre wrote it down for me, I flipped through the other files. There was no one else I recognized. But another curious idea was coursing through my brain with the insistent buzzing of a mosquito. Exactly how much of a coincidence was it that Juliet had been nearby the night Mirelle had died? She had still been a student that January, earning her Ivy League MBA. I could clearly picture her face, squeezed tight with anger. *You ruined my week in Paris, you stupid piece of shit. I wish you were dead.* It wasn't the first time I wondered how far Juliet would go to take control of the business, but my blood had never run that cold when I'd considered the question.

# CHAPTER 26

## Deirdre

I didn't know where to go or what to do after I spoke with Ben. I called Jude on her cell phone and then on her work line, getting voice mail both times. I didn't leave a message, because I was afraid my voice would give me away. Jude had made it clear she was keeping some of my sister's secrets from me. Even so, the idea that Caro had confided in her about criminal activity at the Thraxton business really hurt. That wasn't personal, not like details about her unhappy marriage. It made me feel like Caro had decided she could only trust me so far.

Of course, there was the possibility that Ben was lying. He'd told me about the money laundering. Maybe he'd been the one who told Jude too. He was an evasive character who needed a kick to the head. Taking anything he said at face value felt like a mistake.

I was finishing my water and contemplating whether to take the subway south to city hall and ambush Jude when I got a call from the cops. "Deirdre, we'd really like you to come in to the precinct again. We have to talk to you about some new developments," Villaverde told me.

I couldn't believe it. The cops were calling me? I had the distinct impression that Villaverde thought I was a drama queen when I'd gone in. It was a huge relief to see he was actually following up on the tangled threads of my sister's case.

"I can come over now," I said, sounding like the eager beaver I was. "I'll be right there."

I practically flew to the precinct. I had a short wait when I got there, but a friendly officer took me to the interview room and offered me a soda. When Villaverde walked in, he introduced me to his partner, Detective Gorey, a short, round man with orange hair and freckles. Gorey squinted at me dubiously, staring at my arms as if cataloging my tattoos. When he shook his head, I knew we were off to a great start.

"We need to ask you a few questions, Deirdre," Villaverde said.

"Sure. But first, I have one for you. Did you know that Theo is in Berlin right now?"

They glanced at each other. "No, we hadn't heard," Villaverde said.

"He's free to go anywhere," Gorey said.

"His wife just died, and he's running away, leaving his son behind?" I put my hands out, palms up. "There's something wrong with him. You know, I talked to his father this morning."

"Did you?" It wasn't really a question from Gorey. He sounded bored.

"He admitted that Theo's first wife died. He said drugs were involved." As I spoke, I realized I didn't want to get the old man in trouble. I didn't exactly trust him, but I also didn't want to ruin his life. He needed to tell the cops his story his way. "He also told me Theo came home a day earlier than anyone realized from his last trip. He went to his house early the morning my sister died."

"Look, Deirdre, that's not why we wanted you to come in," Villaverde said. "We want to help you out, but we need some information first."

"About what?"

"You told us your father abused your mother," Gorey said. "But you never said a word about the fact that you tried to kill your father."

Time came to a screeching halt. I could only stare at him, my heart booming like a cannon in my ears. There was no point in belligerently asking what he meant. I couldn't pretend to be innocent.

"I was protecting my mother," I said. "She'd written a letter saying her husband was going to kill her. I found it by accident, and I . . ."

"You what?"

"I had to help her." My voice came out in choked bursts. I'd grown up in a house where the shadow of violence always loomed. For as long as I could remember, it was a place where a casual slap could land on you for not moving quickly enough. The two years Reagan had mostly lived with us had been an oasis of calm, because my parents never behaved like that around other people. But when we were on our own, without eyes on us, our house felt like a feral place. When I was fifteen, things went badly at my father's business, and our homelife really went downhill.

"You stabbed him with a steak knife," Gorey said. "He had organ damage. He could've *died.*"

*Stop being so dramatic,* Caro had told me back then. *This is just what they do.* But I hadn't taken her advice. The week I found the letter, our mother had been wearing a scarf around her neck every day, which was odd. One night, she slipped it off without thinking, and I caught sight of the necklace of bruises circling her pale throat. That was when I'd gone to the kitchen and disappeared a knife into an old tea towel. I told myself I'd act next time I heard them fighting in their bedroom. I hadn't seen the worst of my father's violence, but I'd heard it.

"He was drunk," I said. "He was beating my mother."

I remembered that night like it was a shaky amateur home movie. Maybe it was because I was so rattled when I entered my parents' bedroom. *Get out,* my father had barked at me, but all his fury was directed at my mother. She had started to scream, and he shoved her back. Instead of arguing with him, I'd jabbed the knife into his side.

There was a long silence in the room. "Look, we understand you were in a horrible situation," Villaverde said. "And I'm sorry you went through that. We both are."

His words seemed to nudge his partner along. "No one should ever be in a situation like that," Gorey muttered.

"I was fifteen." The words embarrassed me as they hung in the air between us. Was I using my age as a defense? There was no way to explain to the cops that, in my family, letting outsiders in on our secrets was a crime far worse than violence. Aside from Caro, I had no one I could talk to. Stabbing my father had felt like my *only* option.

"We understand that. We see people all the time who take the law into their own hands. Some of them mean well, but I can tell you their situation never ends well."

Gorey's words were sharp. I couldn't argue. My father had actually refused to call the police or go to the hospital the night I stabbed him. The next day, he'd been so ill he'd passed out with a raging fever. My aim with the knife hadn't been very good, but he caught sepsis, and he ended up in the hospital for weeks.

My mother came to see me as much as she could at Creedmoor Psychiatric Center, where they'd locked me up to see how criminally insane I was. *Why'd you do it, lamb?* she'd asked me gently, in her lilting Irish accent. *That was a terrible thing.*

*He was going to kill you,* I'd told her. *I found your letter.*

*What letter?*

*The one in the Bible.*

She'd crossed herself at that. *That wasn't for you to read, lamb. I'm sorry you saw it.*

*I'm glad I did. He got what he deserved.*

*That's not true. He needs help. I think we all do.*

The memory was making my hands quiver. I clasped them together. "What happened with my father has nothing to do with Caro's death."

"It has *everything* to do with it," Gorey said. "You think men who have bad relationships with their wife deserve to die."

I had thoughts on his definition of *bad relationships*, but I kept them to myself. "I believe in justice."

"But you're out looking for vengeance," Gorey said. "That's not the same thing. I'm not going to pretend I understand what you're going through right now, but you're in dangerous territory."

"I don't understand what ancient family history has to do with this."

"Aubrey Sutton-Braithwaite wants us to file charges against you for what you did to him yesterday," Villaverde said. "We've tried to explain you're under a lot of stress, and—"

"Aubrey?" I was incredulous. "He attacked me."

"You're sitting in front of us, and you look fine," Gorey said. "Meanwhile, he's got two fractured ribs and a concussion."

"He deserved all of it," I muttered darkly. I doubted that his injuries were really that bad. He was probably faking the head trauma.

"What was that?"

It was so tempting to give in to white-hot fury. I wanted to turn the table over, run out of there, hunt down Aubrey, and crack his skull like an egg. But the memory of my mother stopped me.

"Why don't we call my lawyer?" I said. "His name is Hugo Laraya. He's with Casper Peters McNally."

"We know the name," Gorey said. "You can't afford someone like that."

"Yet again, you are wrong," I said. "Where's your phone?"

# CHAPTER 27

## DEIRDRE

I'm not sure what I expected Theodore Thraxton's high-powered lawyer to be like, but it sure wasn't the guy who walked into the interview room. Hugo Laraya looked as if he'd been pulled from a Great Gatsby–themed game of lawn croquet. He was dressed in immaculate white from his pointy leather wingtips to his trilby hat. The detectives stared at him as if he were a storybook character who'd stepped off the page.

"Hi, I'm Deirdre," I said.

"My favorite new client," Laraya said with a smile.

"We were just—" Gorey started to say, but the lawyer put out one hand.

"I know what you were up to," he said pointedly, staring them down. "I've already spoken to an outcry witness to whom Ms. Crawley here described her sexual assault by Aubrey Sutton-Braithwaite."

I blushed at that. Thinking of myself as a victim made me about as comfortable as if fire ants were burrowing under my skin.

"Outcry witness?" Villaverde asked.

"Theodore Thraxton," Laraya said. "The senior one, to be clear." He took a seat next to me. "I spent all of ten minutes researching this Aubrey character, and do you know what I found? Multiple DUIs. A couple of assault charges. Plus, several accusations of sexual assault or rape. Yet here you are, treating one of his victims as if she were the criminal. What are you doing, gentlemen? Where are your heads?"

"Aubrey's dad called the ADA," Gorey said. "He sent over the hospital report. That's how it got to us."

"We knew Deirdre was in mourning for her sister. We wanted to help," Villaverde added.

"Ah, so you were *helping* her by treating her like a perp," Laraya said. "And you wonder why people don't trust the police." He glanced at me. "Let's go, Deirdre."

I was still stunned by what had happened. "I can go?"

"You're not under arrest," Laraya said. "You are most certainly free to go."

Both cops wore the expressions of cartoon characters who'd been run over by a truck. We walked out of the room.

"Let's get out of here before we have a proper chat," Laraya said. "The walls have ears in places like this."

We went out to Fifty-First Street and crossed Third Avenue. Half a block down was Greenacre Park. The name was a bit misleading—it was a fraction of an acre—but it was a green oasis. We sat on a concrete bench and watched the cascading waterfall at the north edge of the park in companionable silence for a minute.

"I don't understand what just happened," I said finally, after I felt calm enough. "Theodore Thraxton gave me your card. I never thought I'd use it. How did you know all that about Aubrey?"

"I did a quick search on the taxi ride down here," Laraya said. "Mr. Thraxton called me, probably just after he spoke with you. He's sort of a strange bird, but he has a tendency to take certain people under his wing."

"It was hard to hear you call me a victim," I said. "I knocked Aubrey on his ass, and he deserved it."

"In the eyes of the law, it's essential that you acted in self-defense. It doesn't look kindly at vigilante justice."

"What do I do now?"

"We need to talk about what happened yesterday," Laraya said. "Then I'll have a word with the ADA. We'll file a police report about what happened to you . . ."

"But I don't want . . ."

"You need to do it," Laraya said firmly. "Don't worry—I'll be able to handle most of it on your behalf. But since he's trying to have charges filed against you, you need to get your side on the record."

"I also told Jude Lazare. She's my sister's friend. She works for the mayor's office—she's in communications. I didn't know where to go after Aubrey slimed on me. I was kind of dazed afterward. He lives a block from City Hall Park, and Jude's office was right there."

"You went there immediately afterward? That's perfect." He looked delighted. "Every witness, every detail is invaluable."

It was helpful, having someone else jog my memory. Through his questions, I remembered I'd told Reagan as well. Then Laraya turned his attention to Snapp.

"You can sue them, you know. They knowingly put you in a dangerous situation."

"They did, but the police just raked me over the coals about some things in my past. I don't want that being dredged up."

"Legally, they can't do that, but of course the law works in funny ways for people with money," Laraya said. "But it's also an option to sue them and settle. Unless they're stupid, they'll want this to go away."

"Wouldn't I be telling the world I was a victim if I did that?"

"They abused you, Deirdre. Snapp was in a position of authority, and they acted like a pimp. They knew what they were sending you into.

There's no shame in speaking up and telling the truth. Silence protects them, not you."

There was a hard knot in my throat that made it hard to answer. "Can I think about it?"

"Of course. I know you've had an awful week," Laraya said. "I haven't even told you yet how sorry I am about Caroline. She was such a warm, lovely person."

"You met her?"

"I was at their wedding," he said.

I didn't remember meeting him there. I'd mostly lurked in the shadows, eventually ducking out early. Jude had been Caro's only bridesmaid.

"Theodore mentioned you're friends with Theo," I said.

"We were best friends in college, but Theo has never forgiven me for doing legal work for his father."

"Really?"

"There's some antagonism between the two of them," Laraya said. "I pointed out to Theo exactly how many Filipino lawyers the white-shoe firm of Casper Peters McNally has: just me. They hired me on his father's recommendation. But Theo sees it as a sort of betrayal. 'You'll get caught up in his web' is how he put it. He says his father always expects interest on any favor he does."

I was tempted to ask Laraya about the money-laundering allegations, but I knew that was pointless.

"Did you know Theo's in Berlin right now?"

"Are you kidding?" He shook his head. "Damn it. That's what I get for trying to help."

"What do you mean?"

"I'm sorry. I should keep my big mouth shut," Laraya said. He was quiet for a minute. "Do you have any idea why things went so wrong between your sister and Theo?"

"Caro never talked about it."

"Well, neither of them talked to me about it." He gave me a small smile. "I always wondered. They were so close at one time."

"All I know for sure right now is that my sister gave me a small fraction of the truth."

"I don't want to sound like a cynical lawyer," he said. "But I think that's all anybody ever gives anyone."

# CHAPTER 28

## THEO

Mehmet Badem's address was in Prenzlauer Berg, an area I knew all too well from my student days. Drugs and fetish clubs existed in every Berlin neighborhood, but if you wanted something dangerous, you were sure to find it there. Badem's address was east of Mauerpark—a reminder of where part of the Berlin Wall once stood—and the charming boutiques and cafés of the Schönhauser Allee.

His building looked industrial, with four boxy floors and an African restaurant on the main level. There were two dozen apartment buzzers, and I pressed them until someone answered. *"Anlieferung,"* I said, hoping that was the right word for *delivery*—my German had always been lacking—and I was buzzed in.

Badem lived on the third floor, and he answered when I knocked. I had immediately recognized his photograph, but if I'd encountered him on the street, I wouldn't have realized it was the same man. He'd been a solid muscular type at one time, but he had morphed into a skeletal wreck. His skin was sallow and sagging, and his eyes were sunken. His dark hair was streaked with gray and slicked back.

It was like looking in a dark mirror. If I'd continued to use all the drugs I'd once been on, I had no reason to believe I'd look any better.

"Mehmet Badem? *Entschuldige.*" I wanted to apologize for showing up at his door unannounced, but I could only get as far as saying *excuse me* in German. *"Ich bin . . ."*

"I know you," he answered in English. He stared at me intently, barely blinking.

"My name is Theo," I said. "You used to work for my family at the Thraxton Hotel."

Badem's eyes widened, and his mouth made a squishy gurgle. "Oh, shit," he murmured.

"I heard you had an accident at the hotel a few years ago . . ."

He stepped back, as if I'd pushed him. I used the opportunity to step inside, quickly shutting the door behind me.

"That's right." Badem took another step back.

"What happened?" I asked him.

"You're a Thraxton. You know what happened," he said, never taking his eyes off mine.

"All I know is that there was an accident five years ago. What kind of work did you do?"

"Security," he said warily.

Of course it was security.

"Cigarette?" he asked me.

"No, thanks."

He retreated further, picking up a pack from the sofa and lighting a cigarette. He may have looked like a wreck, but his apartment was relatively tidy. I took in the big-screen television, video-game console, and new laptop; he wasn't well, but his pension seemed to be supporting him. An annoyed yip came from one of the cushions. A mutt with mottled black-and-white fur sat up and started barking at me.

"Shhh, Snoopy," he chided.

"Cute dog," I said, even though the bundle of fluff was baring its fangs. It was small and probably harmless, but I still had to fight my instinct to flee.

"He gets nervous," Badem said. "Strangers, you know. He doesn't like them."

"I have a few questions for you."

The dog barked again.

"I'll put him in the bedroom," Badem said, scooping the pup into his arms. "Then we can talk."

I walked to the window and stared at the bustling street outside. My first year of school in Berlin, I'd been in Prenzlauer Berg most nights once I discovered it. BDSM clubs were a dime a dozen, but this area was where I'd discovered bloodplay. As often as I could manage, I would pay pretty girls to open my veins. It was how I slipped away. At a certain point, whenever I bled enough, my mind shut down. That was when the voices in my head stopped, when *I am full of hidden horrors* was silenced. No matter how much I worked with Dr. Haven to recover my memory, I never expected to get those moments back—after all, they were dark voids where time and place had no meaning. That had been the entire point.

I stared out the window, wondering why I'd always been so desperate to escape from myself. In my sessions with Dr. Haven, she'd gently guided me into conversations about my parents and how their divorce and my mother's subsequent abandonment of Juliet and me had affected us. But I didn't blame my mother; I believed she'd run away to save herself. My stepmother had said, *Marriage to a Thraxton is sheer misery.* I didn't doubt that.

At that moment, I could hear Mirelle's voice. *What could be more romantic than getting married, Theo? Let's run away and do it. It will be our little secret.* I had agreed immediately because I couldn't imagine life without her. We'd only been together for a short time, but I'd stopped going to clubs because of her; she understood bloodplay and yet was kind and warm and nonjudgmental. But standing in that apartment, overlooking my old bleeding grounds, something about the memory curdled. Mirelle had been everything I wanted, but she never asked for anything back. It was as if she existed for my happiness, and as a young man, I'd accepted that as my due.

Lost as I was in my thoughts, I heard the sharp click behind me and turned away from the window. Mehmet Badem was standing behind me, pointing a gun at my chest.

# CHAPTER 29

## Deirdre

I'd never felt so lost. I didn't have a job, and in spite of Hugo Laraya's assurances, the notion of suing my former employer made me green around the gills. I didn't have a sister anymore, and my conversations with Ben and even Jude gave me a queasy sense that, even though I loved Caro, I hadn't really known her well. I didn't have anyone to talk to honestly about my sister. Reagan cared and wanted to help, but she mostly knew Caro through the filter of what I'd told her. Jude was the opposite: she understood Caro, but wanted to filter uncomfortable information away from me. And Ben had refused to answer my question about their relationship, which only made me believe that my sister really had been stepping out on her husband.

There was only one thing I could think of to do: get as much information as I could directly from Caro herself. I got on the 7 train at Grand Central and headed east.

When I was a little kid, I actually liked hanging out at my father's garage in Willets Point, also known as the Iron Triangle of Queens, a stone's throw from the old Shea Stadium. He let me sit behind the steering wheels, pretending I was a Formula One race-car driver. But it had been a long time since I'd gone over willingly. The place had a newish sign—CRAWLEY'S REPAIRS—soaring above the rusty Quonset hut, but otherwise, it hadn't changed, even though the area around it was being redeveloped. Naturally, my father was the holdout against progress.

I didn't see him as I approached. I was in the broad driveway, breathing from my diaphragm, steeling myself to see him, when I noticed his legs sticking out from underneath a car, the knee-high socks he insisted on wearing rolled down to his ankles, a weird habit he'd always had. It made me think of the beginning of *The Wizard of Oz*, and how the Wicked Witch of the East was crushed.

I tried to speak, but my voice felt rusty. It had been years since I'd said a word to him, and I didn't know how to start.

I hesitated for so long that he had time to finish whatever repair he was making and slide out from under the car. There were smudges of grease on his hands and forehead. He jolted as if he thought I was a ghost and banged his head against the car.

"Deirdre?" he asked, as if I were a mirage. A smile crept across his face. "I'm so glad you . . ."

"This isn't a social visit," I said sharply. "I need to see the last message Caro emailed you."

The smile faded. He wiped his hands on a rag he pulled out of his overalls. It seemed to hold all his attention. "I can't think when that was. We never used email much." His Irish accent was strong, as if he'd just come over from Belfast. Thirty-plus years of living in Queens hadn't softened it at all.

"I know you got a message from Caro the day of her funeral," I said. "I have to see it."

He frowned at me, his eyes squinting in concentration as if taking in a problem he could never solve. "How could she email after she *died*?" He got to his feet.

"She used a service called . . . never mind. Caroline set up some messages to go out in case she died. I got one. You did too."

"I don't have much use for that internet nonsense. But I can check." He tossed the rag on the ground and turned on his heel.

We went through a door that led to a small room at the side of the building. His office was exactly the way I remembered it. There was a small plywood desk and a pair of towering bookcases he'd cobbled together himself. His computer was an ancient beige plastic desktop. It actually screeched when he started it, like a pterodactyl was hiding inside.

"This might take a minute," he muttered, putting on his reading glasses.

On the wall was a framed portrait of my mother on her wedding day. Underneath it was a shadow box with a single red rose. I recognized it immediately. It was one of the flowers that had topped my mother's coffin. My mother had died of cancer just before Teddy was born. I couldn't blame my father for that. But I hated him for everything else.

"Okay, it's fired up," he said.

I edged around the desk so I could see his screen. "Go to your email."

Another minute ticked by while his Hotmail account loaded.

"You still use that?" I asked.

"Why not? It works."

There was nothing from Osiris's Vault in his inbox. True to his minimalist spirit, my father had only a dozen emails in the folder, so it wasn't hard to tell. "Check your spam," I said.

He clicked on that folder. It was empty.

"You must have another email address."

"This is the only one." He made a startled yelp. "Hold on, there's another for the business. Let me try that."

I waited, staring at the walls because it took him forever to log in. "Sorry, I don't usually use this account," he said. I ignored him, examining the framed photographs on his desk. There was one of our family together when I was a toddler and Caro was six, and another of my sister and me hugging.

"Did you put these photos up because Caro died?" I asked him.

"No, they've been there awhile now."

"Why do you have photos of me on your desk?"

He stopped typing and turned his eyes to meet mine. "Because you're my daughter."

"We don't have a relationship."

He turned back to the computer. "That's your choice. I respect it. But it doesn't matter whether you're speaking to me or not. You're still my child."

"Don't try to use the psychobabble you used on Caro with me," I warned. "She was the forgiving type. I'm not."

"You're not going to like this, but you're more like me than Caro ever was."

"Just find the message," I snapped.

"I'm not saying that to hurt your feelings," he added. "I know what it's like to be angry. To not know how to deal with that rage."

"Shut up. You don't know anything about me. We're biologically related, but I don't think of you as my father. To me, you're just the man who used to beat up my mother."

There was a stone-cold silence in the room.

"I was a different man when I was drinking," he whispered. "I can't tell you how much I regret it."

This wasn't a new argument. He'd always blamed alcohol for his rages, even back when he was *still* drinking. He liked to pretend it covered up his true nature, as if it were a disguise controlling the man who wore it. But the opposite was true: Alcohol unmasked the real man and his black heart. It revealed his true identity, like a horror-movie monster pulling off its human mask to reveal slime and tentacles. The darkness underneath was always there.

"Just find the message," I repeated.

I watched him go through company emails. Nothing from Osiris's Vault.

"Maybe it's in the mail at home?" he suggested.

"It's an email! Not regular mail!" I shouted in frustration. "Look, you must have another email address. People sign up for them all the time and forget about them."

"I've used this one for twenty years," he said. "The company one is newer, because I resisted having a website for so long. But these are the only two I use."

Exasperated, I pulled out my phone. "It would look like this. See?"

There it was: Osiris's Vault keeps all your data safe and secure, said the text at the top of the screen. Caroline Crawley wants you to read this letter.

"*That* thing?" He looked astonished. "I deleted it immediately."

"What? Why? What did it say?"

"I don't know. I never opened it. But these vultures were calling me and showing up here asking if Caro was on drugs. I thought it was part of that."

"Open up your trash folder," I ordered him.

He did. There it was: Caro's message. I pushed his hand out of the way and clicked on it myself.

Dad,

This is the hardest letter I've ever had to write. I've always felt like it's my job to be cheerful and upbeat, but the truth is that I have been miserable for a long time. I've always hated face-to-face confrontations—or even conversations about difficult subjects—and that's why I'm putting down these thoughts on (digital) paper.

Having my own child has made me think so much about what influences you when you're growing up. It's made me think about you and Mom—for better and worse. When I think back on my childhood, it's with resentment. There's no way to erase the bad years, but I'm grateful for the ways you've changed. I wish you'd been the man you are now when I was growing up.

I know Deirdre is difficult, but it's up to you to make amends with her. I know you think she hates you and wants nothing to do with you, but it's on you to get past that. We are the way we are because of how you were. If anything happens to me, I want you two to be extensively involved in raising Teddy.

I love you,

Caro

Of all the things I was expecting, that message wasn't it. I gawped at it. When I glanced at my father, I realized he was astonished too. We were a pair of fish who'd leaped into uncharted territory and discovered we couldn't breathe there.

"What do you think she meant?" he asked. "About being miserable. Was that about Theo? She was always a happy person. Caro could light up any room."

"Happy isn't the same as cheerful," I answered grimly. "As she points out in the first paragraph."

"Was she still angry with me? I thought we were on good terms."

If he was looking for comfort, he was searching in the wrong place. I didn't answer. I was too busy seething. *I know Deirdre is difficult.* Caro had always played the role of the good daughter, while I'd been cast as the bad one. Yet there she was, writing that she'd felt the same way I had as a child. We should've been each other's allies. Instead, we'd been estranged for years. Maybe I was the difficult one, but I wasn't the dishonest one.

"What do you think she meant about resentment?" he added. "I thought we were close. I always told her she could tell me if she needed help."

That was the last straw.

"Help, from you? You are literally the last person in the world anyone would turn to for help."

"Deirdre . . ."

"She wanted you to know you were a shitty father who screwed up your kids. Caro played nice and made the best of it, but underneath it all, guess what?" My voice had gotten louder with each breath. I was shouting now. "She hated you as much as I do."

I stormed out of the room and slammed the front door behind me. What Caro had written in her letter was true—she had always avoided any confrontation. I thrived on it. But at that moment, I had to get away from him. I'd hoped to get a clue about what was going on with the Thraxtons. Instead, I'd seen Caro's unvarnished truths about our family. Nothing could have prepared me for that.

# CHAPTER 30

## THEO

"What are you doing?" I asked, staring down the barrel of the handgun. I wasn't afraid so much as bewildered. I had hunted Mehmet Badem down to answer questions about the night Mirelle died, only to learn he'd rather shoot me than talk.

Badem stared at me, his hand quivering slightly. "I know all about you," he said. "I never went to the police. I never talked. Why would you come here? I will not let you kill me."

"All I want are answers," I said, trying to sound confident and blasé, as if a gun weren't pointed at my chest. "About the night Mirelle Beaulieu died."

"I didn't kill her," he said. "I swear to you I didn't."

His words hit me like a tidal wave. I was there to ask him what he'd witnessed; it had never occurred to me that he might be Mirelle's killer.

"I'm not accusing you of that," I said. "But I remember your face. I saw you the night Mirelle died. You . . . I think you carried me. You put me on a plane. My sister, Juliet, was there."

He nodded. "I remember her. She was angry. She said, 'Drop him.' She wanted me to throw you on the floor of the plane, I think. I put you in a seat and buckled you up."

"It sounds like I should be thanking you. Please put the gun down. I'm not here to hurt you. All I want are answers."

Badem stared into my eyes for what felt like a month before lowering his gun. He rolled up the lower half of his shirt, revealing a thin torso with two bullet holes in it. They were old and healed, but the flesh around them had settled in jagged mounds, like miniature volcanoes. "That's what happened the last time I took an assignment from Harris," he said.

It jolted me, hearing the name of my father's trusted lieutenant. My father had grown the business with shady side ventures, and Harris and Klaus were his partners in those crimes. "I would've jumped off a cliff rather than work with Harris on anything."

"I should have done that," Badem said, lowering his shirt. "But for several years, it was a very good living."

"I don't remember the night Mirelle died, and I'm trying to piece it together. I need you to tell me what you remember. Please, will you do that?" There was desperation in my voice, and I believe he heard it.

Badem gestured with the gun for me to sit on the sofa. I took the cushion Snoopy had vacated. Badem went into the kitchenette and rattled around, out of sight for a minute. When he returned, it was without the weapon. Instead, he brandished two glasses and a bottle filled with a clear liquid. He returned to the kitchenette and came back with a bottle of water.

"You have raki before?" he asked me.

"In Istanbul once," I answered. "That was enough."

He chuckled lightly. "It's not poison; it just tastes like it." He poured some liqueur into each glass and chased it with water. Instantly, the liquid became cloudy. He took a drink and made a face. "You too," he said, and I followed suit. It was bitter and bracing.

"Tell me what you remember," I prompted.

"I had been working at the hotel for six, seven years then. It was a good job, the best job I ever had in this country," he said. "One afternoon, Harris came in. He said he needed me to be on call that night."

"Hold on, Harris was in Berlin? We're talking about twelve years ago. January thirtieth."

"Yes, it was Harris. Most of the special assignments I did were for Klaus von Strohm. But the particularly dangerous ones were managed by Harris."

I stared into the pale clouds swirling in my glass. Harris was almost always by my father's side. When I'd called my father, he'd been traveling. Only . . . I didn't actually remember calling my father; I'd been told I called him. What the hell had brought Harris to Berlin?

"Did Harris tell you what you would be doing?"

"No. He said it would be a late night, but it wouldn't be dangerous." He took another swig. "I got his call at three in the morning. I lived in Charlottenburg then; it wasn't a long drive, maybe ten minutes. He picked me up, and we drove to the edge of Mitte, near the zoo. Harris told me to wait for him. I remember it was a freezing night, and he turned the engine off. It was so cold, and he was gone for fifteen minutes."

He was staring into his glass as if a vision of that night were playing out in it.

I was trying to process the details he'd laid out. It chilled me that Harris had been there; I didn't remember that at all. It made sense that my father would send him to clean up the scene—Harris's military background and total lack of ethics would've been assets in that—but I couldn't understand why he'd told Badem to be ready earlier in the day. It was as if he'd known something terrible was going to happen.

Or, perhaps, he was going to make something terrible happen.

"And after you waited outside?" I asked.

"Harris came back and ordered me to come in. He said I had to keep quiet, not say a word. We went to an apartment on the first floor. You were there, lying on the floor. There was a beautiful girl lying next to you." He shook his head and rubbed his eyes with his palms. "She was dead. There was a knife in her chest. Blood was still pouring out of her body. It was getting on you."

"But the knife . . ." My throat constricted; it was almost impossible to choke the words out. "The knife was in my hand."

"Because Harris put it there," Badem said. "You were out cold. After he moved the knife, Harris told me to wake you up. I tried shaking you. Harris told me to stop being so delicate and slapped you a couple of times. It was impossible to wake you up. I told Harris I couldn't, and he said we had to. He said it was the whole point—you had to see this."

A vicious thought had been coiling around my brain as soon as Badem mentioned Harris. I wanted to throw up. I'd spent more than a decade with the awful certainty that I was a killer, only to find out that I had been set up. If Mehmet Badem could be believed, Harris had murdered Mirelle while I was dead to the world.

"You finally came around, and you were very confused. You stared at the dead girl for a long time, like you couldn't focus. Then you screamed 'Mirelle!' over and over. You were crying. You tried to get up, but Harris was holding your head down. I was holding your body in place."

I remembered seeing Mirelle's dead body and screaming. I'd had no sense of time, or how I'd stabbed her. I'd never understood why I'd attacked her in the first place—the voices in my head quieted when violence was done to me, not when I committed it. What I'd struggled to understand was how I'd blacked out from blood loss, yet had enough strength to attack and kill Mirelle. For the first time, the fog in my head lifted.

"I didn't call my father, asking for help, did I?"

"You didn't call anyone. Harris hit you, and you went out cold."

Everything I'd thought I knew about that night was a lie.

"We drove east to a small airstrip. There was a private plane waiting for you. Your sister was already on board. Like I told you, she was furious." Badem gave me a sorrowful look. "I remember feeling worried about you. I didn't understand what had happened, but I pitied you."

# CHAPTER 31

## Deirdre

Leaving the garage, I knew I'd made a terrible mistake. I should never have gone to see my father, even if curiosity was killing me. He was bound to ramble on about how much he'd changed, and I was going to hate him as much as ever. I'd thought I could control it, but seeing what Caro had written to him had put me over the edge.

I was ashamed I'd let the situation devolve into our old, tired battle. We mixed like oil and water. It had been that way between us since the day I'd discovered my mother's desperate letter hidden in the family Bible. I'd hated their fights long before that, but finding the letter gave me a clarity I'd lacked before. Acknowledging my mother was a kind of hostage, living in terror of the man she'd married, changed everything. Before, I'd thought of the fights as *their* fights, as if the battles belonged to both of them and were as routine as dancing on Friday nights. After all, my mother had a sharp tongue, and she wasn't cowed by her husband, no matter how hard he hit her.

I got back on the 7 train, switching to the G at Court Square. The G was the lone train connecting Queens with Brooklyn, and taking it was always a weird adventure as it zigged and zagged. Every so often, I glanced around furtively, worried someone might see a tear glimmering in my eye, but I had little to fear. The G train was half-empty, and nobody who glanced my way looked past my tattoos.

It was an unusually slow train. It took me over an hour to get to Fort Hamilton Parkway. From there, I walked to Green-Wood Cemetery. As I headed in, I wished I had a place where I could visit my mother. I didn't believe in ghosts, exactly, but I didn't *disbelieve* in them either. Energy had to go somewhere, after all. My mother's ashes were, as far as I knew, still in an urn from the funeral home at our father's house. Caro once told me our father hadn't even opened the paper bag; he'd stuck it in a cabinet. I hated my father for many reasons, but the fact he hadn't given my mother any kind of decent resting place was high on the list.

I wasn't sure I could find Caro's grave on my own. I'd driven in with Theo, looping around the twisting roads in a car. On foot, entering from a gate on the far side of the cemetery, I could roam over the grassy hills with tombstones sprouting like toadstools, walking in a crooked approximation of how the crow flies. I was distracted by monuments and mausoleums whispering of grandiose fantasies. There was a lot of beauty in this place, but everything I appreciated was a reminder of another family's loss. I didn't mind the detailed pyramids and castles— even if they felt more like monuments to big egos instead of people— but the statues of sweet children and gentle lambs and doomed lovers overwhelmed me. I wasn't the sentimental type, but the atmosphere of unrelenting grief inched under my skin like dampness, making my bones ache.

By the time I got to my sister's grave, I was ready to lie down beside her. The line from her letter—*I know Deirdre is difficult*—still stuck in my craw, but it wasn't wrong. I wasn't just difficult—I prided myself on it, going toe-to-toe with people I despised. I wondered how, exactly, I'd gotten that way. It had been part of my nature as long as I could remember.

"You could've told me how you felt when you were alive," I said, plopping down onto the grass. "It would've made everything easier."

The gravediggers had filled the hole with dirt, leaving a raised brown scar in the green grass. The small stone marker was covered by a bouquet of white roses with their heavy blooms drooping, as if they'd fallen asleep.

I sat quietly for a while, wishing I could channel my sister's spirit. *Why didn't you tell me what was going on with you?* I wanted to ask her. *Why feed me a handful of bread crumbs after you're already gone?*

In the quiet of the graveyard, I couldn't help but think about the difference in tone between the letter she'd written to our father and the one she'd sent me. The guy from Osiris's Vault, Todd, had said something about different versions of her note to me. Maybe that was because she'd dashed it off early in the morning, less than an hour before she died. Her letter to our father was thoughtful and measured, even if it contained painful truths. Her message to me was rushed and panicked. Something had terrified her.

*Theo killed his first wife and got away with it. Bring him to justice, no matter what you have to do.*

Theo's father had admitted his son had shown up around five that morning, but his visit had been brief. Ben had told me he was supposed to meet Caro near her house, but that plan had changed, with my sister deciding to come down to his neighborhood. I understood that Theo's surprise appearance had rattled Caro—it had to be why she'd dashed off her message to me—but I felt like there was something I was missing, some detail that would thread everything together.

I didn't know what she expected me to do. She'd left me with exactly nothing . . .

Or had she?

All her data in Osiris's Vault was gone, but that wasn't her only digital footprint. I thought of the photographs and the memory card she'd given me. The spreadsheets had been a surprise. What if there was something else on there, a detail I'd missed because I hadn't known what I was looking for?

That thought pricked at me like a thorn all the way back to Queens. I didn't even stop at Kung Fu Tea on my way home. But when I landed on my block, a cop car was parked outside the house, lights flashing.

My landlord, Saira Mukherjee, was on the lawn, talking to a uniformed cop. He was taking notes and nodding. When she noticed me, Saira waved me over frantically.

"We've been robbed!" she yelled.

I hurried over. "What happened?"

"Wilson was in the basement"—Wilson was the human foghorn in the room next to mine—"and he heard some strange sounds. When he poked his head out of his room, he saw your door was open. There was a man ransacking your room."

"You caught him?"

Saira gave me a look that said, *Are you for real?* Wilson hid from his own shadow most of the year.

"The burglar saw him and punched Wilson in the head. He dragged him into your room and messed him up. Poor Wilson's at Elmhurst now." Saira meant the public hospital nearby.

"We're going to need you to do an inventory, see what was taken," the cop said.

I nodded and moved on autopilot toward the house.

My room was a mess. Whoever had broken in had ignored the lock and splintered the plywood door. I didn't own much, but most of what I had was lying on the floor. I sifted through the rubble but couldn't find the envelope from Caro. My laptop was gone. I searched on my hands and knees in case the memory card had somehow fallen out of the envelope, but it had vanished.

# CHAPTER 32

## DEIRDRE

There was no way I could stay at my apartment that night. I gathered up some clothes and toiletries and made my escape to Reagan's house. I felt embarrassed, standing on the porch. There I was, asking for them to take care of me. Again.

"Would it be okay if I stayed here tonight?" I asked when Mrs. Chen answered. "Someone broke into my place."

Reagan wasn't even there—she was working crazy hours as usual. Her mother set me up in what had been my bedroom as a teenager. The window overlooked the street, and the tree next to it was a favorite spot for blue jays. I had no way to thank her enough.

"Who would break into your room, Dee?" Mrs. Chen asked me, perplexed. "You have no money! What could they take? This city is too dangerous now."

I lay awake for part of the night, asking myself the same question. As much as I hated Theo, he was an ocean away. Ben seemed like the obvious suspect—he'd wanted me to hand over the memory card—but another part of my brain was stuck on Theo's father. I'd mentioned the card to him. Even though I hadn't said what was on it, he surely knew Caro had a memory card on her when she died. The cops said it had been given back to her family, so maybe the old man even knew what was on it.

I told myself I was being paranoid. Aubrey Sutton-Braithwaite was definitely out to get me. I could see him breaking into my room and smashing everything I owned for fun. But he wouldn't care about the memory card.

In the morning, I managed to stop Mrs. Chen from waking Reagan up.

"Do you have any idea how hard she works?" I asked.

"Let me tell you about working hard," she shot back. I listened quietly while she regaled me with stories I may have heard a few times before. In the end, I promised to go to Mass with her—on a Saturday, no less—and that mollified her enough to let Reagan rest.

Caro's funeral aside, it had been a long time since I'd set foot in a church. Mrs. Chen attended St. Adalbert's. Growing up, I'd taken First Communion at the Church of the Ascension, another Elmhurst institution. It lay on the north side of the train tracks that bisected the neighborhood, just like my father's house did. St. Adalbert's was on the south side, which meant the odds of running into him were low.

"You have a mask?" Mrs. Chen asked me on our way in. "People still wear them here."

"Always." I pulled one out of my bag and put it on. It had become normal to carry one at all times, especially for taking public transit. That was ironic because New York's subway was better ventilated than most buildings in the city, yet it remained a collective source of anxiety.

St. Adalbert's looked like a church from an old lithograph, with its Gothic bell tower and clean white trim over sandy bricks. It had been founded when the neighborhood was Polish, and that was still part of its identity even in a diverse community—the notice board said the service after ours would be in Polish. My mind drifted as I stared at the stained-glass windows, much as I had as an antsy child. The sermon was about charity, and the word stuck in my brain. I'd been pulling at the threads of my sister's life, but not that one, even though everywhere I went there were reminders of her philanthropy. Mrs. Chen frowned when I pulled out my phone and looked up the Diotima Civic Society. Dr. Adinah Gerstein's contact information was on the site, and I tapped out a quick email, asking if we could talk in person, before mouthing a contrite "sorry" and tucking the phone away.

"Whose butt are you kicking today?" Mrs. Chen asked as we headed out after the service. She was almost my height, which made her unusually tall for a Chinese woman of her generation. She wore her hair in an angular bob, liked to wear black as much as I did, and never left the house without red lipstick.

"Why do you think I'm kicking anyone's butt?"

"It's what you do. Some people need kicking."

"I'm going to see a woman who knew my sister," I said. "Then I'm visiting my nephew. There's a risk my brother-in-law will show up. In that case, you might have to bail me out of jail later."

"Try not to let that happen." She touched my cheek. "You need some rouge."

I rolled my eyes, but inside, I was smiling. Mrs. Chen could drive Reagan crazy with her constant stream of unsolicited advice. Her daughter took it as criticism, but I looked at it differently. Mrs. Chen was one of the only people in the world who actually *cared* if my face was rosy. Or if I lived or died, for that matter. Nitpicking was her way of helping, and the truth was I needed that kind of help sometimes.

"Do you have any with you?" I asked.

"Of course." She dug into her purse, pulled out a little pot of color with blooming flowers and Korean words on the lid, and dotted cream blush onto my cheekbones. "Better," she added, rubbing it in. "Be careful when you're out."

"I try."

"No, you don't. You take too many risks." She patted my arm. "But you are a good person."

"I saw my father yesterday. He definitely doesn't think I'm a good person."

"Did he say that?"

"No. But we fought."

"If you didn't, something would be wrong." She smiled again. "You *are* a good sister. You're doing what's right. *Shuǐ dī shí chuān.* You remember what that means?"

"Dripping water pierces a stone."

"That's right. You are strong. Tenacious. You *will* pierce the stone. Just be careful."

"I'm careful."

"Bad things never walk alone," she warned. "Keep that in mind."

# CHAPTER 33

## DEIRDRE

The Diotima website didn't list a mailing address, but Adinah Gerstein sent me an address in Greenwich Village, at the corner of University Place and Twelfth Street. The building turned out to be doorman-free, so I let myself in and took the elevator up to the seventh floor. A plaque on the door identified it as Dr. Gerstein's suite. The building was on the old and crumbly side, but inside the office was airy and modern, with white walls, framed prints by Frida Kahlo and Georgia O'Keeffe, and flowering plants dotting the reception area. A poster of *The Two Fridas* caught my eye. On the left was the artist in a formal white European gown; on the right she was in a colorful Tehuana costume. The pair held hands and seemed to share a heart that had been cut out of the woman in the white dress, who was holding a pair of scissors and had blood on her skirt.

"Hello, Deirdre. I'm so glad you reached out."

I turned and saw the willowy woman I'd met at Caroline's funeral. Her braids were down, loosely gathered at the nape of her neck, but she looked just as elegant.

"Thanks for seeing me on such short notice, Dr. Gerstein."

"It's Adinah. I'm only 'Doctor' to my patients." She led me into her office and gestured at a plush armchair. "Please, sit down."

Her office was small but cozy, with green plants on every available surface. She returned to her perch behind her desk, making me feel like the doctor was in.

I didn't know how to start. "I feel like I'm going in circles," I said. "I loved my sister, but we weren't that close. And now that she's gone . . ." I took a breath. "I feel like everyone has an agenda when they talk about her. I don't know how to judge what they say, if it's true."

"How much does it matter?" she asked.

I considered that. "Caro wrote me a message to read after she died." There was a hard lump in my throat.

"Delivered by Osiris's Vault?" Adinah asked.

"How did you know?"

"My nephew works there." She smiled, and I wondered if she was talking about Todd. "I've encouraged women to write notes identifying their abusers in case the worst were to happen. But it's not all doom and gloom. Anyone who wants to keep their location completely private can use the service. Or people who want to get something off their chest without having a conversation about it."

"This is what my sister wrote to me." I pulled the message up for what felt like the millionth time and slid my phone across her desk. I didn't want to look at it again.

Adinah read it quietly and slid the phone back.

"Reading that message led me down a rabbit hole," I said. "What Caro says is clear. Her husband wanted to kill her. But the more I dig, the more I find people who . . . people who had their own motives to hurt her. How long did you know her?"

"I met Caroline when she was a student at SUNY. She talked to me for an assignment and ended up wanting to get involved. Diotima's always been run in a decentralized way, so she was able to answer hotline calls from New Paltz."

"Did Caro ever tell you that our father beat our mother?"

"No." Adinah shook her head sadly. "She told me your mother used to hit her."

I was so upset I couldn't answer. "That's not . . ." *That's not true,* I wanted to say, even though it wasn't exactly a lie. *You get away with everything because you're the baby* was Caro's refrain when we were kids. I had dim memories of my mother slapping me, but they were buried deep. *You're lucky. She used to hit me with a hairbrush,* Caro had told me more than once.

"Violence is often part of our family histories," Adinah said. "It's especially painful to talk about, because you feel shame. You have a sense of being disloyal, even though you're not."

She pushed a box of tissues toward me, and I dried my eyes and blew my nose.

"I don't even really know what Diotima does," I said, desperate to turn the thread of our conversation away from myself.

"Have you ever heard of Diotima of Mantinea?" Adinah asked. "She's an important character in Plato's *Symposium.* Her ideas were the basis for the ideal of platonic love. She was a real person, though historians disagree about who she was in real life. I was fascinated by her, and so I borrowed her name." She steepled her hands. "The Diotima Civic Society is dedicated to educating women and men about domestic abuse. We help people get out of abusive situations. You probably know this already, but a great many people who leave an abusive partner in New York end up homeless. They have to navigate the city's shelter system, which is inadequate and even dangerous. Imagine taking your children and leaving your abuser and ending up in that situation. We help people—mostly women, but some men as well—into safe housing."

"Sure." I nodded, glad that she was filling up the air while I recovered.

"A lot of institutions help abusers, not victims. For example, when kids are involved, an abuser has custody rights. The abuser knows where their victim lives. The law pretty much lays out a map for the abuser. Diotima provides assistance that government-funded groups can't."

"Like what?" I asked, throwing the wad of tissue in a bin next to the desk. I'd asked about Diotima because I needed to get my head together, but now I was genuinely curious.

"Have you ever heard the name Deisy Garcia?" Adinah asked.

"No."

"Her case happened a few years back. Deisy went to the police for help with her abusive ex. Only, her report was taken in Spanish and never translated. She made three reports in all, and the police did nothing. Then, one night, her ex came over and stabbed Deisy and their two young daughters to death."

My stomach clenched. I could imagine the woman's desperation, and it made my body shake.

"I didn't know about the case until after she was murdered, but it was like a polestar for me," Adinah said. "I thought, 'What could have saved Deisy?' Some of it is activism, forcing the courts to change and the police to pay attention. But we can't wait for laws to change. Seventy-five percent of women who are killed by their partners are murdered *after* they leave. They need to go to great lengths to escape. Sometimes that means they need fake IDs and other help that's not considered legal."

I was suddenly struck with new respect for my sister.

"These days, you can't get a burner without ID," Adinah went on. "It's an antiterrorism measure, and it makes sense when you look at it that way, but it does no favors to abuse victims who need anonymity. Ours is not an approach most people approve of. They want things done cleanly and legally. But that's a luxury we don't have in every case. Sometimes, it's a life-or-death situation. Caroline understood that. She stopped working the hotline when she finished school, but she gave us a lot of money."

"Thraxton money," I said, but my brain was stuck on the burner phone. Ben had mentioned my sister having one, and I hadn't believed him because I couldn't picture how Caro could get one. Turned out my imagination was lacking.

"Now that she's gone, there's something I should show you. Her message says Theo's the threat, but . . ." She punched a code into a desk drawer, and I heard six beeps. "Caroline asked me to arrange this for her."

She handed me a pair of passports. I opened the first one and saw my sister's image next to the name Deirdre Jane Brooks. The second passport made my heart skip a beat. Teddy's face was identified as belonging to Edward Ryan Brooks.

"What the hell is this?" I asked. "I don't understand."

"She didn't really explain, except that she had to get away from the Thraxtons," Adinah said.

"Not just Theo?"

"The whole family. Her sister-in-law made her miserable. Her mother-in-law . . ."

"Ursula? I thought they got along."

"You know there was some strange issue about Caroline's stuff being moved around, right?" Adinah said. "Caroline blamed Theo for it. But Theo was gone a lot, and it went on. Then one day, Caroline found her mother-in-law in her room."

"Ursula was the gremlin?" It sounded crazy, but Adinah's face was serious.

"Apparently she was going through Caroline's things," Adinah said. "I asked Caroline about it later, and she claimed everything was fine. She and her mother-in-law had talked it out, and they understood each other. She said Ursula was on her side."

"That's something, I guess."

"That was also the day Caroline asked me to get passports for herself and Teddy," Adinah said. "Caroline told me the whole family was like a Greek tragedy, and she had to get her son out of there."

# CHAPTER 34

## THEO

My instinct was to jump on the next plane to New York and strangle Harris with my bare hands. It was easiest to hate him, even though I had enough reasons to know that Juliet and my father had been involved as well. My sister had been there in person, after all, and my father had lied to me about my calling him for help. After being trapped for so many years with the belief that I was a murderer, I felt as if I'd been released from prison. Mehmet Badem didn't know who had killed Mirelle, but I did: Harris. The only question was who had come up with the plan. I couldn't head back to New York with only the word of an ailing drug addict to support my accusations. I needed more.

I hadn't laid eyes on Klaus von Strohm in four years, and while I didn't know where to find him, I knew how to reach him. I dialed a pager number and waited for the call back. One of Klaus's henchmen phoned me within the quarter hour. "This is Theo Thraxton," I told him. "I'm in Berlin, and I need to see Klaus as quickly as possible."

Half an hour later, I received another call. "Klaus will meet you at your hotel at seven thirty. Be dressed for dinner."

As I hung up, I realized that I hadn't told Klaus where I was staying. Not that it mattered. Berlin was his town, and he owned it.

———

A black Mercedes was waiting outside my hotel at the appointed time. The driver opened the door, and I slid inside. The car was empty.

"I take it Klaus is meeting me at the restaurant?" I asked the driver in English as he settled into his seat. He was nineteen or twenty, olive skinned and dark haired.

"Yes, sir," he answered.

The drive into the heart of Mitte took fifteen minutes and brought me back to the Brandenburg Gate—now lit for evening and looking exactly as I remembered it—and to the grand boulevard of Unter den Linden. The driver turned right on Friedrichstrasse and right again on Behrenstrasse before stopping suddenly in front of an alleyway. "Here you are, sir."

"Where's the restaurant?"

"Here you are, sir," the boy repeated. He wasn't going to be of any help. I got out of the car.

The street wasn't well lit, but the empty alley was forbidding. There was a light near the end, and I followed it all the way back. The lighted area turned out to be a loading dock, but it was empty. I stepped inside and followed it to the end. Another alley was to my left, this one filled with blue and red dumpsters. If Klaus wanted to murder me and dispose of my body, this was his chance. I took a deep breath, and my nose immediately regretted it, but I plunged ahead.

Up a small set of stairs near the end of this alley was a metal door with two lights above it. An unmarked buzzer was on the wall. I pressed it and waited. There was a buzz from inside, and I pressed the door; it swung open.

Inside was almost as forbidding. I pushed past the velvet blackout drapes into a dimly lit room. There were two men standing behind a wooden bar.

"I'm having dinner with Klaus von Strohm," I said in English.

"Take the stairs to your right," one of the men answered. "He's waiting for you."

That thought echoed ominously in my head as I followed the narrow staircase up. After the desolation of the street and alleyways, I wasn't prepared for the buzzy dining room. It looked boxy and industrial, but it had been painted white, with silver orbs dangling from the ceiling. Cylindrical lights and candles illuminated the space, and metal pipes ran from ceiling to floor, reflecting the glow. The only art was a giant framed poster with *ficken*—fuck—written in the center.

Klaus was waiting on a red velvet banquette. A smile stretched across his face as I approached. He stood, taking my hand. "My dear Theo, it has been too long. It is good to see you looking so well." His smile faded. "I offer you my deepest condolences about your wife. I only met her at your wedding, but she was such a lovely young woman."

"Thank you."

I looked him over as we sat down, oddly isolated in our quiet corner of the busy restaurant. Klaus was—as far as I knew—the closest thing my father had ever had to a friend. They were roughly the same age—in their early seventies now—and while their personalities were dissimilar on the surface—my father gregarious, Klaus the saturnine former Stasi cop—they were united in being total bastards.

"How did you know where I was staying?" I asked.

"Come on, Theo. Don't I get to be a little bit mysterious?" He was dressed in what I was positive was once a bespoke gray Hugo Boss suit, but it sagged on his frame. Klaus had been close to three hundred pounds at one point, but he had downsized. I wondered how voluntary that was; he looked frailer than I'd ever seen him.

"About that, fine. But not about the night Mirelle died," I said. "You're going to tell me the full story."

"You may find this hard to believe, but I had absolutely nothing to do with that."

"You're right—I find that impossible to believe." I shifted in my seat. "You and my father were always partners in crime."

"Not in that girl's death, Theo." He leaned forward. "I've taken the liberty of ordering everything on the menu. It's all vegetarian—don't laugh, I haven't eaten meat in over a year. Let them bring us some wine, and then we'll talk."

Klaus always had been a control freak, but I couldn't care less about the food or drink. "As long as you answer my questions, I don't care what's on the menu."

The table service took a moment, with a waiter opening a bottle of riesling. Then he was gone, and Klaus lifted his glass.

"To the memories of those we've lost," Klaus said.

We tapped glasses.

"I'm going to tell you what I know, and I want you to fill in the blanks," I said. "I've always avoided thinking about Mirelle because of the horrific way her life ended. But once I started remembering—and looking at the facts in the cold, hard light of day—it all smacked of a setup. Mirelle just landed on my doorstep one day. That wasn't an accident. What I want to know is, how deeply were you involved?"

He met my eyes. "We say we wish to know dark secrets, Theo, but we rarely mean it. The truth is often so ugly we can't look it in the face."

"I need to know what happened."

"If you are certain, then. Your suspicion is correct, Theo: I hired her."

"Hired? She was a prostitute?"

"She was an aspiring actress with a sideline as a dominatrix," Klaus said. "You had a type. Your father was hysterical about the clubs you frequented. About all the drugs. I kept telling him you needed your freedom, that you'd come to your senses eventually. But your father insisted. That's why I hired Nastya."

"Who?"

"You knew her as Mirelle. She was a Russian girl. She was talented with languages, good with accents. You never imagined she wasn't French, did you?"

"No," I admitted.

"I knew she was what you needed just then," Klaus said. "And it worked. You stopped going to those clubs. You used drugs, but not as much. Things were looking up. At least, I thought they were."

"What happened?"

"Your father was angry. He was paying this girl a lot of money, plus footing the bill for her apartment. He didn't want simply an *improvement*; he wanted . . . everything to be his way." Klaus snapped his fingers. "He wanted you to be his creature. You understand?"

"Yes." My father had always wanted a son who would show off his superiority to the world. I was an embarrassment.

"The straw that broke the camel's back was when Nastya took you on that little trip through Alsace for your twentieth birthday. Your father lost his mind when you told him you got married. He called me, ranting about this *Schlampe* trapping his son. I told him to calm down, that the marriage wasn't even valid. But he took it like a shot across the bow. He thought Nastya—Mirelle—had her hooks in you too deep."

"What about my sister? What was her role in all of this?"

"Juliet?" Klaus asked with surprise. "What role would she have? She was still a student then. If she knew of Mirelle, it was only what you or your father told her."

"But Juliet was on the plane that took me to rehab . . ." As the words tumbled out of my mouth, I remembered what she'd said that night. *You ruined my week in Paris, you stupid piece of shit. I wish you were dead.* It dawned on me that nothing about the night Mirelle was killed was accidental. Juliet was in Europe because our father had flown her there. She had likely thought it a treat, a reward for her good grades. It was my father who'd had other plans.

"You're telling me that my father had Mirelle killed," I said quietly.

"To be clear, I am not your father's confessor. He never made a direct admission of guilt to me."

"But you know him. You put the story together."

"He didn't tell me what he was going to do. I would never have allowed it." Klaus stared into his glass. "It wasn't the first job Nastya did for me. I had to tell her parents she was dead. It was . . ." His voice trailed off. "Your father broke our relationship. I couldn't trust him anymore. Say what you will about the Stasi; we had rules. Your father doesn't."

"My father didn't just murder her. He framed me for it. He made me believe I was a killer." The idea was new and raw in my mind. I'd always had an uneasy relationship with my father, but my main antagonist had always been Juliet. I had blamed her for every awful thing. In my mind, she had fangs and horns and a forked tongue. How many times had I complained to my father about how evil she was, only to have him agree with me? It was as if he *wanted* me to hate my sister.

"He wants to control you, Theo. Your father and I have very different ideas about life, but the main one is this: I know I am a criminal. Your father believes he is a businessman. I have always kept my children far from my work. Your father, on the other hand, wants you to follow in his footsteps."

"He convinced my family that I was a killer. Juliet believes it. Ursula. Caroline." My voice choked on my wife's name. No wonder she'd wanted to divorce me. Now that I finally understood the depths my father had sunk to, my brain could barely process all the consequences. Mirelle's death had changed me; I never wanted to hurt anyone again, to be in a state where I could lose control. But it had also damaged every important relationship I had. I couldn't fully trust anyone, ever.

"My sister should know better, after the life she's had with your father," Klaus said. "But Ursula stopped speaking with me long before this happened."

"She once told me you forced her to move into my father's house." My brain was still spiraling around the implications of what my father had done, but I wasn't going to miss the chance to understand this piece of family history. Ursula had been in my life as long as I could remember, even before my mother had walked out.

"I suppose I did. Ursula was young and shiftless, and your mother . . . well, she was always a character, and she had a rough time after you were born. Ursula was supposed to help out with you and your sister," Klaus said. "I never imagined she would have an affair with your father. I certainly never told her to marry him. That was her own mistake."

"She was the reason my mother left," I said. "Juliet despises her for that."

"You don't?"

"Should I? Ursula took care of me from the time I was young. My mother left and never came back. If anyone was at fault for the affair, it was my father." It was true that I blamed him for it. But now there was so much more that I had to condemn him for.

"He was older, but that did not make him wiser."

"My father had you hire Mirelle to pretend to be my girlfriend. Then he killed her and made me think I was a monster," I said. "He deserves all the blame. For everything."

Klaus drank some wine. "I know it is a horrible shock, but I want you to understand it from your father's perspective. He has only one son, and this precious boy was bent on self-destruction. Can you imagine the grief that would cause? The heartbreak?"

"Don't tell me that my father gaslights me because he loves me."

"I don't think your father knows what love is," Klaus says. "It's why he tries to control you."

"He's been holding Mirelle's death over my head for years," I said. "It's how he got me to come work for him."

"That only went so far," Klaus pointed out. "You quit when you discovered he was laundering money through some of the hotels."

"He's using it right now to get custody of my son." Technically, it was Juliet's name on the documents, but as ambitious as my sister was, I understood now that my father's fingerprints would be found on them. He had either put Juliet up to it, or was using her as a shield.

Klaus peered at me. "How? He can't tell anyone what you did. Scratch the surface, and what *he* did will become clear."

What Klaus said was true, but my mind was traveling in other directions. My father had known that I'd come back early from my trip to Bangkok. I'd scheduled it that way so I'd be able to see Dr. Haven with no questions asked by my family, but somehow my father knew I'd stopped by my house at five in the morning. His home was across the street, of course, so it wasn't strange that he might glimpse something out the window. But now that I knew how demented he actually was, I wondered how far he'd gone in invading our privacy.

"Theo?" Klaus prompted. "You look a million miles away. What's wrong?"

"Klaus, do you think there's a chance that my father killed Caroline?"

"What? Why would he? He thought the sun rose and set with her. What reason would he have to do her harm?"

My mind went back to the last time I'd seen Caroline. At five in the morning, I'd unlocked the door to our house, creeping upstairs quietly. I'd needed to pick up a couple of things for my session with Dr. Haven, including the threadbare tiger my mother had bought for me at the Berlin Zoo. To my shock, Caroline had been up. *Do you want to come up now, Ben? I can't wait. We're really doing this, aren't we?*

I'd frozen in place on the staircase, but she'd already heard me. She opened her door. There was fury in her eyes when she saw it was me. *What are you doing here?*

*I live here, in case you've forgotten,* I said.

I didn't want to think about what happened next.

"Caroline was seeing someone," I said.

"I don't think your father would care," Klaus said. "He cheated on his first wife with his second wife, then on his second wife with your mother, then . . ." He took a drink. "The only person I know who hated your wife is your sister."

No matter what Klaus said, an idea was taking hold in my brain. Perhaps my father did care about Caroline; it didn't matter—his affection was like poison. He was using her death to his advantage, and that suggested her death hadn't been accidental at all.

# CHAPTER 35

## DEIRDRE

It was time to head into the lion's den. In the days since Caro's death, I'd seen Teddy exactly twice, including at the funeral. When I rang the doorbell, my heart was divided between a determination to do right by my sister and the crippling weight of guilt. It didn't help that a pair of horned gargoyles snarled at me from the second story. I felt like they were onto my ulterior motives.

The nanny, Gloria Rivera, answered the door, smiling as she recognized me. "Deirdre! It's good to see you." She sounded genuinely delighted to find me on the doorstep. "Teddy will be so happy to see his auntie."

"How's the little guy doing?"

"Okay." She lowered her voice conspiratorially. "He's lonely, poor thing. His father's away, and he doesn't really understand that his mama isn't coming back."

"I have trouble believing she isn't coming back, and I'm supposed to be a grown-up."

"Deeeeee!" shouted Teddy from the top of the staircase. He ran down, stopping at the fourth step from the bottom and jumping, flinging himself onto the landing on all fours.

"Teddy! No crazy stunts!" Gloria scolded him.

"I'm a frog," Teddy said. "Frogs jump."

I hugged him. "Be careful, froggy."

"I can jump from the fifth step," he said. "Want to see?"

"He's always pulling crazy stunts," Gloria said.

Teddy let go of me and dashed up the stairs. "Come play, Deeeeee!"

"I'm going to make some lunch," Gloria said. "It's grilled cheese, because that's all he's eating right now. I can make something else for you."

"Grilled cheese is great, thanks." All the better for my purposes if she was busy in the kitchen. "Where are you, Teddy?" I called out as I climbed the stairs. The house was filled with beautiful archways and moldings, and I'd always wanted to explore it, but Caro usually insisted on meeting at her office or a restaurant. I'd hardly ever been in the house.

"Daddy's room," he answered. I followed his voice, then pushed a heavy wooden door open and found Teddy jumping on a king-sized four-poster bed. "Pirate Island!" Teddy announced.

Theo's room had the dark, wood-paneled charm of a men's club. It felt like there should be mounted stags' heads staring down in disapproval and cigar smoke swirling overhead. The walls were covered in framed photographs that looked like expensively styled snapshots. Theo and Caro sitting on a sailboat. A pair of kids on skis—Theo and Juliet, I figured. Teddy crawling across a manicured lawn with a teddy bear dangling from his mouth by one furry ear.

"That's me!" Teddy said.

A carved wood Jacobin chair with a tall back sat in front of the window, next to a small reading table. Otherwise, the room was disturbingly normal with its chest of drawers and opulently carved bedside tables. It wasn't monastic, exactly, but it wasn't fussy either.

"Does Daddy know you jump on his bed like that?" I quietly opened a drawer and found white undershirts. Another contained boxer briefs. I drifted across the room before checking out the closet. Inside were boring rows of shirts, suits, and shoes, all open shelving. So. Much. Space. I peered through the open door of the bathroom to find a whirlpool tub. The contents of the medicine cabinet had nothing more sinister than face wash and shaving oil.

"Sure. But I can't jump on Mama's bed."

After Teddy was born, it was clear Caro was sleeping in her own room, but I'd never seen it. I'd been given exactly one full tour of the house, and that was three months after the wedding. Caro and I started seeing more of each other after our mother died.

Teddy leaped off the bed, thudding against the floor. There was no carpet in Theo's room.

I heard frantic footsteps downstairs. "Is everything okay?" Gloria called.

"It's fine!" I shouted back. To Teddy, I said, "Wow, I didn't know frogs could be so loud."

Teddy smiled. "You have to jump with me. Ready?"

We hopped out of the room. He bounded ahead of me, his leaps muffled by the carpeting in the hallway. He stopped in front of a closed door. "Mama's room." He touched the knob, but he didn't turn it.

"Let's go inside."

"No." He shook his head firmly, suddenly the world's tiniest martinet. "Can't go in."

I crouched down next to him so we could talk, frog to frog. "Why not?"

"Mama," he said. There was an ocean of heartbreak in those two syllables, a longing and a sorrow that brought tears to my eyes. Keeping the room sealed was like a magic spell, one that promised if everything were done right, Mama might one day return.

"I miss her too," I told him.

His head hung forward so much that his chin touched his chest. He bumped the crown of his head against the door.

"Careful." I put the palm of my hand against his skull. His dark hair was like a silk curtain. "Careful, okay?"

"When are you going to die, Dee?"

"Not for a really, really long time," I told him.

"What about Daddy?"

"Not for a long time either." I hoped Teddy didn't notice my lack of enthusiasm on the subject of his father. I stretched my arms out. "Hug?"

He threw himself into my arms, pressing his face into my neck. There were so many things I wanted to tell him, but he was too young to hear them. Instead, we stayed like that, hugging for a long time.

"Would it be bad?" Teddy asked.

"What?"

"To go in Mama's room?"

"No, sweetheart. Definitely not." I felt like the devil, coaxing a three-and-a-half-year-old into breaking into his mother's room, but I was dying to see inside. It wasn't that I expected a clue to jump out at me. But if I'd learned anything over the past few days, it was that I didn't know my sister the way I'd thought I had. I'd been fooled by the sheen of perfection that hovered around her. Not only had I missed the messiness hiding underneath; I'd never noticed it was there.

I stood and opened the door, instantly inhaling the scent of Caro's floral perfume. Her room was as stereotypically feminine as Theo's was masculine, with a plush bed drowning in pillows, a pair of chairs dressed in pale-rose velvet, and wooden furniture with painted flowers. Bizarrely, it reminded me of her bedroom when we were growing up. I recognized the antique chairs as ones our mother had picked up at a flea market, only re-covered with new fabric. The painted chest of drawers with climbing vines and pink flowers had been plucked directly from her childhood bedroom. The familiarity wasn't comforting. If anything, it was the opposite. Maybe I'd run too far from my own pretty pink childhood room by living in a dark dungeon-like cell, but the fact Caro had re-created her bedroom did not feel emotionally healthy.

There were photographs in ornate frames around the room, and plaques mounted on the walls. One was from the New York City Mayor's Office, another from the Diotima Civic Society. The latter looked more impressive—black lacquer etched with silver—and had a broken column with a female figure standing in front of it. Her appointment book was on her desk, and I sifted through it, but nothing important caught my eye.

Teddy stayed in the doorway, eyes wide like saucers as he took in the room. "Nothing changed," he murmured.

"Did you think Mama's room would be different?"

"Maybe."

I was ransacking my sister's room like a clumsy novice thief. There was no diary, of course. Nothing was ever that easy. But it wasn't a challenge to plunder her cavernous walk-in closet with its ball gown wardrobe. I found a Bible under a shoe shelf. Inside were slips of paper. I grabbed them like winning lottery tickets. In my family, if it was important, it went into the Bible. The one on top was a gold-banded white card written in elegant cursive:

*"The glamour of inexperience is over your eyes," Mr. Rochester answered; "and you see it through a charmed medium: you cannot discern that the gilding is slime and the silk draperies cobwebs; that the marble is sordid slate, and the polished woods mere refuse chips and scaly bark."*

*By making the choice to stay you are participating in a crime.*

I recognized the quotation from *Jane Eyre*, because my sister had forced me to read that book. The line underneath it was what took my breath away. It was unsigned and undated, but I assumed it had to have been from Theo. The spreadsheets Caro had sent me made it clear something was wrong with the family business. Ben had told me the Thraxtons were laundering money. Was that what Theo meant by a crime? Was he the only person in the family who wasn't involved?

"You looking for it, Auntie Dee?" Teddy called out.

"For what?"

"The hiding place."

"Mama had a hiding place?"

I set the Bible back in place and realized there was a small leather box behind it. *Cartier* was embossed on top, and inside was a pair of platinum earrings, panther faces glittering with diamonds, each with slitted emerald eyes that looked surprisingly fierce. A small strip of paper, no larger than a fortune cookie message, was tucked inside. The handwriting was different from the other note, cramped and spidery:

*Caroline, I know you hate extravagance, but I couldn't resist. I am so proud of you and everything you've accomplished. Our family's luckiest day was the one when you joined us. Ever fondly, Theodore*

Teddy bounded into the closet, and I instinctively snapped the box shut and shoved it back on the shelf. "You find it?"

I looked around. Amid the dresses and shoes and hatboxes, I wondered if there was a secret alcove. "Where?"

"There." He pointed at the chest of drawers in the closet.

"In the drawer?"

"No." Teddy sounded exasperated. "Behind it."

The chest of drawers seemed too heavy to move. "I don't understand, Teddy."

"Pull it." He reached for the top drawer but was too tiny to reach it. "Pull."

I pulled it open.

"All the way," Teddy said.

I slid the drawer out.

"See?" Teddy said.

I peered inside. There was no back on the chest of drawers. Instead, I saw a wall safe.

"Do you know the code?" I asked. This was a new low for me, wrangling clues out of a small child.

"Mama said it's secret."

I tried Caro's birthdate, then Teddy's, then our parents', and finally my own. Nothing worked.

"Lunchtime!" Gloria called up the stairs. "Get the grilled cheese while it's hot!"

That made Teddy squeal. "Let's go!"

I slid the drawer back into place and closed the closet door. My heart was heavy as I followed Teddy out of the room. My sister's secrets were tantalizingly close, but they remained out of reach for me.

# CHAPTER 36

## Deirdre

In the afternoon, I took Teddy to the Central Park Zoo. We shared a love of sea lions, so that was a favorite spot. When we got back to the house, the front door was ajar. I paused at the foot of the steps, then turned to Teddy. "Promise to stand right here for a minute?"

"Okay."

I crept up the stairs, wondering what was going on. Then I heard a sharp voice. "I can't tell her not to come here. She has a right. She's his aunt." It was Gloria speaking.

"I am ordering you not to let that woman in here. She is a monster and can't be trusted."

My heart clenched tight. Were they talking about me? At that moment, I noticed Teddy creeping beside me. "Ammy!" he shouted. I followed him in.

"*Liebling!*" A silver-haired woman with bones barely bigger than a sparrow's reached down to hug Teddy. Her printed silk dress hung on her like she was nothing more than a hanger, and her crocodile handbag was wider than her hips. She looked for all the world like a lady who lunches, despite the fact she hadn't been in the same room with solid food in weeks.

"Ursula, you remember Deirdre," Gloria said. "Caroline's sister."

"Yes, of course. How are you, my dear?" Ursula surprised me with a kiss on the cheek. She smelled like pressed powder and juniper.

"Hi," I said awkwardly. After what I'd just heard, I was expecting her to push me down the steps.

"There are cookies," Teddy said, tugging at Ursula's dress. "I smell them."

"I caught the scent as soon as I came in. Gloria is such a fine baker." Ursula said it with enthusiasm, but it was clear no cookie had passed her lips this century.

"How was the zoo?" Gloria asked me.

"Cookieeeeee!" Teddy insisted.

"Okay, but just one. You don't want to spoil your appetite for dinner." Gloria shook her head as he raced by her. "That boy really loves cookies."

"The park was great," I said. "Teddy could hang out there all day, every day."

"Teddy is lucky to have a nice auntie who wants to spend time with him," Ursula said. "Unlike his other auntie."

That made everything clear—they'd been talking about Theo's sister, not me.

"What's Juliet done now?" I asked.

"In English you have this one word, *troublemaker*," Ursula said. "But in German, we say *Unruhestifter, Klatschbase, Provokateur*, about a dozen more. Different words for different trouble."

"Which one is Juliet?"

"All of them," Ursula said. "But I like *Stänkerin* best."

I laughed. I couldn't help it. After what Adinah Gerstein had told me about Ursula going through Caro's room, I wasn't going to trust her. But I'd been pawing through my sister's belongings too. Maybe I couldn't throw stones.

"Auntie Dee, you're coming to dinner?" Teddy called down the hall while munching on a cookie that probably wasn't his first.

"Your grandpa invited me yesterday."

"Don't let her come over here," Ursula hissed at Gloria.

"Okay," Gloria answered uncertainly.

"What did Juliet do?" I whispered.

"There are ongoing conversations about custody," Ursula said, her eyes on Teddy. "Which do not strike me as appropriate."

We crossed the street and walked up the steps to the other Thraxton house, the one I'd never been inside. *It's unbelievable,* Caroline had claimed. *Like a museum. I've never seen anything like it. It's ridiculous anyone lives like that.* She hadn't been exaggerating. A butler answered the door. Past the foyer were a pair of massive stone lions guarding the broad hallway. They looked ancient, like something on display at the Met.

"Trains!" Teddy said.

"Of course, darling," Ursula said. "Go and see the trains. Grandpa has them set up for you."

Teddy skidded around one of the lions and vanished.

"Don't worry—he knows this house inside out," Ursula said. "Care for a drink?"

She led me into a parlor. The house was so much larger than Theo and Caroline's. With the hallways leading east and west as well as north, I was willing to bet this mansion had swallowed real estate on either side of it. This wasn't so much a house as a palace. Oddly, the lighting was turned down low, as if the Thraxtons were watching their energy bill. Because it was so dim, I didn't immediately realize someone else was in the parlor when Ursula walked me in.

"Well, aren't you the little ray of sunshine, Deirdre?" cooed a sly voice from the corner. In the gloom, I spotted Theo's sister on a settee, her plush body spilling out of a tiger-striped dress.

I was wearing jeans and black leather boots with a draped and shirred black top, my version of church-and-family-dinner attire. "If I'd known I was going on safari, I would've worn khaki."

Juliet smiled like she'd caught a canary.

"Why are you still here?" Ursula asked her.

"Because my father is keeping me waiting." Juliet gave her a snooty once-over and looked at me. "Did you know that Ursula used to be our nanny?"

I glanced at Ursula, who was staring daggers at Juliet.

"Yes, she lived in our house, and she loved borrowing all of my mother's finery—her shoes, her jewelry, even her husband," Juliet said.

Ursula made a muffled sound, like a wounded animal, and fled the room.

"Why would you say that?" I demanded.

Juliet shrugged. "Because it's true."

I was never someone who backed away from fights, but I couldn't imagine hurling such nasty words at anyone. "That was cruel."

"How would *you* feel about the woman your father was having an affair with?" Juliet asked. "Especially after he married her and tried to make you call her 'Mommy'?"

"Did that really happen?"

"Your mouth is hanging open, Deirdre. Not your best look. But yes, it happened."

"My sister never told me about that."

"Your sister didn't have a clue." Juliet examined her nails in the low light. "Mind if I ask you a question? Did some part of you despise your sweet sister?"

"How could you even *think* that?"

Juliet shrugged carelessly, clearly delighted to get a rise out of me. "I know we're supposed to love our families, but I find it difficult. I don't even like mine."

What had Ben said? *The entire Thraxton family is a criminal organization.* "Maybe *your* family is particularly unlovable, Juliet."

She laughed at that, holding up her glass as if toasting me. "That could be true," she said before taking a drink. "But if we're honest with ourselves, nature is red in tooth and claw. We're supposed to pretend our siblings are our allies, but the secret is that they can be our worst enemies."

In spite of myself, I was intrigued. "Is Theo your enemy?"

She patted the cushion next to her, signaling for me to sit down. "I'll tell you something about him if you tell me something about your sister."

That was tantalizing, but before I could speak, I heard footsteps in the hallway.

"Sorry to keep you waiting, Juliet. I had to . . ." Theodore noticed me and smiled. "Deirdre! How delightful to see you."

"Thanks for inviting me to dinner."

"Ugh, you roped her into a social visit? Poor thing." Everything Juliet said was dipped in acid, but she gave me her sly smile. "If you ever want to compare notes, I'm game. Call me."

"You could stay, if you want," her father told her.

"No, thanks," Juliet said. "We never had family dinners when I was growing up. I may be allergic to them. But we *do* need to finish talking business before I go, Father. We have a cockroach problem. Again."

"Juliet! I can't believe you said that." Theodore shot me a worried glance.

I had a cockroach problem in my dungeon room, but mentioning it didn't feel helpful.

"We had this exact headache two months ago," Juliet added.

"I apologize, Deirdre," Theodore said. "I didn't realize we'd be delving into such unsavory territory. Why don't you wait with Ursula and Teddy?"

"I'll do that," I said.

I ducked out of the room and walked down the hall. I couldn't slip out of my boots to tiptoe back, so I crept as quietly as I could on the carpet.

"How much did it cost us last time?" Theodore asked.

"A quarter of a million. Caroline said to go ahead and pay it, because we didn't need any bad publicity in this market."

Hairs stood up on the back of my neck. I didn't think they were talking about bugs.

"What's your instinct this time?" he asked her.

Before I could catch Juliet's answer, Teddy popped into the hallway. "You have to help with the trains," he told me.

He had terrible timing, but I couldn't disappoint him.

Ten minutes later, Teddy's grandfather strolled in as the engine was whipping around the track.

"Everything okay?" I asked.

"Fine, fine. Juliet will handle it. She's very capable." He sighed. "I feel guilty, leaning on her as I do. She works very hard. I always expected Theo would join her in the business. But he dumped us all to go adventuring and do what he wanted."

*Maybe he wasn't that into money laundering,* I thought, but I kept it to myself. I didn't know how I felt about Caro's involvement. It was baffling to me. "That's too bad."

"I don't mean to sound bitter." He sighed. "When you have children, you have no way of knowing how they'll turn out. You believe they'll be like you. Your blood is running through their veins. But they can reject everything you taught them and become something you barely recognize."

I wasn't the best audience for this. I had no relationship with my father, and I didn't regret it. "People talk about nature versus nurture," I said. "But I don't think genes predict who you'll be. They give you some characteristics, but they don't define you."

"That's an excellent point. It's been on my mind since Theo ran off. It doesn't seem like he even wants to be a father."

I glanced at Teddy. He didn't look like he was listening, but he was a smart kid. He got every word. "It's a really tough time for everyone right now."

"Of course. But I worry that Theo is going to do something dangerous. What if he took Teddy away to Europe? Can you even imagine that?"

"That would be awful." Teddy was my living link to my sister. I'd never let him go.

"I'm so glad you feel that way," he said. "Juliet is filing some paperwork to keep Theo from taking Teddy anywhere unsafe. It would be helpful to have a sworn statement from Teddy's favorite aunt."

His words sounded sweet, but something sinister twisted beneath them. Hugo Laraya's caution echoed in my head. *You'll get caught up in his web*—that was what Theo had warned his friend. I was starting to sense delicate threads of spider silk attaching themselves to me. Theodore Thraxton had told me terrible things about his son. He had taken my suspicions about Theo and amped them up a thousandfold with the information he'd given me. What if he had done exactly the same thing to Caro?

"Whatever you need," I said blandly, turning to watch Teddy play. Caro had wanted to escape from all the Thraxtons, Adinah Gerstein had said. That included her father-in-law. I was starting to understand why.

# CHAPTER 37

## THEO

My mistake had been in thinking I'd need two days to accomplish what I needed to in Berlin. In reality, I'd only needed one. But the airline wouldn't allow me to change my ticket, which meant I had another day to kill before I could go home.

"I have a particularly strange question for you," I said to Klaus as we left the hidden restaurant he'd lured me to. We were strolling companionably down the zigzagging alleyways.

"Go ahead."

"You know I have scars all over my body," I said. "Some were self-inflicted, but some have been there as long as I can remember. My father always said I was attacked by an animal in a zoo. Did he tell you this story?"

"A version of it," Klaus said. "That you were attacked. No mention of any zoo."

"Then what attacked me?"

"He never said."

"You didn't ask him?" I was startled. "Why not?"

"The reason your father and I have worked together—successfully— for so long is that neither of us asks too many questions. This was one of those cases. He was terrified that you might die. He didn't need me saying, 'Why did you let this happen?'"

We were at the street by that point. "Can I give you a lift?" Klaus asked.

"I'll make my own way back."

"Bon voyage tomorrow," Klaus said. "Will you do me a favor?"

"How did you know I was flying . . . never mind. What is it?"

"Tell Ursula I'm sorry for being a bastard," Klaus said. "I have done many unfortunate things, but that is the one I regret."

"Why don't you tell her yourself?"

"She won't listen." Klaus sounded sorry for himself. "Years ago, she asked me for help, and I refused. I told her she'd made her bed and she had to lie in it. It was wrong of me."

"What help did she need?"

"She wanted to leave your father," Klaus said. "But I cared more about my friend's feelings than I did about hers. I never thought about Ursula's troubles. I told her she had to stay, and she did."

———

It was after eleven when I got back to my hotel, but that meant it was only five o'clock in New York. I called Gloria to check up on Teddy, and then I called Dr. Haven.

"I need to tell you everything I've found out," I said. The words tumbled out of me, with parts of the story in the wrong order, but Dr. Haven listened patiently. At one point, I heard an awful sob and realized belatedly that it had bubbled out of my chest. I was enraged, but I also felt empty and betrayed. I was used to a lack of trust with everyone in my family. I was familiar with the eternal chess games, and I knew that I was just a pawn to my father. But the fact that he would commit a crime and make me believe I was responsible for it was a nightmare I could never wake up from.

Eventually I ran out of words. My face was wet. My breath escaped in tiny gasps.

"Theo . . . this is like something out of a horror movie," Dr. Haven said finally. "I don't know what to say. I've seen family members do terrible things to each other, but this is beyond that."

"I want to make sure that my father never gets anywhere near Teddy."

"There's a lot of talk about grandparents' rights, but they don't exist," Dr. Haven said. "Unless the custodial parent can be proven unfit."

I had no doubt that's what my father was doing. The question pricking at my brain was whether he'd considered Caroline an unfit parent too. He was doing his damnedest to claim my son, and I could only wonder how far he'd go.

"I know you don't feel like you can trust anyone right now, but I want you to listen to me," she added. "You need to trust yourself. Your father—your whole family—plays mind games, but that's not who you are, Theo. Trust yourself."

*That was easy for her to say,* I thought ruefully after we hung up. She didn't have a chorus in the back of her head whispering, *I am full of hidden horrors.* She didn't live with the torment of not knowing what part of your own brain you could rely on.

On instinct, I went into the bathroom. My razor was in my toiletry kit. I retrieved it and cracked the plastic against the marble vanity. The four blades that dropped out were tiny fragments; I held them in the palm of one hand. Each one reflected a small part of my face: an eye, a lip. I appeared as fractured as I felt inside. I'd grown up managing mental pain by balancing it with physical torment, but in that moment, I knew it was futile. I was a bundle of scar tissue, but the agony inside me never abated.

The memory of the last time I'd seen Caroline came into focus. *Do you want to come up now, Ben? I can't wait. We're really doing this, aren't we?*

She was livid that I'd overheard her on the phone. *What are you doing here?*

*I live here, in case you've forgotten,* I said.

*I don't want to be married to you anymore,* Caroline had said. *Why is that so hard to understand, Theo? Get out of my house.*

I'd gone to my room, but I'd forgotten the reason I'd come home. Instead, I pulled the framed wedding photo of Caroline and me off the wall and stormed back down the hallway, smashing it against the doorframe. Shattered glass and wood were everywhere.

*I don't give a damn what you do,* I told her. *You can keep the house, but I will never let you have Teddy.*

Caroline had stared at me with wide, horrified eyes. I went down the stairs and out of the house. That was the last time I saw my wife. The memory of it made me sick.

I dropped the razors in the trash. One day, I would have to teach my son how to deal with pain. I couldn't do it if I hadn't learned to manage it myself.

After sitting for a while, allowing regrets to wash over me, I picked up my phone and looked up a number I rarely called. Of course Juliet didn't answer. I spoke to her voice mail.

"This is Theo," I said. "I'm in Berlin. I came here because . . . I'm trying to understand pieces of my memory that don't make sense. I have a question for you. I know you remember the night Mirelle died. On the plane, you said I'd ruined your trip to Paris. The thing is, you shouldn't have been in Paris. You had school." I took a breath. "Here's my question: Did you decide to come over to Europe yourself, or did Father surprise you with the trip? Because I've discovered he set me up that night. I think he set you up as well."

# PART THREE

He who fights with monsters should be careful lest he thereby become a monster. And if you gaze long into an abyss, the abyss will also gaze into you.

—Friedrich Nietzsche

# CHAPTER 38

## DEIRDRE

On Saturday night, I slept in my own bed in the dungeon room, even though there was police tape on my busted door like it was a crime scene. I taped a couple of black garbage bags together to cover it up and collapsed on my futon. I was too confused about the thoughts churning in my brain to share them. Two days earlier, I'd been ready to nail Theo's ass to the wall for murder. Now, I was looking at him in a different light, just as I was seeing my sister in a new way. I had a tendency to jump to conclusions, and I was realizing I'd leaped to some of the wrong ones.

It didn't help that I woke up Sunday morning to find an email from my brother-in-law: Deirdre, I'm at the Berlin airport now, about to fly. I get in Sunday at noon and I need to talk with you. Could we meet? Thanks, Theo.

I lay on my futon, staring at the message for a while before crawling out of bed at eight. Sounds good, I wrote back. I'd like to talk. I'm free all afternoon. It was four hours until he landed, so I had time for more digging before meeting him face-to-face.

There was no one I wanted to talk to more than Juliet.

I'd never been to her apartment, but I knew exactly where it was. The Thraxtons had their showpiece hotel on Park Avenue, but there was also a smaller boutique property on Crosby Street below Prince. Juliet occupied the penthouse suite, which had its own elevator. On my way to the subway I called her.

"Were you serious last night about swapping sibling stories?" I asked.

"You better believe it," she answered. "When and where?"

"I can be at your place in a little over an hour." Weekend service out of Queens was brutal, but I didn't explain that.

"Excellent," Juliet said. "I'll order mimosas."

She hung up before I could tell her I didn't drink.

I got lucky and caught a train a minute after I walked into the Grand Avenue–Newtown station. The M train practically took me to Juliet's door in forty-five minutes. This Thraxton property was prettier than the glass-and-steel behemoth uptown. It had curving sides wrapped in silver and white metal. Inside was an art gallery, with paintings on display and a cathedral-like ceiling that inspired awe even in a cynic like me.

I asked for Juliet at the marble reception desk and was directed to another counter at the opposite end of the floor. There was a separate elevator bank there, and I noticed a gold plaque designating this one as private. *How very Juliet,* I thought.

"Hi, I'm meeting with Juliet Thraxton. I'm a relative of hers, Deirdre Crawley," I said, thinking how much Juliet would hate to be identified as part of my family.

The concierge hid her disbelief well. "Welcome to the Penelope Hotel," she said, smiling. "Ms. Thraxton's in a meeting now, but as soon as she's free, I'll let you know."

I took a seat in an empty little waiting area in front of the elevators. The plush chair was covered in some kind of fancy sheepskin. It felt almost like a hug, but in a good way. I glanced at the concierge, but she was acting busy. I sat there feeling weirdly comfortable for a couple of minutes, hoping no one would notice.

But the sensation wasn't meant to last. The light switched on over the private elevator. "Miss, would you like me to call up now?" the concierge asked.

"Sure," I said. Then the elevator door opened. Ben Northcutt stepped out.

He looked as shocked to see me as I was to see him. He froze in place, staring as if I had sprouted fangs.

"Ben? What the hell . . . ?"

He bolted before I could finish the question, storming past the concierge and out a small doorway. He wasn't running, exactly, but he was moving fast. I started after him, baffled and alarmed.

"Ben!" I called out a couple of times. He didn't turn back or break his stride. I ran to catch up and then grabbed his arm. He swung around, shoving my arm away. He was breathing hard, and his face was contorted in fury.

"What are you doing, following me?" he demanded.

"I'm meeting Juliet. What are you doing here?"

"Fuck off. I'm not answering your questions."

"I will beat the answers out of you."

"What are you going to do? Stab me like you did your father?"

Heads swiveled on the street. Even my father—the one person who had the right to object to what I'd done—had remained silent on the subject. I felt disoriented, unsure which way to turn.

I was too astonished to be angry. "I was just . . ."

"You know what? There was a reason Caroline didn't tell you anything," he snapped. "Your sister didn't trust you. She knew you'd overreact and do something stupid—like you always do, Deirdre." He clomped off, and I watched him go, feeling like my knees would buckle under me.

# CHAPTER 39

## Deirdre

I didn't understand what had just happened, except that I'd caught Ben doing something he knew was wrong, and he'd lashed out. I walked back to the hotel slowly, chewing on that.

"Ms. Thraxton says you can go up when you like," the concierge told me. She had the same bright smile, as if nothing were amiss. Truly, she belonged in the movies.

"Thanks," I murmured, heading to the private elevator. The trip up took a few seconds. The doors opened, and I stepped into a mirror-covered black-and-white parlor that was like an Art Deco fever dream. At least four Juliets were waiting for me, all wearing black wraparound dresses and satin mules.

"Come into my parlor, Deirdre," she drawled.

"That makes you the spider and me the fly."

"Seems right, doesn't it?"

I moved forward slowly, toward what I hoped was the real Juliet.

"Just so you know, I have a pet python," she said. "He slithers around, but he's on the old and slow side, so don't step on him."

"Cromwell," I said, remembering the name. Caro had mentioned reptilian roommates as one of her sister-in-law's many eccentricities. "Why do you have a python?"

Juliet turned and gave me that funny half-smile of hers. "My father is terrified of snakes. My brother is afraid of large animals, period. Cromwell keeps them out of my space. Now, what brings you to my den of iniquity today?"

"What was Ben Northcutt doing here?"

Juliet raised an eyebrow. "You know him?"

"He's a journalist. I met him a couple days ago."

"Digging up dirt on my family, no doubt," she said. "What did you tell him?"

"Nothing. I didn't like him."

"Most people don't like us either. We're not very endearing," Juliet said. "Do you want a drink?"

She didn't wait for me to answer as she headed into a large room. I followed, stepping gingerly. My boots were made to kick ass, but pythons didn't exactly have butts.

"I was going to order some champagne," Juliet said. "But you seem more like the beer type. No offense."

"I don't drink alcohol." I was staring at the large stone statue of an Egyptian deity at the center of the room. It was a man with the head of a jackal. Anubis, I remembered. I'd always loved Egyptian mythology. Anubis had been the god of the dead before Osiris was killed.

"Really?" Juliet looked me over. "*You* don't need to be on a diet."

"I'm not. I just don't drink."

She blinked at me, for once without insults. "Okay. Take a seat."

"You didn't say why Ben Northcutt was here," I said, sitting down. "I know he's writing about you. Why would you talk to him?"

"It's always good to know what your enemy is up to. Mr. Northcutt considers himself more clever than he really is. Anyway, I thought you were here to discuss our siblings." Her green eyes were catlike, and I realized she thought I was a toy she could bat around. She wasn't an opponent I could beat with force. I'd have to spar on her terms.

"Why did you hate my sister so much?" I asked.

"Oh, are we playing truth or dare?" she asked. "Fine, I'll go first. I hated her because she was the perfect little blonde daughter doll my father always wanted. She was pretty and skinny and eager to please. Father thought the sun rose and set on her."

"Are you fishing for compliments?"

"I know I'm hot," Juliet said. "But I'm the plush, deluxe, sardonic version of that doll. My father started sending me to fat camp when I was eight."

"There's a lot that's messed up about your family."

"Unlike *your* family, I suppose," Juliet shot back. "The untroubled Crawleys."

"Fair enough," I admitted.

"I answered your question. Time to answer mine. What did *you* hate about Caroline?"

That caught me by surprise. "I loved my sister."

"I'm not talking about that," Juliet said. "We've all got mixed feelings about family lurking under the surface."

"I don't. Caro was a good person. She tried to help people."

"If you're going to stay, you have to be honest, Deirdre. Otherwise, you may as well leave now."

I wanted to walk out, but that wouldn't get me anywhere. I liked to think of myself as a person who faced up to the truth, but I had run away from it too many times. "I hated that Caroline stayed close to our father, even after all the times he hit our mother." My mouth was dry, and my heart squeezed tight inside my chest. It felt like it might explode through my rib cage. I put my hands on my knees and leaned back a little.

"I didn't know that. About your family, I mean." Juliet uncrossed her legs and reached for a strawberry from the fruit plate on the ottoman. "I'd say I'm sorry, but that's so patronizing. I wish Caroline had told me that."

"Why?"

"Because it makes sense of her," Juliet said. "I thought she was a little bitch who enjoyed being Miss Perfect. Instead, she was just being the good girl trying to manage every last detail. You get that in families with abuse. Some people think they can create order by doing everything right."

"What is this, Psychology 101?" I tried to make it a joke, but Juliet's words landed hard. When I'd been in the psychiatric hospital at fifteen, I'd had doctors prodding at me, trying to trick me into talking. Nothing made me feel more vulnerable than that.

Juliet shrugged. "I wanted to study psychology, but I had to go into hotel administration. This is as close to a hobby as I have."

"Did you ever have therapy?"

"No. If I had, someone in my family would've bought off the therapist and used my ramblings against me. What about you?"

I shook my head. "It's been suggested, but no. Is this how you got your superiority complex?"

"I've spent more time analyzing my own family than anyone else's," Juliet said. "Thraxtons are dysfunctional. I blame my father as the corrupting influence, but my brother is the worst example."

"Why?"

"Because he wants all of the benefits but plays by none of the rules," Juliet said. "He does what he wants, and yet my father would bring him in to run the business in a heartbeat if Theo would agree."

"Isn't that more of a comment on your father than Theo?" I asked.

At that moment, something behind me clamped onto my neck. I shouted and jumped to my feet.

"Calm down," Juliet said. "That's just Bartleby."

I half-turned and saw a small caramel-colored mammal with rounded ears on top of his head. Its warm amber eyes were regarding me with curiosity.

"He's a kinkajou. They're very affectionate," Juliet said, putting a strawberry in my hand. "Feed him, and he'll be yours forever."

"Where do you get these creatures?"

"His owner was going to feed him to a crocodile," Juliet said. "The creep asked if I wanted to watch, and I said, 'I would prefer not to.'" I must've looked blank, because she added, "You know, like Bartleby the Scrivener."

"Never heard of him."

"It's a short story by Herman Melville. You should read it."

I held the strawberry above the kinkajou's head. He reached for it with delicate sharp-clawed paws and took a bite. His eyes stayed on mine. I petted his head, and his fur felt like thick velvet.

"He likes you," Juliet said. "People are disappointing, but pets never are."

"He's pretty cute. Who would feed him to a crocodile?"

"We do business with some shady characters. But you already know that, don't you?"

"That's what Ben Northcutt claimed." I petted the kinkajou, pretending to be casual. "But he's a liar. He said my sister was a criminal. As if that would happen in a million years."

It was a little bit of reverse psychology, but it worked wonders. Ask a direct question, and Juliet would bob and weave. Praise my sister, and she had to tear her down.

"Oh, you can't imagine dear virtuous Caroline getting her hands dirty," Juliet said. "I'm sure she kept it from you, but Caroline was up to her eyeballs in Thraxton schemes. Your sister loved money."

"She used it to help people," I countered. "She gave an awful lot to charity."

"Hosting galas isn't giving to charity. It's dressing up and showing off so people can admire you."

"Ben Northcutt was the cockroach problem you talked about with your father last night?" At the Thraxton house, I'd wondered what they were really discussing. Insects hadn't seemed likely, especially since Caro had told them to pay out. Suddenly, it made sense.

Juliet nodded. "He's been hanging around for months. He threatens to write a big exposé about us, but he runs away when he gets some cash. He's like a squirrel with an acorn."

"He didn't look happy when I saw him. No acorn today?"

"No acorn ever again."

"I lied when I said I didn't tell him anything," I said. "Caro sent me a message to read after she died. In it, she said Theo killed his first wife. I talked to your dad, and he basically confirmed it. Did you know?"

"I saw Theo the night it happened," Juliet said. "My father told me he'd chartered a plane, and I had to take my brother to rehab. I've hated Theo with every fiber of my being since that night."

"Because he killed someone?"

"Because my father didn't care. He said I shouldn't blame Theo, that it was an accident. It made me ill. He's always excused my brother's bad behavior. I don't know why. Nothing I did was ever good enough." She stared at the Anubis statue, as if it could give her the answers she needed.

"I'm the outcast in my family," I said. "Bet that's news to you."

"What a shocker." She smiled, and it wasn't even her usual smirk. "Theo left me a message last night, and it's looping around my brain. My father used to tell me I shouldn't be so hard on Theo. But the truth is, if anyone screwed him up, it was our parents."

# CHAPTER 40

## THEO

When my flight landed, there was no one I wanted to see more than Teddy, but I headed straight from the taxi into my father's home. The butler who answered the door gave me a frozen smile and led me inside. The air in that frigid mausoleum of a house crackled as if a storm were rolling in.

There was something reptilian in the stone-cold stillness of my father's face as I walked into his study.

"The prodigal son has returned," he said. "How was your trip?"

"I'm here to tell you to go rot in hell."

"That bad?" He kept his tone light. "I always loved Berlin in the spring. We lived there for a few years while I was setting up the European side of the business. You probably don't remember."

It was surreal, listening to his prattle. I was there to confront him, and he was acting as if nothing had changed between us.

"You murdered Mirelle," I said. "You made my life a torment—you made me believe I was a killer! I'm going to take my son to live somewhere far, far away from you."

"You are welcome to try," he answered. "There's no evidence of your being able to provide a stable home. In fact, there's no evidence that you are stable. Let's consider how this plays out in court before you make any rash decisions."

"You killed Mirelle," I repeated. "Don't you have any remorse about that?"

"I didn't kill anyone, Theo. I can prove that I wasn't in Berlin that night." He looked me in the eye, unflinching. "I suppose you met with Klaus on your little jaunt."

"He admitted to hiring Mirelle, at your request."

"How typical of him to foist the blame on me. Whatever he did to that woman, my hands are clean."

I was in awe of his steely nerve. His crime had been uncovered, and he was still confident that he could wriggle off the hook. "I also spoke with the man Harris hired to help him kill Mirelle and stage the scene," I said. "As soon as I heard Harris was involved, I knew what you'd done. Don't embarrass yourself by denying it."

He sighed and leaned back in his chair. "Do you have any idea how difficult it is to have your children disappoint you again and again? Teddy's too young for you to grasp this concept. When he's a teenager, you might understand. Imagine bringing this beautiful boy into the world and then watching him destroy himself with drugs and bad company that encourages his worst impulses."

It was clever of him to mention Teddy, because I'd rather die than allow my son to suffer the pain I had. I couldn't imagine my son harming himself. But I also couldn't envision how cruel you would have to be to create a straitjacket of guilt and force your child to live in it. That was inhuman, no matter the excuse.

"You thought you were going to control me by making me believe I'd killed a woman. What kind of man would do that to his son?"

"It was a lesson in consequences. You needed to understand the danger of what you were doing."

"My entire adult life was based on a lie you constructed. Why did you do it?"

223

"It should've straightened you out," my father said. "And it did, to a point. You stopped frequenting fetish clubs and using drugs. I thought there was hope for you when you joined the business and married Caroline. Sadly, I was wrong. Your feelings got all hurt, and you ran away again."

"What you call feelings are values. Ethics. I know you don't have any. But I told you I didn't want any part of your criminal enterprise. That's why I quit. I was disgusted with you."

"Too bad that Caroline didn't feel the same way," he said. "I think I was far closer to her than you ever were."

I balled my hands into fists. There had always been something unseemly about the attention he'd paid to Caroline, as if he were the one courting her. "It was so satisfying to you, testing her loyalty, luring her to your team. Did you murder her? Was that to protect me as well?"

For the first time since I'd walked into his study, my father's self-possession vanished. "You think I killed Caroline?"

"Juliet told Caroline about Mirelle, and Caroline told her sister. Were you afraid word would spread?"

"You can go to jail forever for all I care. I have Teddy now."

"Did you kill Caroline?"

"No. I loved her," he said quietly. "If you think I harmed her, you're out of your mind."

"I'd be mad to believe there was a person you wouldn't hurt."

He contemplated that. "Caroline was better than my own children. She was the kind of woman who thought before she made a move, considering the consequences not only to herself but to those around her. You and your sister always were a pair of ingrates, you especially. Juliet loves to embarrass me, and she argues over everything. You divorced yourself from this family. Everything I raised you for, everything I made you to be, you abandoned. Caroline was never like that. She was loyal."

"Here's what I think happened. Caroline was distraught to learn about Mirelle. She wanted answers, and when you talked to her, you told her I was responsible. But here's where it gets tricky, Father. I think that dramatically changed her feelings about you."

"What are you talking about?"

"Her dear father-in-law had covered up an innocent woman's murder," I said. "Caroline couldn't accept that. She couldn't live with that. She must've looked at Teddy and wondered what way you would twist him. No wonder she wanted full custody of him. She needed to get him away from this house of monsters."

He watched me impassively, but a muscle next to his eye quivered.

"You killed her," I said. "You murdered Caroline."

"Theo, you're an idiot if you think that."

"You've harmed so many people in your life. You're a poison that seeps through our veins—mine, Juliet's, Teddy's. You have no conscience, no principles. To you, money is the only god. There's no purpose to anything you do except to enrich yourself and hurt anyone who stands in your way. You murdered Caroline because she was going to expose you for the thieving fraud you are."

"Haven't you heard a word I said? That would only harm Teddy, in the end."

"What did you do to Caroline?"

"Nothing! Trust me on that."

"I can't trust anyone in my life," I said. "That's how you raised me, to be always suspicious of other people's motives. You impressed on me, when I was still a child, that the only reason people would want to get close to me was for money."

"It's a good lesson to keep in mind. But Caroline wasn't motivated by money. She believed in family loyalty."

"There's a problem with blind loyalty when you mistake a monster for a man."

There was a thud behind me. I hadn't heard Harris open the door of the study, but his heavy footsteps were unmistakable.

"I heard shouting. Are you all right, sir?" Harris asked.

"Theo's deciding whether he's up to the task of taking me down," my father said. "And—spoiler alert—he's not."

"It's time for you to leave," Harris said.

"This doesn't end here," I promised. "I quit the business for many reasons, but the main one is that I want to see justice done, and I will. For Caroline. For Teddy. For Mirelle."

My father chuckled. "Good luck with that, Theo." He rose and left the room.

After my father left, Harris glowered at me. "I already told you to go."

"I met with an old colleague of yours while I was in Berlin," I said. "Mehmet Badem. Remember him?"

"A drug addict," Harris said. "People like that are better off dead. They're worthless."

I took a step closer to him. "You've been doing my father's dirty work for twenty years now. Does that ever disrupt your sleep? Do you ever feel guilty?"

"You're a fine one to talk. Do you have any idea what hell you put your father through?" he demanded. "He's done everything for you, and you pay him back with betrayal."

The loathing he had for me was so strong I could sense it; it was like steam rising from his skin.

"You've wanted to beat me to a pulp since I was a teenager," I said. "Why haven't you?"

"Your father wouldn't like it if I hit you first."

"Is that all that holds you back?" I asked. "Fine."

I punched him in the stomach. My fist connected with hard muscle, which was exactly as I expected. Harris grunted.

"There you go," I said. "Now you can tell my father that I hit you first."

His eyes lit up. He grabbed my throat with both hands—with the quivering eagerness of a man whose dream was finally coming true—and shoved me against the bookcase. He lifted me up so that I rested lightly on my toes. I'd expected him to draw blood quickly, but he seemed intent on causing more permanent damage.

I grabbed a stone statuette and smashed it into the side of his face. Harris staggered back.

"Sorry, I'm a little out of practice," I said, my voice strained. "I used to do this a lot."

I struck him again, and there was a sickening crunch from his mouth.

"That was for Mirelle," I said. "Believe me, you deserve far worse."

As I walked out of the study, Harris was spitting out blood and a tooth onto the fine Persian carpet.

# CHAPTER 41

## DEIRDRE

The smart play was to head home, rest, and plan a new line of attack for the next day. Or I could go to Ben's and demand answers. Since when had I ever been smart?

I'd tried to get into his Tudor City apartment before and failed. I knew from that first visit there were no alternative entrances. Before I got on the subway, I reached out to the Snapp network of marathoners, asking if anyone had ever dropped off bags at the building. By the time I got to Forty-Second Street, I had a helpful answer. I bought a pair of large paper bags at Walgreens and headed east to Tudor City. I ducked under the scaffolding latticed in front of Ben's building and smiled at the masked doorman.

"Hi, I'm Deirdre from Snapp. I've got a delivery for the Palansky family in 11C. I have keys."

He nodded, and I hurried to the elevator. I headed up to the eleventh floor—where the family lived—and took the stairs up to the thirteenth floor and knocked on Ben's door.

I heard him rattling around inside for a minute before he opened the peephole. We had a silent staring contest—I couldn't see him, but

I knew he was there. Finally, the lock turned, and he opened the door.

"How did you get up here?"

"You want your neighbors to hear this?"

He let me inside. Ben's apartment looked like it was auditioning for a Ralph Lauren commercial. The living room was light and airy, with white walls topped by elegant moldings. A series of arched windows granted a view of the New York Public Library in all its glory. Every piece of furniture looked like an antique; across one wall was a towering row of bookshelves. I expected a Labrador retriever to bound in at any moment.

"Wow, this was your parents' pied-à-terre? Nice digs."

"Who told you that?"

I thought back; it had been Jude, but I didn't feel like revealing that. "Who knows? But you really lucked out."

"I guess anything seems nice when you live in a basement," Ben said.

"You've got no right to be pissed off at me. You're the one who's using information my sister gave you to make money for yourself. I guess the bottom really has fallen out of the journalism business. Why are you still trying to extort money out of the Thraxtons?"

"You are blundering into everything and making a mess," Ben said. "You don't know what you're doing, and you're too arrogant to admit it. Caroline wanted me to do this, and I'm going to do it. You're not going to stop me."

"How does this help Caro?"

"Her in-laws deserve to suffer. Believe me, they're going to." He gave me a dismissive once-over. "All you do is run around and play detective. You haven't figured anything out yet."

"I know this isn't your first try at extortion. You shook the Thraxtons down for money a couple of months ago, and my sister advised them to pay you," I said. "You two were in a scheme together."

"Caroline begged me to help her," Ben snarled at me. "No one else would do it. She wanted to get away from the Thraxtons. Not just Theo. All of them. She said they'd ruin Teddy if they got the chance."

"You extorted a quarter of a million dollars out of them as a nest egg?"

"It's tough to disappear these days," Ben said. "You need a lot of cash to make it happen."

"What are you saying? You were being a Good Samaritan and helping Caro escape?"

"We were going to escape together."

For a moment, everything seemed to freeze. *He has to be lying,* I told myself, but it made too much sense. Caro had used dirty Thraxton money to do good in the world, but at some point she'd realized her son would pay the price for it. Yet, she hadn't said anything to me. She'd sent me those photographs, but . . . I couldn't imagine she'd leave me without a word.

"Caro wouldn't leave me or our father like that."

"Nothing was more important to her than Teddy," Ben said. "She was determined to protect him. But she was getting more panicked and anxious every day. I think when Theo showed up without warning, she lost her mind. She immediately wanted to run away with Teddy."

The real meaning of what he said dawned on me. "But not with you."

"What?"

"She didn't want to run away with you, Ben." I thought of the two fake passports Adinah Gerstein had shown me. One for Caro and one for Teddy. Where did that leave Ben? "My sister was going to run away with her son. You weren't part of that picture."

"Caroline needed me. She couldn't do it alone."

I moved closer to him. "She wanted your help, but she didn't want *you*," I said. "You thought you'd be together, but to Caro you were just the means to an end." It hurt to talk about my sister like that—as if she was willing to do wrong if she thought she had a reason to—but I had to admit the truth of it. The Thraxtons were up to their eyeballs in illicit money, and Caro had been okay with that as long as she could support a worthy cause.

"You don't know that. Caroline made a terrible mistake when she left me. This was our second chance."

"I understand why you want to think that, but you're delusional," I said. "All Caro was thinking about was Teddy. This wasn't a romantic plan to run away, Ben. You know that."

I'd expected him to shout at me, but he got quieter. "She only backed out of it because she panicked."

"Backed out of it?"

"I told you already—she freaked out that morning when Theo showed up. She told me she was leaving with Teddy as soon as she picked up their passports."

"She told you that the morning she died?"

Ben wiped his face and nodded. "She was upset about Theo. She knew he'd been spying on her. She was genuinely afraid of him."

I felt like a ton of bricks had dropped on me. I'd believed Ben when he'd told me he hadn't seen Caro that morning. His story made sense, because she hadn't given him the memory card she was carrying. It had never occurred to me that they *had* met up that morning.

"It never made sense to me, how Caro came down to your neighborhood but didn't give you the memory card," I said, thinking out loud. "I thought maybe someone followed her and stopped her. I blamed Theo, then his father. But it wasn't them. It was you."

"Can you hear yourself talk?" Ben said. "Because you sound crazy."

"You were supposed to come up to Caro's neighborhood. Then Theo showed up, and she came down to yours. You said she never showed up at your building. But this was all supposed to be on the down low. You were meeting her in the park, where there weren't any cameras." That was one of the last scenes on the video the police had, my sister walking out of the park, clutching her head and her chest. It was clear something was terribly wrong. Only it was worse than I'd thought.

"What happened when you saw her, Ben?"

"She told me she was taking off." His voice was low and flat, as if our conversation had hammered him down. "I said I wasn't ready, and she said . . . she said it was just her and the kid."

"What happened then?"

"Do you even understand this, Deirdre?" His voice was anguished. "Caroline led me on. She made me think we would get back together again, if I helped her out with this. I did everything she asked. And she was dumping me. Again."

I was as horrified by his self-pity as much as his words. "What did you do?"

"I grabbed her, okay? I was upset, and I wanted her to come to her senses. But when I let go, she fell back. She hit her head. She was dazed for a minute, but she got up again, Deirdre. She was fine!"

"She was anything but fine." My heart fluttered in my throat like it was trying to escape. "The cops showed me all the video footage. They figured she fell on the steps because of her heart. But she'd *already* hit her head. She was disoriented. That's why she fell. That's why she died."

"I told you, she got up! She was fine!" Ben shouted.

The despair I felt in that moment was like a knife wound. Caro was dead and I couldn't bring her back. It had been brutal to hear she'd had a heart problem she kept secret. But it was only one factor in her death. The first time I'd gone to see Villaverde at the police station, he'd told me the combination of her heart problem and the concussion had ended her life.

"You killed her," I whispered. "You killed my sister."

If there was ever a time I expected rage to course through me, it was then. But all I felt was broken and exhausted. Hitting Ben wouldn't be enough. He needed to be arrested. He had to admit his guilt to the world.

At a cracking sound, my body lit up as if it were on fire. I was on the ground in a second, gasping for breath but unable to draw air.

"Don't deal with an animal without a Taser," Ben said over the buzzing in my head.

He dragged me up by the shoulders and propelled me to the open window. My eyes were still rolling in my head, but they settled on the New York Public Library in the distance.

"Tudor City's had plenty of suicides, people jumping from windows," Ben said. "You'll just be another one."

He shoved my quivering body out the window headfirst. I managed to widen my legs enough to keep from falling out, even though the rest of me was dangling in midair.

"You just had to be difficult," Ben said.

He shot me with the Taser again, and I lost control of my body. For a split second, I was hurtling through the air, and then I was gone.

# CHAPTER 42

## THEO

After my confrontation with my father and his henchman, I rushed to see Teddy. He was coloring at the kitchen table and barely looked up when I walked in. Gloria gave me a silent wave.

"I'm sorry I went away," I told him. "I won't do that again."

He gave me a surly look. "Grandpa says you will."

My blood curdled in my veins. My worst nightmare was already underway. My son was being poisoned by my father's lies.

"I won't," I said, crouching down. "I love you. I'll always be here for you, Teddy."

"Uh-huh," he said, going back to coloring.

"He's in a mood today," Gloria said quietly. "He keeps asking when his mama is coming to get him."

"Thank you for taking care of Teddy while I was gone," I said. "I'm well aware that you are long overdue to have time off."

Gloria waved her hand dismissively. "It's not a problem. It's an awful time for the family. And I love Teddy; you know that."

"I am eternally grateful. Just so you know, I'll be moving Teddy out of this house as soon as I can find a place."

"You're going to stay in New York?"

"I don't want to uproot Teddy and take him away from everyone he knows. Just my father. I am hoping that you'll be willing to move with us, though. I don't know what Teddy or I would do without you."

"And give up living across the street from the man who refers to me as 'the Help'?" She beamed. "In a heartbeat. If you're staying here, we'll figure something out."

"Thank you, Gloria."

I headed upstairs to my own room. I didn't have a plan. All I knew was that I couldn't stay in that house any longer.

That was when I heard a noise from Caroline's room.

I opened the door and found Ursula seated at Caroline's vanity table, a tray of jewelry in front of her. She looked like an eager magpie. "Everything depends on it," she said.

"Ursula?"

"You're back, dear boy." Ursula brightened when she saw me, as if a switch had been flipped. "How was your trip?"

"Awful and illuminating, in equal measure. What are you doing?"

"Sorting some things."

"Why?"

"I put some things out of order," she said cryptically, "and now I need to set them right."

"I saw your brother when I was in Berlin," I said.

"Klaus has been dead to me for years."

"He's not quite as I remembered. He has changed. He wanted me to tell you he's sorry for being a bastard. He said it's his only regret."

Ursula laughed softly. "Ah, Theo, you are a dear boy, but you are gullible if you believe the leopard changes his spots." She moved a couple of rings into a box. "I grew up in the Stasi. My father was a senior officer. Klaus followed in his footsteps. My mother drank herself to death, and now I follow in her footsteps. These paths are set for us when we are young. I often think, if only your mother had taken you and your sister away and started a new life. How different everything would have been."

"My mother got out," I said. "But she left Juliet and me behind."

"No one gets out, Theo. At least not alive."

Ursula loved to make dramatic pronouncements, and it felt like the wrong time to mention that my mother had flown to Guam for a divorce. It had been uncontested by my father because she allowed him to have full custody of Juliet and me. My mother had saved herself, but not her children.

She stared into the mirror. "I am full of hidden horrors."

I shuddered in recognition when she said it. "I've heard that before."

"It's a line from *Medea*."

"But why would you . . . ?"

"It was a line from a play your mother was in. She kept repeating it." She picked up the glass in front of her, only to discover it was empty.

"I don't understand."

"He loved her—I can tell you that. As much as he is capable of loving anyone, which is not much in the greater scheme of things. But he wanted to control her, so he lied and played games with her mind. I am ashamed of my part in it. I was in the house to help with the *kinder*, and instead I slept with their father. No wonder Juliet hates me." Ursula got up from the vanity slowly, with the painful self-awareness of the inebriated. "Of course, he did exactly the same things to me that he did to her. I started losing parts of myself until I didn't even know who I was anymore."

She moved toward me unsteadily.

"Now you understand," she added. "Why I wanted to help Caroline escape. She needed a different life. She and Teddy both did."

What I understood was that Ursula had to be very drunk, and she didn't make any sense. "What does that mean, Ursula?"

"I tried to get away from your father, and I failed. This life is what I deserve. Your father is my penance. But Caroline never did the things

I did. She didn't deserve this. She wanted me to help her, but I can't do what she wanted me to do."

"Which was what?"

"She wanted me to reveal the Thraxton family secrets if anything happened to her," Ursula said. "She wanted the truth to come out. But I can't. It's buried too deep, and I was involved in burying some of it. Teddy . . ." A sob rippled through her chest, but she stifled it. "Poor Teddy does not deserve this."

"Let me help you home."

She waved me away. "I've been doing this a long time, dear boy. I don't want to go home. I don't want to see your father ever again."

She passed me and made her way down the hall, supported by the wall, then down the stairs, leaning heavily on the bannister. I shook my head and went to my room. I sat on the bed for a minute to take off my shoes. It was only two in the afternoon—eight o'clock in Berlin—but I hadn't slept on the flight, and I passed out.

———

I woke up an hour later, woolly headed and cotton mouthed. According to my watch, it was nine p.m., but the sun was streaming in through my window. It took me a minute to realize I'd forgotten to change it from Berlin time.

I put my shoes on and splashed some water on my face. No one seemed to be home, but I heard the television in Gloria's room. I knocked on the door.

"Sorry to bother you, but where's Teddy?"

"Ursula took him across the street to play with the trains," Gloria said.

"Ah." I didn't want to have round two with my father just yet, but I wasn't going to allow Teddy to be in his company for another minute. I hurried out the front door and across the street and rang the bell.

The disapproving butler answered.

"I'm here to pick up my son."

"He isn't here."

"He came over with Ursula."

The butler shook his head. "She's not home."

I was ready to push past him, but he seemed as surprised as I was.

"She said she was going to your house," he added.

"She came over, but now she's gone," I said, panic rising inside me. "They're both gone."

# CHAPTER 43

## DEIRDRE

I was lying in a strange bed, staring at an unfamiliar ceiling. Everything in my line of sight was wobbly, as if I was underwater and staring at ripples on the surface. As my brain shook me awake, the waters parted and my vision cleared.

There was a man in a white coat who didn't look any older than me. He had a scraggly neck-beard and a notable underbite. "It's alive," he said, like I was Frankenstein's monster stirring under a tarp.

I promised myself the first thing I'd do, when I was sure I wasn't dead, was drop-kick this jerk. "Where am I?" I croaked.

"You're in the hospital," he asked. "I'm Dr. Weiss. Do you remember how you got here?"

"I was pushed out a window. Tased . . . twice. Ben Northcutt tried to kill me."

"You have no idea how lucky you are," he said. "You fell three stories and landed on wire mesh. You've got serious lacerations, two Taser burns, a broken fifth metatarsal in your left foot, and a fractured wrist. Honestly, you should buy some lottery tickets when you walk out of here."

"Are you really a doctor?"

He chuckled at that. "Your family's waiting. Are you ready for a visit?"

"Okay," I said, hoping he meant Reagan but wondering if he meant my father. I struggled to sit up. Dr. Weiss put his hands on my shoulders, gently pressing me back, then pushed a button to raise the upper half of the bed. "Where are the cops?"

"They're waiting too."

"Get them in here."

A minute later, Reagan was rushing in and hugging me. "You scared us to death! Are you okay? Tiger Mom wanted to be here, but the hospital only lets two family members in."

Villaverde and Gorey were on her heels. Pulling up the rear was my father, looking pale and anxious.

"You need to haul Ben Northcutt's ass into jail," I said. "He's insane. He tried to kill me."

"Tell us what happened," Villaverde said.

I tried to explain as best I could without mentioning the Thraxton criminal enterprise and Caro's role in it. "He thought he and Caro and Teddy were running away to start a new life, when my sister didn't want anything to do with him," I said at the end. "He admitted he had a fight with Caro the morning she died. He shook her, and she fell and hit her head. He insisted she was okay, that she got up after that, but I told him he killed her. That was when he tried to kill me."

"Which suggests you were onto something," Villaverde said. "I wonder how Theo will take the news his wife was ditching him."

"Theo's already having the worst day of his life," Gorey added.

"What are you talking about?"

"Teddy's gone missing," my father said.

"His stepmother has vanished, and it looks like she took the little kid with her," Villaverde explained. "You know anything about that?"

I was stunned. "Ursula's always been sweet . . . and very drunk. Are you sure she took him?"

"Theo is certain she did. She told him the boy needed a different life."

———

The hospital wasn't thrilled about uncaging me so early, but once I'd signed a bunch of forms saying they were off the hook if anything bad happened, they let me go. Dr. Weiss added his own warnings.

"You need to come back in if you vomit or get dizzy," he said. "You could have problems concentrating, or with balance. You might get angry easily . . ."

"That's normal for some people," my father muttered.

"Wonder where I got that from?" I wasn't sure how I felt about having him around, but if Teddy really was missing, we were going to be spending time together.

"Pot, meet kettle," Reagan added.

We piled into my father's car. Our drive to Theo's town house was tense but speedy, thanks to my father's lead foot on the gas. When we got there, I banged on the door. It was just after seven in the evening. Theo opened it immediately.

"I'm so glad to see you," he said, touching my shoulder. "The police told me you were attacked."

"An old pal of Caro's tried to throw me out a window," I said. "Honestly, I'm more worried about Teddy."

"I'm anxious as well, but I know Ursula loves him," Theo said. "She'd never do anything to hurt him. I think it's just a matter of time until he's found. Please come in—you can wait with me."

I filed in, Reagan and my father following me. Gloria was pacing in the parlor. "I can't believe this is happening," she said. "Ursula has nowhere to go and no money of her own. Where would she take Teddy?"

"It was a good impulse gone awry," Theo said. "I can understand her wanting to get him away from my family."

"Sit down, Deirdre," Gloria said. "Tell us what happened to you."

"I want to hear Theo's story first," I said. "You emailed about wanting to talk. What did you want to say?"

"The day of Caroline's funeral, you accused me of killing another woman. For years, I've run away from that. I tried to pretend it didn't happen. I went to Berlin to finally confront it, and I discovered my father has lied to me all these years."

"I'm confused," I said. "Lied to you about . . . killing this woman?"

"Yes," Theo said. "The condensed version is this: During my second year at university in Berlin, I had a whirlwind fling with a woman I knew as Mirelle. I was a mess at the time, but I thought I was in love." He cleared his throat. "One night, while I was . . . let's just say high . . . this is so hard to talk about."

We were all quiet. Then my father said, "There's nothing more painful than the truth. But it's the only thing that cures you."

Theo nodded. "I don't remember what happened, but Mirelle's body was on the floor—stabbed to death—and my father told me I'd killed her. I believed this for years." He took a deep breath. "I've discovered it was all a lie. The woman was an actress my father hired. He killed her—had her killed—because I married her. It was all a fiction to enable my father to control me."

"How did you get to the truth?" I asked.

"I've been working with a doctor who helps people recover their memories," Theo said. "I've been spending more time in New York because of it, but I didn't want my family to know. The day Caroline died, I came by the house quickly to pick up something . . . the doctor believes objects can help activate your memory." Theo looked sheepish. "I know this sounds like mumbo jumbo, but it's helped me."

"Therapy is like that," my father said. "Unless you're involved, it can sound like nonsense."

"What do you know about therapy?" I demanded.

"I go every week," he answered.

"You do?"

"To group therapy," he clarified. "I've done one-on-one as well. I felt foolish at first, talking so much about myself. I was raised never to do that. But you can't change without understanding what's wrong."

"You need to do something to break bad programming," Reagan said.

"You've done therapy?" I asked her.

"Every so often," she said. "I started a few years after my dad died. I do telemedicine appointments."

"My daughter is in school to be a therapist," Gloria said. "I always said that's just for crazy people, but she's had me do a couple of sessions with a friend of hers. It really helps how you think."

I realized I was completely outnumbered. "Your father told me you'd been to the house in the middle of the night," I said to Theo. "It only made me more suspicious of you."

"I already wanted Teddy far away from my father, but that's imperative now. I think Ursula understands that, too, which is why she took him." Theo paced anxiously. "I want to hear what happened to you, Deirdre."

"I went to see an old friend of my sister's," I said. "A journalist named Ben Northcutt. He was helping Caro extort money out of your family."

"He . . . she . . . what?" Theo blinked at me.

"You know your family is into money laundering, right?" I asked. "That's why I quit."

"Caro was giving him information, and he was cashing in on it. He thought he and my sister were going to leave with Teddy and make a new life together. I made him admit he shoved her the morning she died. Caro fell and hit her head because of him."

243

The doorbell rang. Theo went to answer it and returned with Jude Lazare in tow.

"Your father called me when you were in the hospital, Dee," she said. "I can't believe you're out already." She looked around nervously. "Where's Teddy?"

"He's gone. With Ursula—my stepmother—as far as we know," Theo answered.

"I came over because . . . Ben called me," Jude said. "To be more specific, he threatened me."

"Ben was the one who tried to kill me," I said, feeling a tidal wave of anger rising inside me. It had been weirdly absent in Ben's apartment after he confessed, but it was back. "I'd love to know where he is."

"That's the thing," Jude said. "I knew he was conspiring with Caroline. She'd come to me first, asking me to help her get money out of her in-laws. She wanted to leave, and I wanted to support her, but I simply couldn't bring myself to do it. I know she approached Ben after that. She didn't give me many details, but I knew he did what she wanted." She wiped her eyes. "After she died, Ben started calling me. He told me Caroline wanted to save her son from Theo. Then, in the next breath, he'd say Theo had to be punished for what he did to Caroline."

"You didn't tell the police?"

"I thought he was venting. And I didn't want to tell the police what Caroline had been up to," she said. "But he called me twenty minutes ago. He swore that if I told the police about him, people he knew would kill me. I asked him if he'd hurt Theo, and he said . . ." She put her hand to her lips. "He said it was more important to save Teddy, and that's what he was going to do."

# CHAPTER 44

"I need to call the police," Theo said.

"Do you really think Ben took Teddy?" I asked Jude, not wanting to believe her. "What's he going to do with a kid?"

"Caroline thought her in-laws were an awful influence. She said they would twist Teddy up like they had done to Theo." She glanced at my brother-in-law. "Sorry, Theo."

"Caroline had a point," he answered.

"My sister sent me a message. She sent one to my father, but he misplaced it." I glared at him. "There was a third message." I found it on my phone and read it aloud. "'If I fail, you have to do it. I am putting all of my faith and trust in you. My son's future depends on it.' I showed it to Ben, and his reaction was weird, but he claimed she sent it to him. Maybe he really is doing what Caro wanted him to do."

"Everything depends on it," Theo repeated. "When I came home this afternoon, Ursula was sitting in Caroline's room and saying those words."

My phone started to slide out of my hand. Had my sister put her faith and trust in Ursula? Drunk Ursula? That seemed crazy. On the other hand, Caro had written the message just after five in the morning, right after she wrote mine. By all accounts, she was in a panic and not thinking straight.

"Ursula really did like Ben," Gloria said. "You don't think she would . . ."

"When did Ursula meet him?" Theo asked.

"At the Central Park Zoo, at least a couple of times," Gloria said. "Ursula said she had met him at a gala Caroline hosted." Her face was miserable. "Teddy liked Ben. They talked about animals."

"We have to call the police," Reagan said. "Even if Ursula's not plotting with Ben, he'll have no trouble getting Teddy to go with him. We need to think about where Ben would go."

"My sister sent me a photo of her and Ben—it mentioned a house in High Falls, New York."

"Do you know where it is?" Theo asked.

"No," I admitted. "Just High Falls."

"I know where it is," my father said.

"How?" I asked.

"I had to pick Caro up from there once." He didn't elaborate on why. "His family was well off. They had a vacation home in the Poconos too."

"I'll give the police every lead we have," Theo said. "But if Caroline mentioned High Falls, I think we should head there."

———

We took separate cars, me in my father's and Theo following us. We were mostly silent heading out of the city. It had been a decade since I'd driven anywhere with my father, and it felt uncomfortable because it was familiar and strange at the same time. It was like the adult me had been transported into the past, only instead of stressing about my parents' fighting, we were united in our fears for Teddy.

"What happened?" I asked finally. "The time you had to pick Caro up at Ben's house, I mean."

"She didn't come home for her birthday. Two weeks later, she still hadn't stopped by. It wasn't like her," he said.

"You talked on the phone?"

"Aye, there were some short chats. But very much on the surface, about work and the like." He was quiet for a moment. "She never said anything was amiss."

"What happened?"

"I thought, 'This is too strange.' Your mother believed I was over-reacting. She'd met Ben and liked him. But I didn't think much of him, to be honest."

"Too macho?"

"Too much of a show-off. All these tales of derring-do."

"What happened when you got to the house?"

"Caro was fit to be tied. 'That bastard stole my work,' she told me."

"Ben stole her work? Wasn't he a Pulitzer Prize finalist?"

"Apparently that very story was one Caro reported on and wrote. She got no credit for it." He shook his head. "I thought she might strangle him, but he wasn't in the house. She told me to wait, packed up her things, and that was it. Didn't even leave him a note."

"Stone cold." I stared at the road. "She never told me anything."

"Crawleys are good at keeping secrets, bad at asking for help."

"What I don't understand is why she would have anything to do with him again."

"He was a creep, but I don't think anything violent happened between them back then." He was quiet for a moment. "You wondered the same thing about your mother."

That was true, but my father and I had never talked about it. "I don't understand how she could forgive you. I thought she'd leave you, but she never did."

"I don't understand why she didn't leave me either," he said. "I was a mess. I didn't deserve her."

"Why did you hit her?" That was something I'd always wanted to understand.

"I've spent a long time asking myself the same thing," he said. "When I first went to therapy, it was all about controlling anger. Count to thirty, breathe deep, focus your mind on something else, that kind of thing. But that was like a bandage over the problem. The issue wasn't the anger. It was that I felt entitled to an *outlet* for my anger."

His words resonated with me on a deep level. We'd never talked like this to each other. Maybe it helped that we could look at the road and not each other.

"How do you know you've changed?" I asked.

"I hope I have," he said. "I meet with a group every week. I don't drink anymore, or go to bars, so no more bar fights. The last few years with your mother were really good, but she was sick, so that changed our dynamic. I wonder if I ever got involved with another woman what would happen. Part of me is too afraid to find out."

It had been almost four years since my mom had died. I hadn't realized my father was living as solitary an existence as I was. Part of it was that I didn't trust other people, but I didn't trust myself either. Hookups I could handle. Relationships were terrifying.

"If someone hurts me, I want to kill them," I admitted.

"That's because you're like me." He sighed. "I used to hate my father. He was the cause of so much misery in the lives of people I loved. I dreamed of killing him."

"He beat your mother?" I'd never heard this story before.

"He did. And me, and my brother."

"Did you ever take him on?"

"When I was seventeen," my father said. "I tackled him, and he beat the hell out of me. Then he threw me out of the house."

It was twisted of me, but I laughed so hard at that tears came to my eyes. The similarities between my father and me had always been clear, even when I wanted to deny them.

"Yeah, you enjoy stories about me getting my arse kicked," he commented.

"I didn't mean it that way . . ."

"When you came at me with that knife, that was the thing that changed me," he said. "I know you thought it was because you nicked my liver and I got sepsis. But it was the realization I'd turned into my father. That was the hardest truth I ever faced."

He wiped his eyes with the back of his hand. We were off the highway now, on a scenic country road, passing elegant nineteenth-century houses with gingerbread gables and turrets. It was tough to make out numbers and signs in the dark.

"I need to slow down," he said. "I remember the house was completely hidden from the road. It's on a large patch of land with a creek at the back. The house was a bungalow with a large addition—a sidesplit, I guess. There's a screened-in porch at the back."

"Great recall, but you said it's completely hidden from the road. Do you remember any signs?"

"There was one for a restaurant," he said. "A big white board. There was a house across the road, on a much higher parcel of land. They had a couple of barky dogs and an electric fence."

"I'll keep my eyes peeled."

We kept driving, Theo on our tail. We passed a house on the right that was elevated high above the road.

"Stop," I said. "I didn't see the driveway, but this could be the right area."

We drove into a turnoff on the right. Theo followed. We all got out of our cars. The house on the hill had its lights blazing. A pair of huskies watched us from a broad window. One of them yowled, and the other joined in.

"That's the house," my father said, pointing to the opposite side of the road.

When I looked carefully, I could make out the openings for a semi-circular driveway in between the thick tree line.

"You're the only one who's been to the house," Theo said to my father. "How should we do this?"

"The back porch would be the easiest way to get inside," my father said.

"I'll head back there," Theo said. "I'll signal you if I need a distraction at the front."

"The house has a strange layout," my father answered. "The staircase up is hidden. The door to the cellar's in an odd place. I need to go in myself."

"Then we'll go in, and Deirdre can drive up if we need a distraction," Theo said.

"This seems like a bad time to tell you I don't know how to drive," I admitted.

There was a moment of silence for their dead plan.

"I'll circle back to the porch with my father," I said. "I'll text you if we need a distraction at the front, okay?"

Theo nodded.

"Let us get a head start," my father said. "I don't want to get too close to the house until we're behind it."

We crossed the road and sidled along the edge of the property. It was quiet, except for the sound of crickets chirping. I was limping in the boot they'd given me at the hospital.

There was no way of knowing how much security Ben had. My hope was that he hadn't outfitted the place with booby traps.

"Do you think Ursula is with them?" I whispered.

"I hope so," my father answered. "She might be drunk, but she loves Teddy."

Behind the house was an expansive yard that sloped down to the creek. On the other side of the water was a golf course, but no one was playing in the dark.

As we crept toward the house, I saw movement inside and heard the crash of Teddy's steps. He was running.

"Ice cream!" he called out, delighted.

I could hear a man's voice, but it was indistinct.

My father moved to the screened-in porch, which allowed him to see into the living room. I took the window that peered into the kitchen. Teddy was sitting at the table, greedily devouring a pint of ice cream. "This is my favorite," he said.

I gestured to my father that we'd found our quarry. I tried the kitchen door, but it had a pair of solid locks on it. My father shook his head silently. He went back to the porch, pulled a box cutter out of his pocket, and slashed the mesh. He unlocked that door and padded up the steps.

"Where's Mama?" Teddy asked Ben.

"She wants to be with you more than anything," Ben said. It was a different voice than I'd ever heard come out of his mouth. Kinder, warmer. "But we've got each other, so that's pretty great, right?"

"Sure," Teddy said. "Where did Ammy go?"

"She stayed in New York," Ben said. "But she sent you with me because she loves you."

It was deeply weird, watching Ben act like a caring parental figure. I wasn't even sure he was pretending. The man who tried to kill me a few hours earlier had a gentle, fuzzy side.

We watched in silent surprise.

"We need to get you ready for bed," Ben said.

"I forgot my toothbrush," Teddy noted.

"That's okay. I got one for you. Let's go upstairs."

They retreated from the kitchen, and Ben turned out the light.

I texted Villaverde that we'd found Teddy with Ben. I didn't have an address to give him, just general coordinates. It was awkward to type with my damaged wrist, yet preferable to letting my father handle anything tech related.

"What's that sound?" my father asked.

"What?"

I kept typing. A heartbeat later, my father shoved me to the ground as a gunshot rang out.

"I can hear you," Ben called, his voice no longer sweet. "Come out wherever you are."

NOW, I texted Theo. A moment later, I heard his car roar into the driveway.

"What the hell?" Ben muttered. Footsteps clattered away.

"Wait here," my father whispered.

"Where are you going?"

He vanished, and I cursed myself for not being able to chase after him. I could hear shouting at the front of the house and Teddy screaming. Then there was another gunshot.

# CHAPTER 45

## THEO

Years ago, I'd paid good money for people to abuse me at fetish clubs. Knives were sharp, but nothing had ever cut into me with the precision of a gunshot that pierced my side. It didn't even hurt at first. As I tumbled to the ground, I saw the stars shining above me, and I heard footfalls.

I'd rushed out of the car when I heard Teddy scream, but then I'd heard his voice. "Grandpa!" Teddy said. "What are you doing here?" His clear, delighted tone came to my ears like the sweetest music. My boy was safe.

The man who'd shot me dragged me into the house. My blood left a trail on the pale wood planks. He shoved me through an open door, and I tumbled down a splintery staircase, falling into a heap at the bottom. I was lying on cool, damp earth, and the smell of it filled my head.

A light went on, a dim bulb on a wire hanging from the ceiling. "How did you find us?"

"You must be Ben," I said. "What a way to meet."

"Yeah, well, I'm the man your wife was actually in love with."

"You don't seem lovable," I observed. "You abducted my son. You tried to kill my sister-in-law. And you killed my wife."

He sank his foot into my ribs—the side without the wound.

"I've always hated you, Theodore Thraxton. From the moment I first heard your name."

"It's Theo," I said.

"You're the reason Caroline is dead," he spat.

"From what I heard, you shoved her and she fell and hit her head. That makes *you* her killer."

"You don't have a clue." He kicked me again. "You showed up at the house and terrified her. It was your fault she wanted to get away immediately. This is all on you."

I laughed, even though it hurt.

"What's so funny?" he demanded.

"There's nothing worse than a man who won't take responsibility for his actions," I said. "That's the story of my father. Everything he does—every evil thing—he blames on other people. It's always their fault. No one loves a man like that. Caroline might've been willing to use you, but she was never going anywhere with you."

Ben's face loomed above mine. "We'll see how philosophical you feel after I'm done with you," he rasped. "I spent years writing about the worst people in the world. I'm going to use what I learned on you."

# CHAPTER 46

## Deirdre

Teddy was safe. That was the most important thing. But Theo was in danger, and I didn't know how to help him, especially in my mashed-up state. I called the police as soon as we got to the road. My father led Teddy across to his car, and I hobbled after them, out of my nephew's earshot. Teddy got in the back seat, and I clambered in after him while my father reclaimed the driver's seat.

"What's going on?" Teddy asked. "Where's Daddy?"

"He went to the house to rescue you," I said.

"From Ben?" Teddy looked perplexed. "I had ice cream."

Whatever Ben had done to him, it didn't seem to have fazed Teddy. For that, I was grateful.

"Did the police say how long it would be?" my father asked me.

"Fifteen to twenty minutes."

My father turned around to look at the house. "I should go back in."

"Don't," I said. "I thought all he had was a Taser. I was wrong."

I texted a quick group message to Reagan and Jude and Gloria, who were back at Theo's house. Teddy safe. Theo in danger.

"What happened to your wrist, Auntie Dee?" asked Teddy.

"I hurt it on a window."

"Ouch," Teddy said. "Kiss." He leaned forward and planted a gentle smack on my bandage. "All better."

"Wow, it feels better now," I said, and I meant it.

As I was speaking, a couple of dark SUVs pulled up in front of the house. Several large men in black T-shirts and cargo pants piled out of the vehicles.

My father's head swiveled around. "I thought you said—"

"That's not the police," I answered. It was a clear night, but tough to see details. "That looks more like a SWAT team."

I stared at them as they conferred.

"Let me see what's going on." I kissed the top of Teddy's head. "I'll be right back."

I got out of the car and crossed the road again.

"Hey!" I called.

A big, bald-headed guy turned around. I'd seen him before, but I couldn't remember his name.

"Theo's in the house," I said. "I think he's been shot."

"Have you seen the boy?"

"Teddy? He's safe," I said. "He's with my father."

"Where?"

"In that car." I pointed across the road.

"Gentlemen," the man called out. "Stand down. Put away your guns. The boy is safe."

The five men in black reacted immediately, stashing their weapons as quickly as they'd retrieved them.

"But Theo's been shot," I said. "He was dragged inside the house. Ben is a psycho. He killed my sister. He tried to kill me. He's going to murder Theo."

"Mr. Thraxton couldn't care less about what happens to Theo," the hulking man said. "As long as Teddy is safe."

He marched across the road and to my father's car, me trailing in his wake. I tried phoning Theodore, but no one answered.

"How did you get here so quickly?" I asked.

"There are tracking devices in all of Mr. Thraxton's vehicles," he said. He opened the back door of the car. "Hello, Teddy."

"Hi, Harris," Teddy said, clearly unenthusiastic. "Where's Daddy?"

"I'm going to take you home, Teddy," Harris said. "To your grandpa."

"His grandpa's right here," my father said.

Harris ignored him. "Come on, Teddy."

I didn't want him to take Teddy, but I knew that was selfish. We were sitting ducks out there, and Ben was armed. "It's best if you go home right now, Teddy," I said. "But I promise we'll see you soon."

My nephew reluctantly slid out of the seat. "I want to see Daddy," he said.

"Your grandpa will let you play with the trains," Harris said. "There will be cookies and ice cream."

"I want Daddy," Teddy answered decisively.

"You have to help Theo," I said to Harris. "You can't leave him in that house."

"I have my orders," Harris said. "We're only here for the boy. Theo can rot."

He lifted Teddy and carried him off. I started after him, but my father touched my shoulder.

"We need to let Teddy go with them. It's the safest thing for him," he said. "Now we have to do what we can to help Theo."

# CHAPTER 47

## THEO

"When you think about it, Caroline ended her own life," Ben said, cuffing my hands together in front of me. "By making too many bad decisions."

"You killed Caroline because she wouldn't run away with you." I was grateful Deirdre had given me the outline of the story already. I was in no small amount of pain, but it was clear that listening to Ben's version of the story would be intolerable. I was inoculated against anything he claimed.

He kicked me again, then dragged me farther into the cellar. He attached something to the cords that bound my wrists.

"You smug bastard." Ben pushed a button, and my wrists jerked upward. In the dark, I hadn't seen that I was chained to a pulley attached to a beam running along the ceiling. It lifted me to my feet, then went farther, raising me until I was off the ground completely, dangling from my arms.

"I see. Now you're going to torture me." I sounded jaded, even to my own ears. "That's your masterly plan? Should I beg you not to hurt me?"

"I will show you fear in a handful of dust," Ben said.

"If you're going to quote T. S. Eliot, why not start at the beginning of the poem? It's more impressive. 'April is the cruelest month, breeding . . .'"

Ben punched me in the solar plexus. "Quote more poetry, asshole."

"The police are going to find you," I said as soon as I got enough breath back. "Why don't you run while you can?"

"You ruined everything. I would've been a better father to Teddy than you ever could've been. Now, I don't care what happens. Caroline's dead. What does it matter?" He picked up a metal box. "But first, we have some business to take care of. I'm going to make you wish you'd never been born."

He pushed the button again, pulling my shackled hands into the air a little higher, then dropping me suddenly. My arms rattled in their sockets. It felt as if they were about to be pulled from my torso.

"How does it feel to be completely powerless?" he asked.

"I've had worse days."

"You're the reason Caroline is dead. If she'd left you for me, she'd still be alive." Ben looked me over. "She didn't give a damn about you."

"You can't blame me for her death," I said. "You'll have to live with the guilt of that for the rest of your life."

He pulled a black plastic object out of his pocket and took aim at me. As the hooks sank into my skin, I realized it was a Taser. The electricity that flooded through me was like a fire. It crackled through my brain, forcing my eyes wide and making me gasp.

"Admit it. Caroline never loved you. She was only with you for your money. Caroline was a climber. She used you as a stepping-stone," he taunted.

I didn't answer. He charged up the device again. The pain was overpowering, almost magnificent. Fire raged through my body again. I'd been here before, so many times, so many years ago. It was the oblivion I'd always craved. It was the reason I'd been with Mirelle and the reason I'd wasted endless nights in awful places and the reason I'd poured dangerous substances into my body. In the darkness was perfect stillness.

"Caroline stayed with you as long as she did because of Teddy. But she hated you, Theo. She really did. Caroline knew you murdered a girl years ago. She thought you deserved the worst."

Those words truly hurt. They were the last nail being hammered into my coffin. Because Ben was right about this single thing: Caroline *had* believed the worst of me. I'd always been afraid she would learn the truth and hate me for it. The horrific irony was that my fear kept me from investigating what really happened that night. Caroline died believing that I was a killer. I would never have the chance to make matters right between us.

What made me want to die was that Caroline had gone to her grave hating me.

"I would've prepared better if I'd known I'd be entertaining guests here. I want this to be as painful as possible," Ben said. "I've got strychnine, which is supposed to be the worst poison of all, thanks to the convulsions. I wish I could hang around for three hours to watch you die. But I have to go out and shoot your accomplices now."

"Teddy . . ."

He punched me in the face. "You ruined everything, you know that? If Teddy gets hurt, that's on you."

That lit a rage inside me that pushed the void back. Falling into the soothing blackness was a luxury I didn't have. I had to fight for my son.

"Caroline . . . told . . . me . . ." My breath escaped in short bursts, as if I were still being rattled by amateur electric-shock therapy.

"What's that?"

"Caroline . . . told me . . . about you." My head drooped forward as if the life had already bled out of me.

*I am full of hidden horrors.*

The voice scratched across my brain, far worse than anything in Ben's limited repertoire. Ursula claimed the words were from a play; I wasn't certain that I believed her. They had taken on a life of their own inside me.

"What did she say?" He stepped closer to me and then, as if reading my intent, he fired up the Taser again. My whole body convulsed, loudly rattling the chain.

I whispered something unintelligible.

"What was that?" Ben was impatient now, and he came so close I could smell his shaving lotion. He was desperate for any token, any sign indicating that Caroline had thought of him at all.

My lips brushed against his throat when I finally spoke. "You underestimated my ability to tolerate pain," I whispered.

Before he could step back, I sank my teeth into his throat, right into his jugular.

# CHAPTER 48

## THEO

I would have been satisfied to die in that darkness. I wasn't afraid. Ben was no longer a threat to Teddy. My son would be safe. I hadn't thought I was capable of saving anyone, but at least I'd done that. It didn't matter if I died now.

The scar that ran down my chest burned as if a beacon lay inside my flesh. Perhaps that was Death's way of letting me know he was close. Blood blanketed me from top to bottom. The metallic tang of it lingered in my mouth. I'd killed Ben Northcutt, and the dreadful shame I was supposed to experience over taking a life was nowhere to be found. That man had deserved his fate.

For reasons I couldn't explain, I had the sense that Caroline was in front of me, touching the scar on my torso. I couldn't see her, but I could feel her presence as surely as I could catch the scent of her perfume in her bedroom. We were caught in twilight, neither living nor dead.

*I am full of hidden horrors.*

I had never wanted to face that voice. It was better believing that a tiger had slashed me to pieces. That was a comfort compared to reality.

*I am full of hidden horrors.*

Dr. Haven had told me I needed to re-create smells and sounds and tactile sensations to bring my memory back. She was right. In that horrific basement, time unspooled. I was no longer an adult man, but a three-year-old boy, lying in a cold cellar. The ground was dark with blood. My blood.

I floated outside of my body, watching myself at Teddy's age. Feeling Caroline's presence beside me was the only reason I was strong enough to do it.

My mother was kneeling over me with a knife in her hand. She was reciting the same lines, over and over, as if casting a spell for an unbreakable curse. *I am full of hidden horrors.*

I'd known the story of Medea long before I'd ever heard of Euripides at boarding school.

I'd heard my mother's voice taunting me all my life. I knew I must have been the worst kind of monster there was to make my mother want to murder me. All my life, I'd been haunted by that broken shard of a memory. As she stabbed me again and again and the blood drained from my body, I imagined I was being purified. If I died, it meant I deserved to die. I felt an odd sort of liberation in knowing that I'd been a sacrifice rather than a target. My mother hadn't wanted to kill me because she thought I was a monster but because she knew my father was.

My mother had tried to destroy me, just as Medea killed her own sons. Medea had done it to spite her unfaithful husband; perhaps that was what my mother had in mind, as well. Only I hadn't died.

In my memory, there was an oubliette guarded by steel traps; I wasn't supposed to venture in that direction, ever. A black fog swirled in the air above it; brushing against it left me light-headed and sapped my energy. Backing away from it, my memory cleared, but it only picked up several years later when my mother had vanished and Ursula was suddenly my stepmother. But Ursula had been there, in the house, for a long time. She had been in the house that very night my mother tried to kill me.

Caroline's soul was still beside me, giving me the strength I'd always lacked. My mind returned to that oubliette and—for the first time in my life—I peered inside it.

I saw my father running into the basement. My mother screamed at him, and he wrestled the knife away from her, then shoved it with all his might into her stomach. She screamed, collapsing beside me on the floor, covering me in her blood.

For the first time in that darkness, I screamed.

# CHAPTER 49

"Maybe we should wait for the cops," I said.

"*You* should wait for them," my father said decisively. "You almost died already today. I'll do this."

"Like hell," I said. "I'm going with you."

We trudged across the road again and down the driveway, the broken bone in my foot aching. The headlights of Theo's car were still on, and I saw blood on the three steps up to the house and wood slats in front of the door. My father tried the front door, but it was locked.

"We can get in at the back," my father said.

My phone rang, but I ignored it as I hurried around the side of the house. The porch door was still hanging open, its torn screen blowing in the breeze.

The door to the house was still unlocked.

We stepped inside a mudroom. To the right was the kitchen, where Teddy's abandoned pint of ice cream was melting over the table. To the left was the living room, with a large fireplace. To the left was a step up to a hidden door that blended with the wood paneling. It must've led into the addition, presumably upstairs.

"No blood trail," I whispered.

We crept to the foyer. Blood was streaked over *that* floor. The path ended at a closed hallway door. We stopped, listening for any sound. There was nothing.

"That's the cellar," my father whispered.

"We need a weapon," I said.

"We need to hurry."

My father pulled something out of his pocket and started to jimmy the lock open. I rushed to the kitchen and grabbed the biggest knife in the counter block. By the time I'd run back to the hall, my father had the door unlatched.

"How come you never showed me how to do that?" I whispered.

"Like you didn't get yourself into enough trouble growing up."

He opened the door a crack.

No voices, just an eerie creaking sound.

He opened the door wider, and an earthy smell filled the air. Something metallic was behind it. Blood, I realized.

No one shot at us. It felt like a good sign.

There was an odd rasp, then a soft moan.

"Someone's alive," he said.

We crept down the dimly lit stairs. A man was hanging from the ceiling, swaying slightly on a chain.

"Theo?" I said, and he groaned.

My father found the light switch and turned it on. Theo was soaked in blood from his face down to his bare feet. If he was alive, it was only barely.

"We have to get him down," I said, but my father was frozen in place. He pointed at the floor, and I realized Ben was lying there, eyes wide, mouth open, and missing most of his throat.

# CHAPTER 50

## Deirdre

The first state trooper who walked into that basement scuttled out like a cartoon character, legs pinwheeling on the stairs.

"What d'you want to bet *he* puts in for early retirement?" my father commented.

We'd managed to get Theo down from the ceiling, but his arms were still looped in chains. Even on the ground, they were stuck in position, as if he were a doll broken by an angry child. By the time paramedics made it there, he was murmuring like a fever victim. I tried to pick out words and failed.

Finally, some cops arrived on the scene and ordered us out as they set up floodlights around the perimeter of the house. We stood as near the action as we could, watching the parade of uniforms march in and out with the grim tenacity of ants.

"Pity," my father murmured.

"Because we don't get to settle our score with Ben?"

He nodded.

"I know what you mean," I admitted. "But I'm grateful Teddy's safe, and hopeful Theo will survive."

My father stared at me for a moment before nodding. "I am too."

Our impulses were dark and raw. That didn't mean we had to follow them.

The cops stationed out front wouldn't let us back in, even though we'd already been inside the house and had contaminated the crime scene. "Believe me—you don't want to see it anyways," a grizzled cop with a florid face told us. "It's like Ivan the Terrible's torture chamber down there."

They brought Theo out first on a stretcher. His arms were still dangling above his head, and his mouth was open in what looked like a scream, but he was alive. The next gurney rolled out with a big bag of Ben-sized remains. They left it in front of an ambulance with open doors, but disappeared without loading it. Dead was dead, after all. It wasn't like Ben was on a schedule anymore.

My phone buzzed again. It was Juliet. I answered this time.

"Deirdre, what is going on?" she demanded. "I was told Teddy was missing, but now he's safe? And Ben Northcutt tried to kill you? And Ursula tried to throw herself in the East River?" Her voice was brittle and agitated. Every sentence came out like a question, as if she had doubts about reality.

"Yeah, it's been a day," I said, too emotionally exhausted to react. "Is Ursula okay?"

"Who cares? They're putting her in a mental hospital." Juliet gulped audibly. "What about my brother? Gloria said he's been shot and might be dead?"

"Theo's in bad shape. He was shot and tortured and . . . it's bad."

"Is he going to live?" Juliet's voice was very small.

"I don't know," I said. "Your father's men showed up ready to attack, but when they realized we'd rescued Teddy, they took him and fled. They left Theo behind. On your father's orders, Harris said."

There was a choked sound on the other end. I wondered if she was crying.

"Juliet, Theo's going to need your help if he's going to survive this," I said. "Can you do that?"

"I don't know."

"From what Theo told me, your father has been gaslighting you your entire lives," I said. "Have you ever thought about what would happen if you stood together against him?"

# CHAPTER 51

## Theo

They moved me from one hospital to another; I might not have noticed except for the color of the walls. "You're *certain* Teddy is safe?" I demanded each time I woke. "Also, no opiates. I'm an addict."

"Your son? Yes, he's fine. He's with your family."

That set off alarm sirens in my head. "Not my father!"

"Your sister, I think? Dark hair, tattoos . . ."

"My sister-in-law," I said, relaxing. "That's good."

I drifted off again. The next thing I knew, a small voice was calling, "Daddy?" Instead of jumping, Teddy bobbled up to the hospital bed like a curious little duckling. "Does it hurt?"

"No," I lied.

"Really?"

"Maybe a bit," I amended. "But now that you're here, everything is better."

"Kiss," Teddy said, lifting his arms in an unspoken demand to be picked up. Juliet appeared and lifted him, allowing him to kiss my cheek. He considered my arm, a mix of old scars and new damage. "Looks bad," he said finally, kissing it too.

"We can only stay for a little while," Deirdre said from the doorway. "Doctor's orders."

For a moment, I thought I was hallucinating. Deirdre came up to Juliet and whispered something; my sister nodded. "Give your father a hug, Teddy. We're going down the hall to see where they keep the cookies around here."

"Cookies?" Teddy's interest was piqued. "I get one for Daddy!"

When they left, Deirdre came closer. "How are you really feeling?"

"Half-dead." My throat crackled as if someone had scrubbed it down with sandpaper. "You saved me."

"You saved yourself," Deirdre replied archly. "Turned out you didn't need help."

"Yes, I did. A lot of help, actually." I took a breath. "I thought I was going to die, in that basement. I know this sounds dreadful, but I wasn't sorry about that."

"You have to stick around. Teddy needs his dad."

"Does he? I can't decide how I feel about that. It's as if I'll damage him by being there, yet I'll also harm him if I'm not. I've caused him enough damage already, don't you think?"

"You're not the cause, Theo," Deirdre said. "I wish you could've been honest, but I'd say the same thing about myself. Caro and I both tried to ignore our past. We pretended it never happened. But it was like a wall that divided us. We never dealt with it, so we never got beyond it."

"My father always says what's past is past. I thought I could keep everything buried. I *wanted* to keep it buried. I never wanted anyone to know the truth about me, least of all Caroline. She would think me a monster."

Deirdre gave me her reluctant, lopsided smile. "The wonderful, terrible thing about Caro was that she could love a monster, even knowing he was a monster."

"You think we would have reconciled?"

271

"Maybe you would've found your way back to each other." Her face turned serious. "If you'd told me a week ago I'd be spending time with my father, I never would've believed you. I've never really trusted that people can change. I think maybe he has, or at least he's trying to. Reagan said something that blew up my brain. She asked me what it would take for me to forgive him, and I said I would if he died." Deirdre paused, as if contemplating it anew. "And Reagan said, 'You believe he deserves the death penalty?' And something clicked in my brain. I mean, I believe in rehabilitating people—at least theoretically. I still haven't forgiven my father. But I also want to keep talking with him."

"I'll never forgive my father," I said.

"I wasn't suggesting you give a sociopath another chance to destroy you," Deirdre said. "But maybe you should talk—really talk—with your sister. I wish Caro and I still had the chance."

"Cookie for Daddy," Teddy said, running back into the room with a sealed packet in his hands.

"Sorry," Juliet said to Deirdre. "I know you wanted privacy, but we bumped into a vending machine, and a certain someone's a bit too good at spotting cookies."

"That's okay. We got to talk." Deirdre patted Teddy's head. "We need to get you back home. Daddy and Aunt Juliet need to talk."

It was disturbing, watching Juliet have a normal conversation with another human. In my mind, she was forever the antagonist, swiping at Caroline, clawing at me, locking horns with our father. I'd seen her kindness to animals, but I'd always believed that was where her sympathies ended.

"It's almost like you and Deirdre are conspiring together," I said, after they left.

"She's a tough character. I like that in a woman," Juliet said. "How are you feeling, now that you've cheated death again?"

"Like I've been dragged through hell. Why do we never talk honestly to each other about anything?"

"It's never fun to poke at raw wounds," Juliet said. "That's why we avoid it. But your weird voice mail made me think back to my trip to Paris. I've been talking about it with Deirdre. The timing was terrible—I had exams coming up—but Father insisted that I go. It was unusually generous of him. I should've guessed he'd have an ulterior motive."

"There always is, with our father," I said. "Now I want you to tell me what you remember about our mother."

"Father made it clear I was never supposed to talk about her. Not ever." Juliet's red mouth tightened. "I was seven when she vanished. I couldn't understand what had happened—I went to bed one night and everything was normal. When I woke up the next morning, our mother was gone and you were badly injured. Father wouldn't take you to the hospital, but there were a pair of doctors buzzing around, and Ursula was barking at them in German. I didn't understand a word. Father told me that our mother had tried to kill you before she ran away. He told me I couldn't tell anyone, or our mother would go to jail forever, that they might even execute her." Her eyes were damp. "Even then, I knew he was lying. And he made me lie to you. He said it would be better if you thought a wild animal attacked you. He made up a story about you being torn up by a tiger at the zoo. I know it sounds horrible, but I went along with it. He always reminded me what would happen to our mother if I didn't."

"Our mother was already dead," I said.

"On some level, I think I knew she was gone, but I clung to anything that let me pretend she was alive," Juliet said.

"What else do you remember?"

"I know Ursula went away for a long time, and I was so glad—you know how much I always hated her—but then she came back, and they got married. In my mind, she was the wicked witch who got rid of my mother."

"Father's the one we should blame. He killed our mother."

Juliet perched on the edge of the bed. "How can you be sure? You weren't even four when all of this happened."

"You don't have to trust my memory," I said. "Ursula's been dropping hints that she can't live with herself. I believe she knows most of what happened. The question is if we can get her to admit it."

Then I told her everything.

# CHAPTER 52

## THEO

When I got out of the hospital a week after I went in, I returned to the cursed house my father had bought as a present for a doomed marriage. But I also quietly made the preparations I needed to. It wouldn't do to make a move until I was ready.

By the time I came home, Ursula had been moved from a mental hospital—to ensure she didn't attempt to kill herself again—to an alcohol-detox facility upstate. She wept when I drove up to see her. "I'm so sorry. I thought I was helping Teddy," she said. "That was all I cared about."

"I know you did," I told her. "And you still can. You told me Caroline wanted you to reveal the truth. I need you to do that."

"I don't know if I can. I did awful things, Theo . . ."

"I have faith in you," I told her. "So did Caroline."

When my stepmother finished her weeklong program, she opted to stay with Teddy and me, telling my father she didn't feel ready to talk quite yet. She asked him to come over late on a Thursday afternoon.

When my father arrived, he clapped me on the back, as if he hadn't spent my entire life gaslighting me. "You're looking well, son." He grinned at me, and I attempted to smile back.

"Come sit in the parlor, Father. I can't even remember when you last visited. What can I offer you to drink?"

"Something celebratory. Sancerre—or even champagne," he answered.

"Ursula just got out of her detox program," I said. "Do you really think that's a good idea?"

"Let's be realistic," he said. "She'll never be able to stop drinking. Why pretend?"

"It's strange how you like to say what's past is past, and yet you think people should be trapped by their history," I said. "I believe people are capable of far greater change than you realize."

He shrugged. "You're setting yourself up for disappointment, son."

"Perhaps," I said. "Perhaps not."

There were footsteps behind me.

"I heard a request for sparkling," Juliet said. "Theo has a fine assortment of imported waters. Shall I pour you a glass?"

"I'm not keeping alcohol in the house these days," I explained.

It took our father a moment to recover. "Well, I *am* surprised to see you here, Juliet."

"Why? My brother and I have been discussing history lately. It's a subject we both enjoy."

"I know," our father answered casually. "But it seems like just the other day you were telling me you wished your brother had died instead of Caroline."

His basilisk eyes stayed on hers. Juliet faltered, freezing in place. Divide and conquer. That had always been our father's strategy. He controlled the two of us by fueling our long-standing rivalry.

"I wouldn't blame Juliet for that," I said. "I've wished the same thing myself."

My sister glanced at me, amused and maybe even slightly relieved. It seemed to propel her forward. "What's that saying of yours, Father? 'A liar has to have a perfect memory.' Yours is impressively sharp."

276

"I can recall my Shakespeare, at least. 'How sharper than a serpent's tooth it is to have a thankless child.' Or, in my case, two thankless children. After everything I've done for the pair of you, this is how you repay me?"

"Don't even start," Juliet said. "I've devoted my life to running your company. I've done everything you ever asked of me. You owe me answers. You owe us both."

"Haven't you told me, time and time again, Juliet, that I owe your brother nothing? That I ought to cast him out on the street because he's worthless?" It was clear that our father saw my sister as the weak link, the one who would crack under pressure. I'd spent years defying him; Juliet had always been eager to please him. If he could, he would twist her loyalty back to him and break her with it.

"I've deserved to be called worthless," I said.

"Believe me, he has called you far worse than that," Ursula said from the doorway. Her voice was cool and crisp. She was simply dressed in a white shirt and trousers, but her eyes were brighter than I'd ever seen them. "He called you a killer. He made all of us believe it."

"Was this your plan? The three of you ganging up on me? Because I don't have time for this shit." My father got to his feet. "I'm also giving you notice to vacate this house, Theo. I own it. You're just a tenant. You can live on the street for all I care."

"You don't want to leave just yet," I said. "You'll want to hear our exciting news about the family business."

"What news?"

"I've decided to return to Thraxton International."

He peered at me as if I were a curious artifact he couldn't decide was real or counterfeit. "Are you serious? You want to work with me?"

"Definitely not. I'll be working for Juliet." I glanced her way. "What's my title again?"

"Senior vice president of global operations, ethics, and compliance," Juliet announced grandly.

"Is this some kind of joke?" Our father's head swiveled to look back and forth between us.

"Theo and I agree that a nicely downsized hotel business is the way of the future," Juliet said. "Our future, at least. No money laundering. No crime-ing at all. Can you even imagine it? Don't answer that, Father, because I know you can't."

"You think you can *quit*?"

"We're not quitting anything," Juliet said. "We're firing *you*."

He broke out in laughter. "You two are incredible," he said finally. "You barely have a penny to your names. How are you going to take the business away from me?"

"Because you'll be in jail," Juliet said.

He shook his head. "If *I* go to jail, honey, *you* go to jail. There's no way to implicate me in any crime without implicating yourself. Theo might be able to wriggle off the hook, but the name Juliet Thraxton is on documents from here to Moscow."

"Actually, Theodore," Ursula said, "Juliet is quite safe. You're the one who'll go to jail for murder."

My father blinked at his wife, suddenly uncertain about how much the ground was shifting under his feet. "Murder?" He glanced at me. "Sorry, Theo, but you don't have a shred of evidence about Mirelle. None of you have anything you can prove. Klaus would never testify against me. I've always kept my hands clean. The men who work for me are well paid for their silence."

"That doesn't matter anymore," Juliet said. "We have Mother's body."

"You have no such thing." My father was eerily confident, as certain as if he'd buried her himself. For all I knew, he had.

"Pardon me—what I meant to say is that we have Mother's body double," Juliet said.

My father's face was ashen as he turned to look at Ursula. "You wouldn't."

"I did what you ordered me to do," Ursula said. "I flew to New York, dyed my hair black, and packed a couple of suitcases full of your dead wife's clothes. Then I flew to Guam and hid in a hotel there for three months so you could have an easy divorce that stayed out of the spotlight. A fake divorce, which seemed appropriate for a man who is such a fraud in every aspect of his life."

I was watching out the window for the NYPD, and two vehicles pulled up at the time we'd agreed. "Look, it's the police," I said. "This part will be amusing."

My father's head swiveled. "They can't arrest me. They don't have a warrant. They don't have jurisdiction. They don't have—"

"Shhh," I said. "It's not your turn. Yet."

We watched in silence as they banged on the door of my father's house and poured inside. They knew Harris was ex-military and had guns, which made him a serious threat. But his takedown was surprisingly peaceful. He exited with his hands cuffed behind his back, his bald head bowed low.

"What are they arresting him for?" my father cried. "He had nothing to do with your mother! He didn't even work for me then!"

I thought about telling him that the case of Mirelle's death had never been closed by the Berlin police and that Mehmet Badem had confessed to his part in a sworn statement. I had no doubt that Harris had committed no end of illegal acts on my father's behalf and that he would never see justice for most of them. But he would be spending his upcoming years in a jail cell, and that was important. I would've worried about Ursula's safety if Harris were free.

My father looked shell-shocked when he turned away from the window. "You can't do this."

"Your reckoning has been long overdue," Juliet said.

"None of you would have anything without me!" My father's face twisted like a gargoyle's as he shouted in impotent rage.

"You really need to sign these papers." Juliet opened a large leather attaché case on the table. "Hugo Laraya was kind enough to draw them up for us. You'll be signing over the company and the various properties you own."

"Why would I do that?" my father demanded, eyes bulging. "You can all go to hell."

I looked out the window. One of the NYPD vehicles had ferried Harris away, but the other was still there.

"You can sign now, before Interpol arrives," I said. "Or you can wait until all your stolen property has been seized by the government. This isn't even about the money laundering. Yet."

"What are you doing? You're pulling apart everything I ever built."

Juliet tossed the papers at him. I handed him a pen.

*I am full of hidden horrors.* My mother's voice ran through my head. I could forgive her—if anything, I empathized with her torment—but I could never forgive him. The horrors belonged to him. As he finally realized his empire was collapsing, his eyes filled with tears. It was the only time I ever saw my father cry.

# CHAPTER 53

## DEIRDRE

Two weeks after Theo got out of the hospital, Reagan's mother decided to host a family dinner. For as long as I'd known Mrs. Chen, her response to any situation, happy or sad, was to cook. "It's her primary way of expressing affection," Reagan told me. "She might criticize what you're wearing, what you're doing, and every choice you make, but if she makes roast duck, that means she loves you."

Mrs. Chen went all out, cooking for two days straight and shooing me out of the kitchen when I dropped by to help.

"Start one little kitchen fire and no one trusts you anymore," I grumbled.

"If it was only one, it would be okay," she answered. "You're too good at breaking things."

Dinner was set for six o'clock on Friday, which was as early as Reagan could get home from work. Teddy and Gloria got there early. "It smells SO GOOD," he said when he skipped into the house, endearing himself forever to Mrs. Chen. She let him into the kitchen, putting him to work as her official taster.

"He's been excited about this for days," Gloria told Mrs. Chen.

At five thirty, the bell rang. My father was on the doorstep, clutching a bouquet of orange lilies and a big bag from Joe's Sicilian Bakery in Bayside. I'd invited him on impulse. His words about regrets had been circling in my head. I wasn't ready to forgive him. I wasn't sure I ever could. But I was open to finding out how much he'd really changed. More than that, I took Caro's last words seriously—she wanted both of us to be deeply involved in raising Teddy, and that meant I couldn't shut him out of my life.

He seemed suitably uncomfortable.

"You look like you're trying to impress," I told him at the door.

"Caro gave me this blazer," he answered. "Does it look ridiculous?"

"I meant the bag from the bakery. The jacket's fine. Theo probably has the same one. Maybe he'll wear it tonight."

It was strange being in the same room as my father. For years, he'd loomed large in my imagination. In person, he had a shy curiosity and awkwardness, like a penguin who'd been let out of the zoo on a day pass. Jude came in, and he relaxed a little. Then he pulled me aside and handed me a paper bag, first pulling out a small, shiny box. "This is yours," he said.

Inside was my mother's gold locket, all delicate Celtic scrollwork dangling from a gleaming chain. I cracked it open. Inside was a photograph of my family, taken when I was eight.

I had a lump in my throat the size of the Empire State Building.

"There are some other things in there," he added. "But I know you loved that locket. I've been meaning to give it to you. Caro refused to do it—she said I had to give it to you myself. I asked Jude to do it at the funeral. I'm sorry I held on to it for so long."

I nodded. "I appreciate it."

He patted me on the shoulder. "Don't get all snuffly."

"I was admiring the brown paper bag. So classy."

"You always had such a mouth on you," he said. It wasn't entirely without admiration.

"Pot, meet kettle," I told him.

"I found something else too," he said. "It came up while the cops were investigating. I talked to someone at that Egyptian company."

"Osiris's Vault? They're not Egyptian; they're in the Bronx."

"Whatever." He handed me an envelope. "For you to read whenever you're ready."

I went out for a walk, curious but apprehensive. When I'd braced myself, I opened it up. The first page said:

Deirdre,

I'm terrible at emotional conversations (like everyone in our family) so I wanted to put some thoughts down in case I never get to say them in person. I keep thinking of Mom, and of how things were when we were growing up. I've always regretted that we lost touch for a few years, and I wish

The letter stopped there. I turned the page, but it was blank. For a minute, I was confused, until I remembered the day I'd stormed into Osiris's Vault. The one employee who'd helped me had mentioned that there were earlier versions of Caro's message to me. That was what I was holding: her earlier drafts. My hands shook as I scanned the next one.

Deirdre,

I keep thinking of Mom, and how you never believe you're going to end up like one of your parents, until you do. For so long I've wanted to talk to you honestly about our lives growing up, but I can't seem to do it in person. I used to be angry at you for doing what you did. But the truth is I'm angry

at myself for doing nothing. I don't think I ever told
you how much I admire you.

Like the first one, it stopped suddenly. The last one was very short.

Dodo,

You are a kind of a monster who kicks everyone's
ass, but I love you anyway.

I read each one over again and again. It was a strange gift, seeing my sister's words—and hearing her voice in my head—after she was gone. Caro had never finished exactly what she'd wanted to say, but I knew her well enough to get the gist of it. I circled the block, dried my eyes, and went back to the house to be with our family.

# ACKNOWLEDGMENTS

I've said before that writing a novel is a solitary adventure, but that was especially true in lockdown and quarantine. I signed the contract for this book in November 2019, but by the time I turned it in, in June 2020, the whole world looked a lot different. For all the friends, family, and colleagues who made pandemic life bearable, I am eternally grateful.

I want to give my heartfelt thanks to everyone on the Thomas & Mercer team for making the publication of this book such a joy. That's especially true of my wonderful editor, Megha Parekh, who got incredibly excited when I first told her about my idea for this book; she has been a tireless champion for it ever since. Thank you to my developmental editor, Charlotte Herscher, who always asks smart questions that help me find deeper possibilities in the story. I'm grateful to editorial director Gracie Doyle for her incredible support, and to author relations manager Sarah Shaw for brightening my day whenever we interact. Thank you to my copyeditor, Susan Stokes, for fixing my (many) mistakes, and to my proofreader, Bill Siever, for his amazing attention to detail. Thanks, too, to the exceptional marketing team, especially Gabrielle Guarnero, Kyla Pigoni, Erin Mooney, and Lindsey Bragg, for their dedication and help, and to publicity manager Dennelle Catlett and publicist Brittany Russell for all their work to promote this book. There are so many amazing people who worked behind the scenes to get this novel into your hands, including production manager Laura Barrett, cover designer Lindy Martin, and art director Oisin O'Malley. I know I'm missing a few names here, and I apologize for that. The truth is that working with everyone on the Amazon Publishing team has been a privilege and a pleasure.

I also want to thank my agent, Mitch Hoffman, who has read this book more times than any other human and is the world's best sounding board for ideas. I'm grateful for his wisdom, enthusiasm, and friendship. I also appreciate the support of the entire team at the Aaron M. Priest Literary Agency.

My entire extended crime-fiction family deserves thanks, but a few people deserve special shout-outs (in alphabetical order): Megan Abbott, Ed Aymar, Nancie Clare, Angel Luis Colón, Libby Cudmore, Matthew Farrell, Kim Fay, Lee Goldberg, Rachel Howzell Hall, Jennifer Hillier, Chris Holm and Kat Niidas Holm, Susan Elia MacNeal, Brad Parks, Gavin Reese, Joe Reid, Hank Phillippi Ryan, Alex Segura, Sarah Weinman, and Holly West. I couldn't imagine a greater group of shady characters, and I'm lucky to know each one of you.

There are so many friends I want to thank, especially Stephanie Craig, Helen Lovekin, Ilana Rubel, Trish Snyder, Kathleen Dore, Deena Waisberg, Ghen Laraya Long, and Beth Russell Connelly. You guys know where the bodies are buried.

Rest in peace, Mark DeWayne Combs; you will be very much missed.

Pandemic life canceled my last book tour and made conference attendance impossible, but it's also opened up a world of possibilities via virtual events and podcasts. I'm so grateful to Jane Kulow of the Virginia Festival of the Book, Carrie Robb at the St. Louis County Library, Barbara Peters and Patrick Millikin of Scottdale's Poisoned Pen, Pam Stack of Authors on the Air, and the wonderful crew at Queens's own Kew & Willow Books. Thank you all, and I owe you drinks when I see you next. (I should add that I can't wait to visit my usual haunts—Toronto's Ben McNally Books, Houston's Murder by the Book, Denver's Tattered Cover—as soon as possible.)

Last, but certainly not least, I owe many thanks to my family, especially my parents, John and Sheila Davidson (that's doubly true for my mom, who reads all my books early and gives me feedback; my dad is forced to wait, since he can't keep a secret). My aunts—Amy, Evelyn, and Irene—are the world's best cheering squad. Most of all, thank you to my amazing husband, Daniel, for his endless encouragement and support; no one gets to hear all my crazy ideas like he does. I couldn't do this without you, my love!

# ABOUT THE AUTHOR

*Photo by Anna Ty Bergman*

Hilary Davidson is the bestselling author of *One Small Sacrifice* and the winner of two Anthony Awards. Her novels include the Lily Moore series—*The Damage Done, The Next One to Fall,* and *Evil in All Its Disguises*—and the stand-alone thriller *Blood Always Tells*. Her widely acclaimed short stories have won numerous awards and have been featured everywhere from *Ellery Queen* to *Thuglit*, as well as in her collection *The Black Widow Club*. A Toronto-born travel journalist who's lived in New York City since October 2001, Davidson is also the author of eighteen nonfiction books. Visit her online at www.hilarydavidson.com.

11042381R00183